Trish —

I so admire you — and your tutelage in writing. Thanks for your friendship. Enjoy!

Emmett

Window on Death

a novel by

Emmett K. Smelser

This is a work of fiction and any similarity to any actual places or persons, living or dead, is strictly inadvertent and unintentional.

Copyright 2013, Emmett K. Smelser

All Rights Reserved

ISBN-13: 978-1518761898

ISBN-10: 1518761895

Window on Death

Chapter 1

An hour back in the office from my hiking vacation to the Grand Canyon, my still-tender stocking feet were perched on my desk's open file drawer. (The boss hated it when I used the desktop. "Slovenly" he called it.)

The trip to Arizona was a chance to decompress and reconnect with an old Indiana University journalism school chum who works at the *Arizona Daily Sun* in Flagstaff. Our seven-mile descent to Phantom Ranch, two-night stay by the calming flow of the Colorado River and vigorous ascent back to the rim provided a welcome, needed respite from the relentless deadlines of a daily newspaper. Now, back in the frozen flatlands of central Indiana, I was looking forward to a leisurely morning catching up on the past week's papers. Then the phone rang.

"Mr. Andrews?" The voice was female, frail, high and hesitant. "Is – is this – uh -- Brock Andrews, the police reporter?"

"Yes. What can I do for you, ma'am."

"I – I – don't want to be critical, Mr. Andrews, but we need you to look into an error in your story and…" she hesitated, "and make a correction -- if possible."

"A correction?" A disagreeable tingle of adrenalin surged up my spine. I hate errors and after 15 years in the newspaper business I like to think I make damn few of them. Even more than I hate errors, few as they are, I confess I hate having my own called to my attention. "A correction, ma'am? When? What story?"

"The story that said my husband died because of his accident. We're sure that's not right."

"Ma'am, I'm – I'm sorry. Sorry for your loss. But can you help me out here? I've been on vacation and need to get connected again? What's your name?"

"Georgia Owens – uh -- Mrs. Raymond Owens. My husband died almost two weeks ago and your story – it had your name on it at least – said he died because of his accident. We called before but they said you wouldn't be back until today."

The details rushed back. Owens. Single vehicle crash, late January morning, icy roads. The driver, 59, headed home alone in his pickup after working the night shift at a local factory. Skidded off the rural highway, tipped over and, without a seatbelt, was thrown into the ditch.

"Yes, I remember the accident. Again, I'm sorry for your loss. But what do you feel was in error?"

"He didn't die from the accident. I'm – we're -- sure of it. He was – he was progressing so well – in the hospital for over a month. And then suddenly they call and say -- he's dead." She paused, keening sobs stifling her words.

I let her cry, using the seconds that ticked by to recollect details of the stories I'd written. Routine – if any fatality can be called routine. The accident report from the county cops listed serious multiple injuries -- broken leg, arm, shoulder and collarbone, probable concussion. A one-week update on the victim's condition said he was improving. Then, after several weeks, the funeral home called in an obit and the sheriff and coroner said he died of his accident injuries. Routine.

The crying stopped and there was dead air. "I'm sorry, ma'am. But the sheriff's department listed it as the county's second traffic fatality of the year."

"I know. I know," she sobbed. "But they're wrong. We know they're wrong."

"Why do you say that?"

"Because he was getting better. Don't you see? Something must have happened in the hospital. We're sure of it." The sobbing began again and then there were muffled words in the background.

"Ma'am? Are you all right? Do you have someone there with you?"

"Yes, yes. I'm sorry. It's just so hard. My children are here, and they saw their father. He was so much better and then …"

A new voice came on the phone, this one male and insistent. "Look, my mother's right. My dad's injuries were healing. I mean, he still felt like crap, but who wouldn't. And then suddenly he's dead? They said a stroke, but we're not buying it. The hospital must have done something to him – wrong medication or something. We're asking you to find out what really killed my dad. That's your job, isn't it? Reporting what actually happened?"

I didn't like the son's tone. But I'd learned it never pays to argue with people on the sharp edge of grief. It wasn't the first anguished call I'd gotten from bereaved family. When the news isn't good, emotions are raw and survivors are hyper-sensitive. Any hint of error, indelicate word choice or unfavorable nuance could easily launch the bereaved into tirades against the messenger.

A third voice, this one soft and calm, said, "Mr. Andrews, this is Teresa Owens – er, Wilkerson. I grew up here but my husband and I now live in Louisville. I'm a nurse and we're just baffled by my father's sudden death. No warning of complications. His doctor can offer no explanation. Just suddenly a massive cerebral hemorrhage and he's gone."

"Yes, I see now. But I'm not sure what I can do. Have you contacted the sheriff's office? We have to rely on the accuracy of the police reports."

"We're not *blaming* you," she said, barely audible. "I'm sorry for my brother's abruptness, but John's upset. I hope you can understand. Can you just look into it for us? Please?"

"Okay, okay. Look – uh – Mrs. Wilkerson, I'm just back from vacation, and it'll take me a little while to get back into things. Can I call you in a day or so? I see your number on my phone. Is this where I can reach you?"

"Yes, please. I'll be here with Mom for a couple more days. But if it's after that -- let me give you my cell number, too. And – thank you."

She recited ten digits and then said goodbye, leaving me to wonder, *What is this? A grieving widow unable to accept death of a spouse? Supportive children seeking to put blame on anyone but their non-seatbelt-wearing father? An insurance angle? A screw-up at the hospital? Or something else?*

Chapter 2

"Andrews, get your butt over here."

It was Jerry Snyder, the crusty managing editor who regarded it as his mission in life to keep his reporters humble. Actually, the abrupt summons was among the mildest in Snyder's lexicon. And normally I wouldn't have minded even his harsher demands. But just back from vacation it was harder to take. Not bothering to slip back into my shoes, I crossed the carpet to the quadrangle of desks that served as the newsroom's editing hub.

"Whattaya want, old man?" I said to the back of the editor's head. Sparse white wisps of his remaining hair struggled to approximate a comb-over. He sat hunched in front of his computer.

"Don't call me old man," Snyder growled back, the words escaping around the gnarled pen gripped fiercely between his jaws. Computers had replaced pen and paper more than 30 years ago, but all Jerry was missing from the green eyeshade era was the eyeshade. He spun in his chair to peer up at me with a jowly scowl. Even at 7 o'clock in the morning, his frayed collar was unbuttoned and an equally disreputable tie was askew.

"Oh, sorry, boss. I didn't realize you were *sensitive* about your age." It was a long-playing ritual between us – half jocular and half serious. Jerry was almost five years past normal retirement and tried hard – sometimes too hard – to merit his reputation as resident curmudgeon, both mentor and menace to neophyte reporters. I would be 36 at my next birthday and, despite the nearly 35-year gap in our ages, we were the veterans of *The Chronicle's* newsroom.

Fifteen years in this place and he's still talking to me like I'm a fresh kid. "Whattaya got, boss?"

"You were on the phone. Scanner sounds like cops are working a homicide. Better give 'em a call."

"Will do." *Homicide? Wonder why Danny didn't call.* Sgt. Danielle (Danny) Morgan was my favorite unnamed source (and longtime girlfriend) on the Kenton Police Department. *Is she still pissed at me for not taking her with me to Arizona? You'd think she'd have forgiven me by now.*

Kenton, Indiana, had not had a bona fide homicide in more than a year. *At least you'd think she'd have called me on something as big as a possible murder.*

I punched in the speed dial for the KPD non-emergency line. "Kenton Police Department," the friendly female voice answered. "Is this an emergency call?"

"No. Hi, Kelly, this is Brock."

"Hey, Brock. Back from vacation already, huh? How was it?"

"Great, thanks. Hey, what's going on? Heard you've got a homicide?"

"Right. Give me a sec." There was a rustling of papers. "Yeah, here it is. Officers are still on the scene so I don't have any paperwork yet. But the address is 5145 West Cass Street."

"Okay, got it. Thanks. Talk to you later. I brought you a little something from the desert."

"Oh, yeah? What? Not a snake or scorpion, I hope."

"No, nothing like that. Just something sweet for the sweet. Gotta run."

I'd loaded up my checked bag with jars of cactus and pepper jellies for my favorite sources. "Nothing of significant value" said our ethics code about gifts given or received. Neither I nor any of my sources in the cop shop or courthouse was going to be compromised by a jar of jelly, but a touch of thoughtfulness went a long way in easing conversation. I'd wrapped each jar carefully in thick hiking socks and amazingly they'd all made it intact through baggage handling at Phoenix and Indianapolis.

***

So much for my planned gradual immersion back into the maelstrom. I headed to my car. I'd been with *The Chronicle* since college, turning an internship and the premature death of the paper's long-time cops reporter into what was threatening to be a life sentence. I'd thought of leaving many times, but I'd come to cherish the creative freedom granted by the paper's editor and owner. Well – former owner, Bill Graham, before he sold out to Mega Media. But that's another story. And so's my firm attachment to a certain KPD cop.

I slid to a stop mid-block before Cass Street dead-ended into corn field, the foot of the street clogged by an armada of cop cars. The white one-story in question was the last house on the left. It sat to the right of a long gravel driveway blocked by three KPD black and white Dodge Chargers. Lining the street were two black state cruisers and two unmarked but conspicuous Crown Vics. Despite the early-March morning chill, the ground had thawed and I gingerly parked on the right shoulder opposite the drive to the house down the block – a good 100 yards from the subject property. My ride is a new electric blue Camaro and the last thing I wanted was to get mired in the mud.

The house drawing all the attention was set on a double lot some 100 feet back from the pavement. It was bordered on the right and rear by cornfields now still in winter stubble -- about as remote as it got and still within Kenton city limits. What had ostensibly been a simple two-bedroom postwar bungalow had been greatly expanded and updated. The siding was wood-look white vinyl, the asphalt roof shingles mimicked wood shakes, and a new looking detached three-and-a-half car garage flanked the house to the left. Above the garage's pedestrian door at the far right was a sign that read, Stanley Gordon, Photography. A vinyl white picket fence surrounded the house and yard. The front and side along the driveway were wrapped with barren morning glory vines. Yellow police tape was draped across the gravel drive, side gate and narrow concrete sidewalk that ran to the front door.
■■■

Across the tape at the drive apron stood Sgt. Danny Morgan, all 5-foot-10 of her in black – slacks, nylon bomber jacket, uniform hat and service oxfords. A black leather belt and holster with a black Glock 9mm completed her ensemble. She lifted the tape as I approached and smiled, "Welcome home. Glad you picked up on it. The report came in just as the shift changed and I didn't have time to call you."

"No problem." I had to restrain myself from grabbing and kissing her right there at the crime scene tape. It's the same temptation every time she's near. Tall and athletic, she had been a volleyball spiker at Kenton High and then at Indiana State where she got her criminal justice degree. Now back in her home town, she was an imposing figure with a reputation as a no-nonsense, take no crap patrol officer for KPD. For other reasons entirely, she was an imposing figure to me. *God, she's gorgeous,* I thought, habitually appraising assets that refused to be hidden by her utilitarian dress. I reminded himself how lucky I was we were still together.

Following my eyes, she smiled and tossed her long black pony tail as an invitation to duck under the tape. "Good to see you too."

"What've we got?"

Man of about 40 – apparent skull fracture. Found by his wife when she returned from an overnight stay across town with her mother."

"Motive?"

"Maybe robbery. Too soon to tell. The wife is pretty shaken, but we've asked her to do a quick inventory to see if anything is missing."

"Weapon?"

"None in evidence. Blunt force trauma to the left temple. Not much blood, so death was pretty quick."

"Where'd it happen?"

"Master bedroom. Back door glass broken as the apparent entry point. But no sign of an extended struggle. So the assailant might have startled the victim from his sleep."

"Okay for me to look around?"

"You know the drill. Just stay out of the way. Leave your shoes outside."

Chapter 3

I saluted the two uniforms at the front door and slipped off my shoes. None of the cops would mistake my beat up brown loafers as their own.

A narrow porch enclosed in louvered glass spanned the front of the house. Fake grass carpet supported two faux-wood Adirondack chairs to the right of the door and an upholstered slider settee on the left. Ceramic planters lined the outside wall, the stems of whatever they contained last summer now brown and brittle looking.

Modest as the neighborhood was, the house's interior was surprisingly well-appointed. The living room stretched the width of the house, a probable joining of the original small living and dining rooms. A designer touch showed in both the brocaded furniture and the elaborate drapes and valances at the windows. Down a short center hallway was a full bath on one side and a small bedroom/office on the other. Next to the rear was another full width room that consumed space probably once occupied by a kitchen and another bedroom. It now was an open great room. At far right was a gleaming kitchen with stainless steel appliances, cherry cabinets and black granite counter tops. The raised granite counter above the sink island was ringed by bar stools. A sliding glass door led onto an expansive flagstone patio at one end of which sat a large hot tub. At center of the great room was a formal dining area and at far left a sitting area with side-by-side fireplace and built-in nook housing a large flat-screen TV.

Seated on a magenta leather sofa were two women, one whom I knew as a plain-clothes detective and the other the apparent wife of the victim. Two young uniformed guys and an older one in plain clothes were picking their way meticulously around the room. My initial thought was that, given the reputation of the local constabulary – Danny excepted, of course -- they'd likely be bitten by a clue before they'd notice it. I shook off that judgment (have to maintain journalistic objectivity, you know) and paused a moment to listen to the females officer's questions of the widow. Sensitive, leading but not demanding. A reporter's impatience would get to the point quicker, but then might well miss the nuances picked up by a trained investigator. I decided to cut the cops a break. Besides, I knew better than to inject myself into a crime scene if I didn't want to get ejected from the house.

At the far left rear of the family room was a door at which another two uniforms hovered, and several voices inside indicated that was the location of the body. I leaned across the uniforms' outstretched arms as far as I could to get a glimpse of the death scene. Again, the home's expansion was evident. The master suite also stretched across the entire rear of the house. The bedroom was carpeted in light green plush and the centerpiece was a large mahogany sleigh bed bracketed by matching night stands against the rear wall. A small sitting area was on the left around a fireplace set into the rear wall. A mirrored dresser and high-boy chest adorned the inside wall, and at far right a wall of closets and a door that gave onto a brightly lit tiled bathroom.

The KPD photographer was bustling about the room shooting from every angle and a crime scene tech was dusting for prints. The body was not visible, but the bulky Wilkes County coroner, Buster Bradshaw, was bent over behind the king-size bed, an unbecoming expanse of pink backside showing above his belt.

The bed obviously had been slept in, because the top sheet and blanket were tangled and a folded-back quilt sagged onto the carpet. The mattress was slightly askew on the box spring, but the only other sign of a possible struggle was that one of the bifold closet doors was off its track and hung open attached only by its top hinge.

Bradshaw looked up, saw me and ordered, "Don't come in here. We're not done."

"No problem, Buster. Just getting a feel of the scene."

"Well, get it out there," he barked. "You know the rules."

The rules, as they were articulated by the sheriff and police chief, granted news reporters and photographers presumptive access to crime and accident scenes as long as they didn't get in the way and obeyed all orders of official personnel. But that access could be revoked at any time at the discretion of officers. I retreated to a corner of the great room and watched as the widow was asked the same questions several different ways.

The story, as I pieced it together, was that the wife, Valerie Gordon, had come home about 7 a.m. to find the back door glass broken. She figured her husband Stanley, who often mislaid his keys, might have locked himself out and had to break in. Then she found her husband lying face down on their bedroom floor. She tried to wake him and, when there was no response, she turned him over and saw his left temple was caved in. She said he was cold to the touch so she knew he was dead but called 9-1-1 immediately.

No, she said, they didn't keep anything but pocket money in the house, nor any precious jewelry, guns or electronic equipment. And, while she hadn't had a chance to look carefully, nothing seemed to be missing. She said she not yet had a chance to check the garage photo studio.

The coroner exited the bedroom, replaced by ambulance personnel with a gurney. Jim Rogers, *The Chronicle's* chief photographer, saluted me as he hustled to the bedroom door where he also got stopped. I watched as Jim juggled lenses and got wide-angle overviews of the bedroom from the door. With the EMTs already bagging and escorting the body of Stanley Gordon out the door, the photographer was spared our paper's no-no's – no blood, no bodies.

Only hours into my day, however, I had two of the latter, both wrapped in shrouds of unanswered questions.

Chapter 4

With hours before KPD's formal incident report would be ready on Kenton's first homicide in 18 months, I still had enough to get started. Barring a natural disaster my story would surely lead the next morning's paper and my deadline wasn't until midnight.

I pulled into the crowded parking lot behind *The Chronicle* and nosed into the slot marked Police Reporter, third from *The Chronicle's* back door behind only Publisher and Photographer. I'd long since gotten used to that coveted perk for staffers constantly rushing against deadline.

I stared up at the second story newsroom windows of the aging red brick *Chronicle* building while I planned the rest of the morning. Jerry would want a complete rundown on the homicide, but I always prefer to advance my own story strategy first instead of letting him dictate one. While long on experience, he's sometimes short on imagination, relying on familiar formulas and less open to new approaches. Not that Kenton afforded all that much practice on major crime stories, but I wanted to do it my way.

Mounting the rear stairs to the newsroom, I deliberately dodged the news desk where Jerry would stop me for an update. There would be time for that later. First, I wanted to type up my notes while the words and images were still fresh.

I took the long way around the half dozen clusters of desks that formed *The Chronicle's* various news departments. Labels corresponding to each section of the paper swung from chains above each cluster – four desks each in Features, Sports, and my section, Metro, plus smaller groups for Arts & Entertainment, Business, Photo & Graphics. My desk was just across the aisle from the window-enclosed corner office housing her royal highness, Executive Editor Sarah Goldman.

Silently passing behind Jerry's back, I hesitated half a beat at the sight of my new deskmate. Jennifer J. Jermaine was tall, maybe as tall as Danny but without Danny's kinetic intensity of a dedicated athlete. Jermaine was slender and graceful in an almost balletic way, her long reddish blonde hair sweeping her shoulders as she bounced enthusiastically from one assignment to another. Only a few months out of Indiana University, she had none of the dowdiness of most print journalism students, the pretty ones usually migrating to broadcast. Instead, she was both attractive and the very image of dressed for success in a crisp gray pantsuit. She had been assigned to the desk next to mine only days before my vacation.

It was one of the bright ideas of our new editor, Goldman, to pair the newcomer with the staff veteran. *But a feature writer, for god sake?* "Cross pollination" was what Goldman called my orientation of Jermaine in the newly created assignment of news features – the stories behind the breaking news. Pain in the ass was what I called it.

Oh, Jermaine was a decent enough writer and no doubt bright. She had a BA in journalism from Northwestern going right into an MBA at Indiana that she hoped would land her at *Business Week* or *The Wall Street Journal*. But in a tight job market and with student loan payments looming, she'd jumped at Goldman's offer -- in features for Kenton's *Chronicle.* All book learning and no experience besides an internship with an Indy business magazine. Plus, she bore this irritating co-ed perkiness that was accented by her choice of byline. I know I shouldn't be irritated by such things, but she'd taken a perfectly memorable, alliterative name and begged an impression of superficiality by rendering it Jeni. Sorry, but gag me with a sorority pin. And her handwriting – her notes all loopy letters with a circle over the "i." *Christ! Might as well have been a weather girl. Gimme a frickin break!*

"Hey, Brock," she chirped. "Bet you're glad to be back from vacation, right?"

"Yeah. *De*-lighted."

"You don't have to sound so happy to see me."

"Oh, it's not you, Jeni," I lied. "I'm just back from a murder scene."

"A *murder?* No *kidding?*" Her "oh, gosh" exclamation at almost every new incident was a reminder of why she rankled me. Well, maybe that and the fact she appeared to be Goldman's new favorite.

"Yeah, Jeni. No kidding. Right here in little Kenton, Indiana."

"Okay, I get it. You want to be left alone."

"Just got a lot of work to do. Talk to you later, okay?"

"Yeah, sure." She went back to straightening several already neat stacks on her desk – one each for phone messages, news releases, newspapers and magazines. Her compulsive orderliness, I was sure, was calculated by Goldman to shame me into attacking the tattered uni-stack that took up most of my desktop and always seemed on the verge of sliding to the floor, which occasionally it did.

It wasn't that I felt threatened by this and other members of the cyber generation – their interminable and intermingled streams of phone calls, text messages, photos, videos and e-mails to family, friends and story sources alike. *Don't these people ever just shut up and think?* Not that I'm cocky about it – well, maybe -- but I figure I have a right to be. The box of state press association plaques and certificates under my desk offer modest evidence of that. As the veteran, I'm easily the most prolific writer at *The Chronicle.* But aside from using the internet for research and a cell phone for convenience, I've got little tolerance for newer staffers' fascination with electronic gadgetry. And certainly not their use of smiley-face on-site video feeds to the paper's website and local cable station. Call me old fashioned, but I'm a written-word journalist and intend to stay that way. Well, I have agreed to posting early versions of my stories online.

That thought spurred me to check the phone directory. White pages verified the Gordons' address and a small yellow pages ad proclaimed the photo studio was now in its eleventh year. I wrote up several paragraphs from facts picked up at the scene.

A 41-year-old Kenton man became Wilkes County's first homicide in a year and a half, the victim of a possible home invasion.

Kenton Police have identified the deceased as Stanley A. Gordon, of 5145 W. Cass St. Determination of exact cause of death is pending a coroner's examination, but appeared to be a severe blow to the head, police said.

Gordon reportedly was home alone at the time of the attack. His wife, Valerie Jean Gordon, told police she had stayed the night with her mother across town. She returned about 7 a.m. to find her husband with a head injury and unresponsive and she called 9-1-1.

The home is in a quiet neighborhood of older but well-kept properties adjacent to the west city limits. Gordon ran an independent photography business out of his garage.

Mrs. Gordon reported that the rear door to her home was unlocked when she arrived and a rear door glass has been broken. Police have not speculated about a motive for the attack. An inventory of the property was being taken to determine if anything of value was missing.

There. That would give web-savvy readers more info than they'd pick up on local radio and cable Channel Six until the full story came out in the morning. *But I'll be damned if I'll pose if front of the crime scene and do one of those hokey talking-head promos.* "*Full details on I'mwitless News at six and eleven.*" *What bullshit.*

"Andrews!" Jerry's basso boomed. "Whattaya got? I need a couple grafs for the website."

"Already in your queue, boss."

"Oh -- uh, good," was the only reply. *Did I hear a backhanded thanks? The old man must be getting soft.*

***

The computer archive of previous *Chronicle* articles provided additional details to enrich the story once the police report was complete.

Stanley Gordon was an Ohio native who had come to Kenton some 15 years before as manager of PixQuik, a strip mall retailer of cameras, photo supplies and film developing and printing. A couple more business items showed his transition to a photography business of his own. A social item showed that two years after arriving in town he had become engaged to and then married the former Valerie Jean Blaine, a Kenton High graduate who at the time was employed as a dental hygienist with Dr. Howard Schmidt. Apparently she still was because a year old brief reported her being a monthly nominee for the Chamber of Commerce annual Good Citizen award for her volunteer work with the Dental Society's free exams at local schools. From their graduation dates, it appeared Stanley was two years older.

A check of past city directories indicated the couple had lived in the same house for at least 10 years, although the photography business had moved to the residence only three years ago. *Probably about the same time the garage was added. The photo business must have picked up. Or maybe dental hygiene pays a lot more than I thought.*

Chapter 5

"Man murdered in home invasion" screamed the banner headline over my story on the next morning's front page. I had argued against use of the *"home invasion"* claim in the headline because, while police had theorized that might be the case, they hadn't stated it categorically. Using it un-attributed meant *The Chronicle* was saying it – and by implication I was saying it.

As the paper's new top editor, however, Goldman insisted on reviewing all Page One stories and headlines. She thought "home invasion" was more of a grabber to lead the paper than "westside home." Only a fourth of city residents lived on the west side, she argued, but all readers have a home. *Ah, preying on the fear factor. So much for factuality.*

I admit my relationship with Goldman was an uneasy one. The short, dark-haired news executive was pleasant enough, and attractive in an aloof, austere way. But she had this sort of frantic energy, reflected from her gray eyes that often bored into her staffers as if endowed with x-ray vision. She seemed to genuinely appreciate my work. But her goals often seemed, if not opposite, at least perpendicular to mine. My focus was on fast, factual and accurate reporting. So far, she appeared to be fixated mainly on sexing up the paper with huge photos and sensational headlines to help meet her corporate bosses' ambitious circulation goals.

The Chronicle is now owned by Mega Media, a conglomerate that bought the paper some two years ago from long-time publisher Bill Graham. I vividly recall the day the sale was announced. Mega's matching Gulfstreams swooped into our little airport and parked dramatically nose to nose on the tarmac. You'd have thought they were royalty as the entourage descended the steps and ducked into limos for the drive to the paper.

So to me, Goldman appeared to be a corporate gypsy, a new breed who, in contrast to the relaxed attire of traditional newsrooms, were crisply coifed and dressed managers seemingly more at home in their offices poring over budget spreadsheets than in the hurly-burly of newsrooms. Two years my junior, she already had worked at five papers before *The Chronicle*. She hadn't spent more than two years at any one -- barely enough time to learn the street names, let alone how a town really worked.

Goldman was named top editor of the paper a year ago. Old man Graham had stayed on for a year of transition, and then he announced his retirement as editor and publisher and that his son, W. Damron Graham, would be succeeding him as publisher. That made room for an editor, and Goldman transferred in from Mega's corporate news staff.

Not that *The Chronicle* couldn't use an infusion of new ideas to compensate for Jerry's inherent inertia and lack of imagination. But of the two, I felt more comfortable with and confident in the old-school motivations of my immediate boss.

Jerry and I agreed on a follow-up for the next day, a Wednesday, but there was a nagging lack of new information. The story was pretty much summarized in the first paragraph: "Kenton police are still seeking a motive and the identity of the person or persons who killed a westside man in his home late Sunday."

Danny had confirmed for me off the record that detectives of her department were literally clueless about why Gordon had been killed. An inventory of the home and photo studio had found nothing missing. Nor had they found anything that approximated a weapon that might have caused Gordon's fatal injuries. And that invoked the entire range of possibilities: The killer could be a total stranger committing a random homicide – or, someone driven by something far more personal. The problem with the latter speculation, however, was that neither the widow nor the police could come up with any cause for a killing of passion. The victim had lived a relatively quiet life outside of the public eye, and police interviews had determined he had no recent disagreements or confrontations with neighbors or customers of his photo business.

I was again kicked back at my desk, staring at the ceiling and deep in thought when my field of vision was interrupted by a quizzical tilting of the head of the blonde whose desk abutted mine. "Hey, anybody home in there? Where have you been?"

"Oh -- oh, just thinking about where to go on this murder."

"You need any help? I'm on a lull between stories – waiting for call-backs."

The thought of turning Gee Whiz Jermaine loose on a murder story was faintly amusing. A hint of a smile rippled across my lips, but I was relieved she seemed not to notice. Then inspiration seized me.

"You know what you *can* do for me? Won't take but a few minutes. Can you go down to the county health department and get a copy of a death certificate? Raymond Owens."

"But that's not the name of the murder victim, is it?"

"No, but it's another story I'm working on. It'd be really helpful to me while I try to sort out where to go next on this homicide."

"Oh, sure," she said, grabbing her shoulder bag and heading for the door. Fifteen seconds later she was back. "Health department? Where is that?"

"*County* health department? Courthouse?" I answered.

"Oh, yeah," she said, shooting herself in the head with her cocked thumb and forefinger.

Stroke of genius. Get her out of the office, give her some exposure to real news gathering, maybe even get some brownie points with Goldman for "mentoring" the rookie. And – did I mention -- get her out of the office?

Resuming my deliberations, something in the back of my mind tickled my curiosity about the Gordons.

I was still trying to define that thought when Jeni returned from the courthouse with a triumphant smile. "Hey, that was fun."

"Good. How'd it go?"

She pulled a photocopy of Raymond Owens's death certificate from her shoulder bag and waved it as if she'd just won a Pulitzer Prize.

"No problem – after I told them it was for you. Guess they don't want to give these out to just anyone."

"First lesson in covering government. To bureaucrats, paperwork is power. Most guard it jealously. That's why we need laws assuring access to public records."

The death certificate explanation of cause for the passing of Raymond Joseph Owens was terse: "massive cerebral hemorrhage." Not much doubt there. Stroke. Pretty cut and dried. But that wouldn't make it any easier to return the call to Teresa Owens.

When I looked up Jeni was still standing there expectantly. I mentally slapped myself in the forehead and said, "Uh, thanks, Jeni. Good job. This helps." Dodging her suggestion we go out for lunch, I did accept her offer to bring me back a sandwich.

I returned to wondering about Stanley and Valerie Gordon. *When in doubt, lean on your friends.* I decided to call a long-time ally of the paper and professional photographer who occasionally had done freelance work for *The Chronicle.* Rudy Lipscomb had been a combat photographer toward the end of Vietnam and returned to his home town to build Kenton's most successful photography business.

"Hey, Rudy, Brock here."

"Hello, Brock. To what do I owe the honor of a call from the Fourth Estate?"

"No honor, just a question."

"Shoot. You're in luck. I feel real smart today."

"What can you tell me about Stanley Gordon? Business-wise.

Personal-wise."

"Stan? Yeah, too bad about him. Jeez, you never know do you? Here one day, then …. But, to your questions. Decent photographer. But -- not to speak ill of the dead -- people skills left something to be desired. Started out okay, even for a time had a studio downtown. Family portraits, wedding photos, some commercial stuff. But his business sort of withered on the vine."

"Why was that?"

"What little I heard – from former customers -- was he was hard to get along with – didn't like to take suggestions from his clients. Which is hard to do when they're paying the bills. Wanted to do his thing and be left alone. Word got around, I guess."

"But he still had a studio at his home."

"Yeah, I'm not saying he couldn't support himself. He did get work – family stuff, anniversaries, plus corporate jobs, executive portraits, catalog, brochure and website stills -- that sort of thing. He just wasn't a major player, that's all."

Hmm, must've been very frugal to pay for all those additions and remodeling.

"Anything else? Personal stuff?"

"Don't know much about him. But Valerie is a local girl – classmate at Kenton High with one of my daughters. Worked hard in school, won a scholarship to the community college and got herself an education."

"They have any kids?"

"Not that I know of."

"They ever win the lottery, get a big inheritance or anything?"

"You'd have heard about the lottery. But inheritance? Again, don't know about him, but her definitely not. Raised by her mom -- dirt poor."

"What's she like?"

"I know her only from my dental checkups. Kind of a mousy thing. Very pleasant and soft spoken. But not hard to look at from the dentist's chair – if you know what I mean."

I didn't know what Rudy meant – at least until I looked more closely at the archive photo. *Rudy, you horny old goat.*

Valerie Gordon's image in the photo of her dental society volunteer role was pretty much as Rudy described, with one exception. Something I had totally missed as she was being grilled by the cops. As she leaned over a kindergarten student to check the child's teeth, the otherwise demure woman bore a bodice-full. *Maybe I should start getting my teeth cleaned more often.*

Chapter 6

I was confident I'd gotten all there was from the police report for my initial story on Raymond Owens's accident. But to at least give lip service to his widow's request, between bites of the reuben Jermaine had brought me I left messages for both the Wilkes County sheriff's deputy who investigated the accident and the paramedic who took Owens to the hospital.

When they returned the calls, the deputy's report was as I remembered it. The paramedic was no help either but more voluble in his response. Although patient records were private, the ambulance outfit was a private contractor for the county and hence more PR conscious than a public agency. Plus the paramedic liked to talk about his job. He confirmed that, while the injured man had shown no outward sign of head trauma, concussion was suspected. "He was bound to have been banged around pretty bad when thrown from the truck," he said. "Sometimes these things don't show up immediately."

One more call to make – cantankerous coroner Buster Bradshaw. Never the easiest guy to talk to, Buster proudly lived up to his name by ball-busting anyone he deemed his inferior, which included reporters. Although it was the coroner's legal responsibility to investigate all deaths from accidents or violent means, he didn't take kindly to questions about how he did his job.

"Whydya wanna know?" he demanded in response to my "just checking" query about Owens's cause of death.

"Because, Buster, the widow and her kids were convinced their old man was getting better. Maybe somebody missed something that should've been caught?"

"What, they talkin' lawsuit, I suppose?"

"No, not that I know of. They're just pretty distraught and trying to understand. They needed some hand-holding. I guess mine was the nearest hand."

"Well, you can set their minds at ease. Lotsa times blood vessels are weakened by the trauma of an accident and give way later. Delayed rupture in the brain. I'd say that's probably what happened with Owens and it killed him."

"*You'd* say? Wasn't there an autopsy?"

"Nope, didn't see the need for one. They're optional – and expensive. Doctors, ya know."

That made me roll my eyes and shake my head. Indiana coroners are elected officials, and in most counties it's rarely a physician. More often than not it's a politics-minded mortician like Buster.

"Besides," the undertaker said, "the guy had been badly injured and the hospital diagnosed it as a massive brain hemorrhage. Good enough for me."

"What happens if what's good enough for the coroner isn't good enough for the family? What are their options?"

"Well, goddam it, I suppose people could exhume the friggin body to try to prove me and the hospital wrong."

"Hey, Buster, take it easy. I'm just asking. It's my job, you know?"

"Yeah --sure. I guess. But, anyway it's too late for that now."

"Why's that?"

"Bradshaw & Sons didn't handle the funeral arrangements, but if I recall what I read in your paper, Raymond Owens was going to be cremated."

***

Mercifully, the Owens home had an answering machine, and I hoped the message I left sounded sympathetic. "Hello, Mrs. Owens. This is Brock Andrews at *The Chronicle*. As you requested, I've checked again with the ambulance service, sheriff and coroner and they all say there's no reason to change their earlier conclusions. I hope this provides the closure that you're looking for."

I was not, however, going to get off that easily. Hours later, sitting at my desk pondering whether to shop for groceries or carry home some Chinese for supper, Raymond Owens's daughter phoned to renew her family's request.

"Thank you, Mr. Andrews, for following up with us. We appreciate your efforts. But did you check with the hospital? We've asked for details, but we just keep getting the same story. I think they're tired of hearing from us."

Maybe because that's all there is? I thought, but said, "No, honestly I didn't. Both the death certificate and the coroner's office confirm that the cause of death was cerebral hemorrhage."

"But can you double-check with the hospital? They're not returning our calls anymore."

"The coroner based his report on the hospital's conclusions. I think that's where it's got to stand."

Only soft breathing came from the other end of the line, and then finally, "Well, thank you again."

Teresa Owens Wilkerson clearly wasn't happy with the result of my inquiry, and I suppose I couldn't blame her, but there was scant else I could do. I must have said that out loud, because Jermaine, who had been quietly clicking away at her keyboard, said, "What?"

"Oh, nothing. Just another dissatisfied customer." I explained to her the significance of the errand she had run earlier in the day. "Family's naturally upset. Can't say I blame them. Must be tough to lose someone you almost lost and then thought had pulled through."

"Yeah, that's terrible. You know, I've got a friend in PR at the hospital. Maybe she could find out something to get the family off your back."

"They've already gone the hospital route and still aren't satisfied. But thanks; I'm done chasing this one."

"Well, okay. But -- hey, how about some Chinese later?"

"Just thinking about that myself," I said and immediately regretted my candor. My quiet dinner alone was at risk.

"You been to the new Great Wall buffet?" she asked.

"Yeah, but actually Mr. Wong's is my favorite," I said, hoping she'd take the hint and go her own way.

"Oh, I like that one too. I'll meet you there. Six o'clock?"

Her maroon Corolla pulled into the crowded parking lot just seconds behind my Camaro.

Once seated, she said, "I want you to know I appreciate your letting me help you today. I mean, I'm not dumb, I know it was just a go-fer errand, and maybe you were just testing me – or getting me out of your hair. But I also know I've got a lot to learn about real journalism."

Suppressing a strange urge to confess, I just nodded and said, "Hey, you're a smart woman. You'll do fine. It'll just take some time to pick up on sources and all."

The waitress brought hot tea and we ordered – hot and sour soup and General Tso's chicken for me, extra spicy, and egg drop soup and cashew chicken for her. Alone again and crunching on a crisp cheese-stuffed wonton, she laughed, "Well, at least I learned about death certificates – and where the health department is."

"Look, Jeni, you strike me as the kind of woman who knows what she wants and will figure out how to get it. What's the cliché nowadays? Strong, smart and bold?"

"That's what they always told us at the girls club," she laughed.

"Well, my main advice is to learn all you can while you're here, because the next step up you'll be expected to know it already along with everyone else."

"I appreciate that. I also learned something today about reader relations. You went beyond the call to try to help the Owens family. Even though they're disappointed with the results, I bet they're grateful for your being so considerate."

"Yeah, maybe. Hard to tell. Most times they just forget or take it for granted. Sometimes remembrance of a good deed will come back years later. Works both ways."

"Well, to show you how grateful I am, after we talked this afternoon I called my friend Angie. She's community relations assistant at Wilkes Memorial. She was finishing up undergrad at IU when I was working on my master's. I thought maybe she could give you some comforting platitudes to get back to the Owens family with."

Only her obvious enthusiasm quelled my initial urge to tell her to mind her own business. But I'd opened the door to my beat by asking her to get the death certificate. Instead, I said, "I'll bet that was enlightening. Memorial isn't exactly a model of media cooperation."

"Well, maybe this time it'll be different."

"And your friend said?"

"That's the strange thing. She didn't know anything specific but she said it was weird – her word. She'd heard the family had been pestering the staff about the cause of death. And when she asked her boss about it, she was basically told the subject is off limits. All questions are being referred to the hospital's president."

Chapter 7

Angela Lawrence was a relative newcomer to her community relations position at Wilkes Memorial, but she knew her place. If her boss, Ruth Johnson, said a subject was closed, it wasn't likely to be career enhancing to defy her wishes.

The massive hospital served a multi-county area of central Indiana and Angela felt privileged to work there right out of college. She held her boss in something approaching awe. As the director of community relations and development, Johnson was the very image of the professional woman Angela aspired to become. Trim, attractive, confident and highly involved in the community, Johnson had recently been recognized by the Chamber of Commerce as one of the local Women of Distinction. And Johnson did report directly to the hospital's chief executive. If James M. Blanchard Sr. ruled an issue was his province, so be it.

But now Angela was caught in a dilemma. While Johnson made the decisions, as media relations assistant Angela was responsible for the actual delivery of information about the hospital to the public via the media. And her new best friend in town, Jeni Jermaine, had made a specific inquiry about a recent death at the hospital.

The two didn't know each other all that well, but as fellow IU grads they had immediately formed a bond when Jeni showed up at Angela's hometown paper. And it had been a kick for her to help the two-year-older Jeni with some contacts at the hospital for a couple features.

Like Johnson, Jeni embodied everything Angela envied -- tall, athletic, attractive and self-confident, in contrast to Angie who was short and constantly at war with her weight and innate self-consciousness.

Now, while a newbie, Angela was smart enough to know that newspaper reporters don't have time for idle questions. She needed to let her boss know.

"Uh, Ruth, do you have a minute?" she asked as she stood poised in the director's doorway.

"Sure, Angie. What is it?"

"Well, you know that subject you said the other day had to be referred to Mr. Blanchard?"

"Yes?" Johnson said, lifting her eyes from the papers on her desk to meet her assistant's. "What about it?"

"I got a call yesterday from a reporter at *The Chronicle.* Jeni Jermaine? She said she was helping their police reporter follow up on the death of a man named Raymond Owens."

Now Johnson's eyes blinked wide. "What did you tell her?"

"Just -- just what you said. Questions were being referred to Mr. Blanchard."

"Oh, my."

"What? Did I do something wrong?"

"No. No. It's okay. It's just that this obviously is something very sensitive. In all my years of working with Jim he has never taken over media relations, even on rate increases or asking the county to pay for our care of indigents.

"We have to be careful with *The Chronicle.* The family is being difficult -- out of grief, I'm sure, which is understandable. But people under stress sometimes jump to conclusions and say things that are untrue but damaging to others. We have to think about the hospital's reputation."

"Yeah, I can see that. Okay. Well, that's what I did."

Chapter 8

I returned to the office the next morning to find a white letter-size envelope on my desk with my name printed on it in red pencil. Inside was a third of a sheet of lined notebook paper. Scrawled in block capitals in red was: RE: STANLEY GORDON – CHERCHEZ LA FEMME.

"Hey, Jermaine," I said. "You take French? Your name's French isn't it? What's this mean? Something like 'beware of the woman?'" I shoved the piece of paper across to her.

"No, that's too loose a translation. Actually it means look for -- or seek -- the woman."

"So, someone's trying to tell us that a woman killed Gordon?"

"Or that there's a woman behind it – maybe as the instigator – or cause. Like maybe a love triangle?"

"I dunno. From what I've seen, Valerie Gordon doesn't seem like the kind to excite murderous impulses. Or to hire someone to kill her husband."

"Wouldn't have to be the wife, would it? Maybe Mr. Gordon was sporting around with another woman – like, someone else's wife?"

"Or maybe," I mused, "none of the above and this little slip of paper is just meant as a diversion by the real killer. Or more likely just some prankster yanking our chain."

"What are you going to do with it? Show it to the cops?"

"Probably should." I turned my chair around and shouted across the newsroom. "Hey, anybody see who dropped this envelope on my desk?" Half a dozen heads turned and stared blankly with shrugs or head shakes of denial.

"Nobody's been here since I arrived," Jeni said. "Maybe it

was just shoved through the mail slot downstairs and whoever found it delivered it to you."

"Probably. It's so vague I'm not sure the cops will be interested, but maybe they can check it for fingerprints. I just happen to know exactly who to take it to."

***

"Dammit, Brock," Danny said when I handed her the envelope across the table at Applebees. "Once you saw what it was you shouldn't have handled it."

"Yeah – I know -- sorry. But I didn't know what it was at first. And it maybe nothing. I just thought you might get some brownie points with the chief for coming up with a possible clue."

"Well, I can use all the points I can score, but I think you're right. This is probably too generic to be of much help to the detectives. We always know there's the possibility of a woman being involved somehow – especially the wife. Unless there are some usable prints that lead to the culprit. But as you say, it could be just a prank."

"Well, for what it's worth, it's in your hands now. Speaking of the wife, your folks come up with anything that might seem unusual? Like their house? Seemed pretty fancy to me given their apparent earning power."

"Yeah, we noticed that, too. But you can't tell how people spend their money. With no kids, and no apparently lavish lifestyle – cars, vacations, etcetera -- maybe they just plowed it all into their home."

I was skeptical. "How do you know about their vacations?"

"Well, to start, we asked" she said, tilting her head and raising her eyebrows as if to say "duh." "Where had they traveled? And if they had met anyone who might be inclined toward violence. Plus, there were no pictures around to indicate they'd been to Tahiti, wherever. Plus, I'm sure the detectives have been checking bank and credit card statements to verify, or see any other unusual spending pattern."

"And the wheels?"

"His was a four-year-old Dodge minivan – registered to the business. Hers is a Chrysler Sebring convertible – even older vintage."

We were seated opposite each other in a back booth at Applebees, sipping iced teas while waiting for our salads. Hers was the half-size oriental chicken and mine the full size southwestern. Unless business intervened, it was a weekly ritual after our Thursday night workouts at Fitness First. Hers was a session on the elliptical machine followed by a weight circuit. I lifted free weights – as much as allowed by the separated shoulder that had sidelined me as a freshman walk-on wide receiver at IU. Afterwards I'd worked up a mighty sweat in a pickup basketball game. We caught showers at the gym and met for a light dinner.

We'd been seeing each other – almost exclusively -- for nearly three years. The cop and I had gotten to know each other when our schedules collided at late night accident and crime scenes. We both had lost our first spouses – mine to a car accident and hers to war. No children. We agreed we had had ideal mates, so neither of us had been in any hurry to risk disappointment in a second marriage. Compatible companionship had given way to close friendship and then to benefit of consort. But we recently had talked about more – or at least I had.

I ran through with her the possible "la femme" scenarios I had discussed with Jeni.

"That about covers the range of possibilities," she said. And then, "You like this girl?"

"Who, Jermaine? Jen-eye?" I spelled it out with an extra emphasis on the "i."

"Yeah, Jen-eye. You seem to talk a lot about her."

"Well, that's pretty hard to avoid when she's plunked right across from me and I'm supposed to be her – *men*-tor. She's okay. Green, but smart. She'll be good someday. Why, do I sense a touch of jealousy?"

"Jealous? Moi? Of practically a teen-ager? C'mon."

"Well, you needn't worry. She's not my type. You are. You know I'm *very* attracted to *older* women. Well – at least one."

"Yeah, I've sort of noticed. You coming over tonight?"

"I dunno. Maybe I *should* go back to the office."

"Up to you."

"Well, now that you asked."

Chapter 9

James Blanchard was fiftyish, a tall, handsome man but balding and with a good start on a case of beergutitis. He self-consciously pulled his suit jacket closed over his girth and cleared his throat as he appeared at Angela's open doorway.

"Uh – Miss Lawrence – Angela. I need to speak with you for a moment."

Uh-oh, Angela thought. *Am I in trouble?* Blanchard was friendly but had seldom said more than hello to her directly, usually going through her boss. There had been rumors of staff cutbacks, and Blanchard's appearance at her door couldn't be good news.

"Uh -- of course, Mr. Blanchard. What – what can I do for you?"

He paused while he fixed her with a blue-eyed stare. "I understand from Ruth that you've had an inquiry from *The Chronicle?*"

"Yes -- yes, from Jeni Jermaine."

"Please tell me what she said."

"She's working on a follow-up to the death of a man named Raymond Owens. But I told her she had to speak with you – just as Ruth said."

"Good, good. You did the right thing." His voice was reassuring but his smile was tight. "Did she say what kind of follow-up?"

"No, just that she was helping their police reporter, Brock Andrews, look into the cause of death for the family."

"Well, it's understandable when some people have trouble accepting loss of a loved one. But there's no reason for us to get dragged into that. If they call again, just be sure to transfer them directly to me."

Chapter 10

"Mr. Blanchard, this is Brock Andrews at *The Chronicle,*" I said into the phone.

"Uh – yes, Brock. Good to hear from you. It's been quite a while."

"Yeah, it has. Say, I'm doing a courtesy for the family of Raymond Owens. They claim my story was inaccurate about his death being from injuries suffered in his truck crash. So I'm just following up and was told I need to speak with you."

"Oh, of course. Yes, well, I assume you've talked with them? As I'm sure you have sensed the family is, understandably, very distressed over the loss of their husband and father. They have been insistent in their communication with Memorial staff that something other than his accident injuries must have caused Mr. Owens's death."

"And *was* there anything else that contributed?"

"No." He paused, and then said, "Not at all. But the family has had such difficulty accepting his passing that they've made some very rash statements – as if the hospital were at fault. The need to find someone to blame is not all that unusual – especially after it seemed he was getting better. But we take any such assertions very seriously. That's why I've asked for any questions to be directed to me."

"Sure, I can see that. So there was nothing untoward about Mr. Owens's cause of death?"

"No, I can assure you I've looked into it personally. Mr. Owens died of a massive cerebral hemorrhage as a delayed result of his traffic accident."

"Well, I appreciate that confirmation. Thank you for your time." We said goodbye and hung up. I looked across the desks at

Jeni and said, "You heard?"

"Yeah, You gonna get back to the family?"

"Nah, this about covers it. I think I'll leave well enough alone. It does seem a bit odd that a call from the paper gets bounced to the CEO of the hospital. But maybe that's to their credit -- that they take such things seriously. The Owenses will just have to let time heal their hurt."

***

Two weejs since Stanley Gordon's slaying, police still had no clues to why he was killed or who might have done it. After daily follow-up stories the first week, I was now doing a weekly piece on police progress. Or non-progress -- just more of the same – a brief recounting of the crime and more confident proclamations from KPD Police Chief Ernie Caldwell. The cops were still sifting through all available information about the victim, his business and personal life and expected to have a break in the case soon.

The vacuum of news, however, had to be filled with something and the rumor mill obliged. As we lay together in her bed after our weekly workouts – before and after Applebees – Danny and I went through the latest.

"My mom says she heard at the beauty parlor that Gordon was gay and was probably done in by his male lover when he refused to leave his wife," Danny said.

"Yeah? Well, our grapevine obviously is of the opposite gender, because the barber shop skinny is that it was the wife who's gay and the murderer was her *lesbian* lover because Mrs. Gordon wouldn't leave her husband – or he wouldn't let her go."

We laughed and I asked, "Was there really any evidence at the home that either one of them went the other way?"

"Detectives don't tell me everything. But not that I've heard. No sex toys of either gender, just condoms and lubricant in the night stand. Birth control pills in the medicine cabinet."

That caused me to do a double take. "Condoms *and* birth control pills?"

"Can't be too careful, I guess. They probably didn't want to start having kids at their age."

I shook my head. "The rumor mill in this town is really amazing. It just churns on and on. Can't people just let anyone be straight anymore? Guess hetero isn't sexy enough."

As usual, she had the last word. "Oh, yeah? Haven't heard you complain."

"Speaking of kids, you given it any more thought?"

"What, giving birth or adopting?"

"Well, yeah -- that -- and us."

"You think I need *you* to have a baby?" She laughed and jabbed me in the ribs as she swung her leg over and straddled me.

"No," I said, her cobalt eyes playfully inches from mine. "Not to have one – but maybe to raise one."

"You're sweet," she laughed again. "If I ever decide to have a baby, I'll make sure you're the father."

"I'm serious, Danny. You know I love you. And neither of us is getting any younger."

Her expression darkened. "I don't need you to remind me of that." Her marriage to another cop had ended with his death with the National Guard in Iraq nearly five years ago. She is now 32, which by today's standards isn't old for starting a family. But with me four years older, I don't want to look like my kid's grandfather when he – or she – enters high school.

I lifted her by the shoulders. "Look, we've talked about it a hundred times. Don't you think it's time to act?" I'd been single since my wife and unborn child died when a drunk driver rammed them head-on. We had been married only three years and that was over eight years ago. Understanding of our mutual loss was partly what had drawn Danny and me even closer.

"I know you love me. And I love you too. You know that. I'm getting there, but I'd like to make detective first. Just give me a little more time," she said.

"Well, just so you know. I'm ready any time."

She wriggled her hips against me and said, "Yeah, I can tell."

Chapter 11

"You folks up there better get your bosses to come clean or you got a load of trouble comin' your way," the muffled and gravelly male voice said into Angela's ear. She was checking the community relations department's overnight phone messages. "Cain't hide somethin' like that very long."

Calls came in after hours almost every day, from news media, hospital donors, one of the hundreds of volunteers, or occasionally the odd patient complaint that got misrouted to her instead of to the patient relations rep. Angela would jot on pink call slips the topics, the callers' names and return numbers and forward to her boss those that needed her attention.

This one, however, she hesitated to pass on. *Hide what? The caller left no name, no number. And, maddeningly, no specifics. The voice was unnaturally husky – obviously to disguise his identity. And what did it mean, "You guys up there." Up where?*

As a word person, she was a confirmed non-techie. Since coming to Memorial she had decided it was better to play dumb about such things and get the geeks in IT to earn their keep. Besides, calling for help with computer reboots and copier failures gave her an excuse to talk with Russell Cunningham, the hunk assistant in the IT department who she thought was anything but a geek. *He is such a flirt.* They hadn't dated yet, but she knew he was single. *A girl can hope.*

"Hi, Russ. This is Angie. Can you do me a *big* favor?"

"Hey, for you, sweet cakes, anything. You name it."

He called all the single women *sweet cakes*, and some of the married ones too. *A bit sexist*, she thought. *But he is so cute, nobody's going to think harassment.* Perhaps least of all Angela who hadn't had a real date since returning to her hometown after IU graduation. She knew she shouldn't, but she secretly savored the young man's uninvited familiarity, even if it was spread indiscriminately across the female staff..

"Could you run the phone log on incoming calls to our department from closing time last night to eight this morning?"

"Sure, won't take but a few minutes. What do I get for my trouble?"

"We'll talk about that some other time." She enjoyed the chance to be a tease.

An hour later, when she returned from her daily rounds among the hospital's departments, she found the log on her desk. The mysterious voice mail had been the last one received. But when she zoomed to the bottom of the list, something was wrong. The last number on the log was one left by the next to last caller.

She punched in Russ's number again. "Hey, Russ, got a problem. I've accounted for all the numbers from voice mails, but the last one before I came in this morning isn't there."

"What time did it come in? I ran the list from 5 p.m. to 8 a.m."

"Three-thirty."

"Hmm." He paused a moment and then said, "Oh, yeah. That's not a problem. The system tracks only calls from outside lines. Your caller must have been inside the hospital."

Inside the hospital? The light dawned. *"Up there," the guy said.* She mentally ticked off the hospital layout. *First floor is reception, gift shop, security, emergency, admitting and outpatient services. Admin and accounting, radiology and pathology are on two. Surgery, ICU, and general medical/surgical patient rooms on three, obstetrics, pediatrics and NICU are on four. The basement! Everything is "up" from there.*

Angela wasn't fond of going into Memorial's basement aside from the cafeteria that lay just outside the elevator. Other than her orientation tour she had resisted venturing into the long dark corridors that seemed like catacombs: kitchen, mechanical rooms, storage, laundry, and maintenance and janitorial staff.

She had, however, befriended night janitor Oren Williams. He was black and nearly toothless, of indeterminate age and even less certain education. But he was a hard and steady worker and always had a friendly greeting. He was legendary around the hospital for looking after the female employees that he called "my ladies." More than once after late nights at work he had escorted "Miss Angie" across the shadowy parking lot to her car. Whatever his limitations, he was unfailingly kind and courteous and regarded by many as a substitute father.

To Angela, he was sweet and always knocked softly at her door when she worked nights. "I don't want to startle you, miss," he said the first time they'd met. "But I has to empty your wastebasket if you don' mind." He welcomed her to Memorial, offered to help her with anything she needed, and thereafter always had something nice to say. How was she feeling, how was she getting along, or offering her a compliment. "That's a mighty pretty outfit you got on today, Miss," he'd often say. He was without a doubt the nicest person she'd met in a uniformly friendly workplace.

Could the caller have been Oren? He doesn't have the best grammar, and he has a deep voice, and maybe if he intentionally muffled it, he could sound like that. She made a mental note to speak to him that evening when he came in. But then, of all times, an hour before quitting time she got a call from Russ.

"Hey, sweet cakes. A couple of us are going for beers at that new microbrewery. You wanna join us?" She couldn't turn down an invitation like that. She'd catch Oren tomorrow.

Chapter 12

Danny plopped a thick manila envelope onto her kitchen table in front of me. "I shouldn't really have these, but I persuaded one of the detectives to let me review them overnight. He knows I'm studying for the exam, so he figured he'd be nice to me."

"I hope that's the only reason."

"Now who's jealous?"

"Damn right. I've seen the way your fellow officers look at you."

"Well, no need to worry. I only have eyes for you."

"So the song goes. But you mean you have eyes *only* for me. Others might have eyes for me, too."

"You wish," she said with that playful sideways glance that drives me crazy. "Whatever. But will you please stop correcting my grammar?"

"Just thinking of your advancement," I said. "The future chief of police needs to be a model to the department and an example for the youth of our community."

"I don't think there's any danger of me becoming chief."

"Actually, it's *my* becoming. Possessive."

"Oh, give me a break already. I just want to pass the detective exam."

Danny was two courses shy of completing her masters in criminal justice from ISU. She'd joined her hometown department right out of undergrad and desperately wanted to ascend to detective.

"You really sure you want that? You've enjoyed the variety of patrol so much. And probably meet a better class of people than the detectives do."

"Yeah, that's true," she said. "But investigation is where the action is — more skull work, less sitting on your butt in a car."

"And fewer doughnuts to go to your …."

"Ha, ha. Haven't heard you complain."

"And you won't either. As butts go, yours is *very* nice."

"Like, you're an authority?"

"In all modesty, I've seen my share." Now, I know when a topic is spinning out of control, so I said, "But, I hasten to add, yours is not only gorgeous, but the only one I'm interested in."

"Well, that's a relief – I *guess*. But can we get off the subject of my behind and back on *my* becoming a detective?"

I raised my hands in surrender. "Well, since you insist."

"Actually, there's less danger than patrol," she said. "Fewer crime-in-progress calls and hot pursuits -- or domestic fights to break up. Not to mention another five hundred a month. Here, let's have a look at these pictures." She shook out the contents of the envelope.

I had seen only newspaper shots of the Gordon crime scene, shot by Jim Rogers. The police photos were far more complete and graphic. Stanley Gordon's body, in boxers and a tee shirt, lay face up on the floor to the right of his bed. A closeup of the head showed an asymmetrical depression at the left temple. The sheet, blanket and spread were thrown back and the mattress was askew to the left, as I'd seen. After the body was removed, a small dark circle was visible on the carpet, presumably blood where the victim's head had lain. And beyond the bed to the right one of the white bi-fold closet doors hung loose from a single hinge.

"Why's the closet door broken? It must be at least six, eight feet from the bed," I said.

"I don't know. The supposition is that the victim was awakened and when he arose was struck on the head. From the looks of the bedding, though, there might have been a brief struggle. Either the victim or the assailant might have been thrown against the door or the bed. Hard to tell from the physical evidence."

"What's that spot on the door? Victim's blood?"

"I doubt it. There wasn't much bleeding. With a caved in skull death was pretty instantaneous. Maybe just a chip in the paint."

"Any more information on the weapon?"

"Nothing showed up at the scene or a search of the vicinity." She pulled out a stapled sheaf of papers. "The autopsy report says only that death was caused by brain trauma from a blunt object. Something long and thin like a pipe, according to damage to the skull and surrounding flesh. Definitely not as small and defined as a hammer, or as thick as a baseball bat."

We shuffled through the photos several more times until at last she shook her head and scooped them back up into the envelope.

"So, what's all this leave you with?" I asked.

"Not a thing. Certainly nothing to impress them I'm ready for detective."

Chapter 13

"Tomorrow" for Angela faded into a week and, caught up in what she hoped was a developing relationship with her heart-throb from IT, she all but forgot about her mysterious phone call.

Her source, however, was not so inclined.

One morning as she was sorting through the department voice mail, the same raspy voice said, "Patient fell outa the window. He dead. How long that be covered up?"

Oren? Can that be Oren?

She headed to the basement to talk to him, but once in the elevator had to remind herself he didn't come in until the evening. She stopped at 1 instead and headed to Security. The second cutest single guy at Memorial had been two years ahead of her in high school. Willy Bostic, a jock at Kenton High, had gone into the army and become an MP. Now he was deputy chief of security at Memorial. And he was no longer Willy; just a would-be-cool Will.

"Hey, Angie. Good to see you. Comin' to tell me you'll finally go out with me? How about a movie this weekend?"

He'd asked her out several times. But even off duty the guy wore black cargo pants and sleeveless black tee-shirts to show off his muscles and tattoos. His blond hair was buzzed flat on top and cropped close on the sides military style. Too much macho swagger for Angela's taste.

"Well – uh – can't, thanks, but I was kind of hoping you could tell me something. You know – just between you and me?"

"Sure, Angie. Whatever ya wanna know."

"Did someone recently fall out of a window here at Memorial and die?"

"Huh," he scoffed. "Where'd you hear that?"

"Oh, just an anonymous phone call."

"Well, that oughtta tell you something," he said, more loudly than necessary. "Someone just spreading vicious rumors."

The vehemence of his denial made her suspect he wasn't being totally candid. "I notice you didn't say it didn't happen," she said.

"Oh – uh – sorry," he said more softly. "I didn't mean to be so vague. No, nothing to it." He waved his hand dismissively.

This time she was sure he wasn't telling the truth. She kept at him. "Come on, Willy. We've known each other since grade school. You can tell me."

His denials continued until finally she said, "You know, Willy, it's my job. If something might hurt the hospital's public image, I need to know about it – be prepared instead of surprised."

"Look, Angie, I'm sorry. I don't know what more to tell you."

She shook her head, still unconvinced, but there was nothing more to be gained by pushing it. And, she didn't want to have to dodge more overtures for a date.

Chapter 14

Late that afternoon, Jerry called me into Goldman's office.

"Look, Brock," Snyder said. "We've just met with the publisher. He heard you've been doing some digging with the hospital into that traffic death last month. Raymond Owens?"

"Yeah, the family is pretty convinced something happened in the hospital to contribute to the death. Owens seemed to be getting better and then just died." I paused to consider why the sudden interest in what I'd already concluded was a non-story. "What's the publisher got to do with it? It's a dead issue – if you'll forgive the pun."

Goldman said, "Well, I'm glad to hear that. Graham got a call from the CEO of Memorial. He wanted to make sure the hospital's name wasn't going to be dragged by the paper into – in his words - - a needless controversy that has no substance."

Publisher W. Damron Graham. The worthless wastrel son of Old Man Bill Graham. The position of publisher had devolved to the son -- a condition, rumor had it, the old man had insisted on during the sale to give his unevenly motivated son a steady income. The father had been just "Bill" to his employees, but W. Damron insisted on everyone at *The Chronicle* calling him "Mister Graham." That touch of phony formality in a traditionally relaxed newspaper atmosphere was emblematic of the younger Graham's insecurity as publisher. He'd grown up in the business and had done the obligatory one-year tour through each of the departments. As the third generation of his family to inhabit the corner office, young Graham liked the money and the public profile the position gave him. But when he wasn't vacationing in Florida he was usually too busy playing golf, serving on a bevy of nonprofit boards, or seeking favorable coverage for his cronies to pay much attention to the daily operations. Mega Media's unrelenting focus on profits, however, had made him highly sensitive to any controversy that might affect advertising revenues.

Invoking the nickname that irreverent news staffers – well, I -- had pinned to our dilettante publisher, I said, "Well, I trust you told Dam-Gram to tell Blanchard to mind his hospital and leave us to decide whether a report has any substance."

Snyder just scowled at me, but Goldman said. "Now, Brock. Don't get on your high horse. If you think the rumor has no merit there's no reason to get your back up."

I explained my recent conversation with the hospital CEO and said, "I didn't think there *was* any merit to it. But with all the high level attention it's getting, kinda makes you wonder, doesn't it? It does me."

Chapter 15

That same afternoon, Ruth Johnson called Angela into her office. Blanchard was there too.

"Angela," he said, "You've been with us for nearly a year now, and we're very pleased with your performance. We want you to know that."

"Oh, thank you," She blushed at the unexpected praise. "I really enjoy working at Memorial – and Ruth has been wonderful."

"Well – yes -- thank you," Johnson said. "We do make a good team." She paused and looked to her boss who nodded and she continued. "Mr. Blanchard and I have spoken today and we wanted you to know that we appreciate your work. It's not time for your annual review, but this week we'll be putting in a $20 raise in tangible recognition of your progress."

"A *week*?" Angela almost squealed. Johnson smiled and nodded, and Angela said, "Oh – oh, thank you." She was mentally calculating what another thousand dollars a year could mean to her stressed budget and paying off her student loans. Or maybe replacing her clunker Ford Escort.

"We appreciate your loyalty as a member of the Memorial management team," Blanchard said. "If things continue as expected, there could very well be a possibility of greater responsibility."

Sitting in her office hours later, Angela had time to wonder about the timing of her raise. She'd already had her six-month review several months before -- along with a $20 a week raise. And now another $20 on top of that? She felt she had done well, but didn't realize her worth to the hospital had become that well recognized. At length, she concluded, *Whatever. A thousand bucks is a thousand bucks. It's nice to be appreciated.*

She spent the rest of the day burying herself in news releases and planning the annual volunteer recognition banquet. Her return home for the evening, however, was met with a faint uneasiness, a sparse appetite and finding herself too wired for sleep. At 11:30 she headed back to the hospital unsure of why. Something just didn't feel right. By the time she got there she had decided. She headed off in search of Oren.

Chapter 16

At my desk the next morning, a Friday, the nearly blank computer screen stared back at me. So far, I had entered nothing substantial under the column headings on the daily story budget form that Goldman had instituted: "Tomorrow, Next Day, Weekend, Next Week, Long-Term."

Police beats – now more grandly labeled "public safety" -- can be feast or famine. And right now the cupboard was about bare. Aside from the daily grind of minor accidents, fires and petty crime reports I picked up twice a day, city police and fire departments right then were pretty quiet. The same held for sheriff's office and volunteer fire departments out in the county. There were no trials of moment in county courts, and county budget wrangling was months away. That left me temporarily bereft of breaking news and feature ideas, and there wasn't much hanging aside from the stalled Gordon murder investigation.

I was still pissed about Blanchard's going over my head to the publisher, and maybe there was something to the Owens death after all. But I couldn't get a handle on what it might be, or for the moment how to discover it.

The buzz of the phone interrupted my funk.

"Hi, Brad. It's Tommy Wallace."

"Yeah, hi, Tommy. How's it goin' in the world of high powered, overpriced cars?"

Wallace laughed. He was a salesman at the Chevy store and had sold – well, taken the order for -- my new Camaro late last year. "Picking up soon with warmer weather, I hope," Wallace said.

"Well, sorry, but I'm not in the market. You drained my bank account last fall, remember?"

"Yeah, well, that car was made for you. But, say, you got time to meet me for lunch? There's something I need to talk with you about."

"Yeah, what's that?"

"I'd rather not talk about it on the phone. What say I pick you up at 11:30?"

"Sure, Tommy. No problem. I'll be waiting outside."

What in hell can Wallace want? Whatever, there'd better be a story in it to keep Jerry off my back.

***

Wallace's choice of restaurant was far from my favorite – a poorly lit tavern out along a gaudy strip that the car dealers liked to grandiosely refer to as the "auto mall." Pete's Joint was known for its gigantic, greasy hamburger and fries baskets and not infrequent police calls on weekend nights. Fistfights and cuttings were not uncommon. But at noon on weekdays it drew a less violence-prone if no more respectable crowd from the dealerships.

Wallace chose a rear booth and shouted to the bartender orders of beers and the Triple B (Biggie Burger Bundle) before I had a chance to scan the menu for something less likely to trigger an instant coronary.

"Thanks – thanks for seeing me on short notice. I – I need to know this is just between us – okay? Like an anonymous source -- you know?"

I resisted telling him that, since I knew his name, he was no longer anonymous. And so far at least he wasn't a source. "Confidential. Confidential source. Depends on what a source tells me. Like if they just committed an ax murder -- no, I can't promise I won't reveal their name. But, yeah, in general I can say I won't disclose my sources."

"Well, it ain't nothin' I done, so you don't need to worry

about that. But I can't have my name mixed up in it, okay?"

"Mixed up in what?" I said. The beer tasted great.

"Might be nothin' but I been readin' your stories on the murder of that Gordon fella."

"Yeah. So far, Kenton's finest have pretty much drawn a blank."

"Well, again, it might be nothin'. But they might wanna be lookin' at Mrs. Gordon."

I caught my breath mid-sip and had to choke back a mouthful of beer. *The second subrosa reference to a woman connected to the Gordon killing. And this blunt instrument of a car salesman doesn't figure to have written "cherchez la femme."*

"Why do you say that?"

"Again, it might be nothin' but you know she works as an assistant for Dr. Schmidt the dentist."

"Yes, I've heard that."

"Well, pardon the expression, but she's got this great set a knockers, ya know, and she ain't bashful about showin' 'em off." The waitress had arrived, frowned down at both of us, shook her head and slapped the baskets down in front of us.

"So she's proud of her boobs," I said quietly after the waitress departed. "What's that got to do with her husband's murder?"

"Well, one day I was in the chair gettin' my teeth cleaned, ya know, and her top is unbuttoned a couple notches and I'm gettin' an eyeful. She catches me lookin' down her blouse, and I feel like a dumb shit and jerk my head away. But she just kinda smiles and keeps leanin' over me, ya know. And so I continue to enjoy the view and before long she puts her hand on my arm, smiles and says, 'Wanna see more?'"

"No kidding," I said. Tommy was licking his lips like a porn flick was playing behind his eyes. I felt like leaving, but he had driven, so I said, "And you said?"

"Well, I'm as horny as the next guy, but believe it or not I'm a happily married man second time around and I wanna stay that way. So I just shook my head and closed my eyes."

"Yeah, sure you did. And?"

"End of story. I even thought about tellin' the dentist, like that's not the kinda thing oughta go on in a professional office. But then I thought, 'Nah, leave it alone.' She seems like a nice gal and maybe she just liked me – or has one of them hang-ups like -- ya know – showin' herself off?"

"How long ago was this?"

"Oh, it was better'n a year ago."

"Well, have you gone back to the dentist since?"

"Yeah, the wife and kids and me still go to Dr. Schmidt, and it never came up again. I mean, she still has this nice rack, but she has never, ya know, showed 'em like that again. Like I said, she's a nice gal."

"So why are you telling me this now?"

"I dunno. Just thought maybe someone should know. If she still has a problem like that, she coulda come on to the wrong guy. I wouldn't feel right if I didn't say nothin' and it happened again."

There's no accounting for taste -- or for how some women dress nowadays. But something's out of synch here. I've already heard about Valerie Gordon's chair-side skin show from Rudy. Maybe she's just a lousy dresser. Or maybe Tommy's just fantasizing -- wishful thinking. Sitting on your ass waiting for a tire-kicker to come into the dealership be mind-numbing. So maybe he's just getting off putting himself in the middle of a murder case. He doesn't seem like the kind of guy to excite a woman into exposing herself – much less risk her job or marriage. Sure, she was in shock when I saw her at her home, but that mousy middle-aged woman didn't really seem like the exhibitionist type.

I pushed aside my half-eaten greaseburger and fries and shook my head. "Stranger things have happened, I guess. Thanks for the tip. Lunch is on me." I paid the bill and Tommy seemed satisfied he'd done his civic duty.

He dropped me back at the office and I decided that no matter how far-fetched it was, I'd pass it on to Danny when I saw her that night.

***

But Danny called to say she'd volunteered to pull a double shift to fill in for an officer on sick leave. That left me at loose ends for a Friday evening, so I sought action in a roundball game at Fitness First. Afterwards, I accepted the guys' invitation to catch happy hour at The Keg. Considering the lunchtime lipid overdose, I opted for Diet Coke and a chopped salad. Danny would be proud of me. But I drew the line on self-punishment by letting the waitress tempt me into bleu cheese and bacon crumbles.

Eleven o'clock found me back at the office, kicked back in Jerry's absence with my shoes off and feet on top of the desk. I was just pondering whether to turn Jeni loose again on her hospital source when the phone rang.

"Brock? It's me. Oh, thank – thank goodness you're – you're there."

The words were a little indistinct.

"Jeni? Is that you? You okay?"

"No -- not -- not reeeally."

"Where are you?"

"Downtown. The Brass Rail. My friends have left and I need a ride home." But it sounded like "Braa Srail," and "frens haf lef" and "raad hooome," the slur now self-explanatory. "I'm a little – a little drunk."

"Yeah, I can sorta tell. Be right there." My watch said 11:17.

The yuppie bar was less than five minutes from the paper, and when I pulled up to the curb the weightlifter who wore the nametag "GREG Guest Services Manager" (a.k.a. bouncer) eased Jeni into the passenger seat.

"I'm shorta meshed up," she giggled.

"Yes you are. You're not going to hurl or anything are you?" *Not in my new car, dammit.*

"Don' think sooo. I'll be okay in little whaaale. Jush gemme home. But drive – drive schlow, okaaay?"

Five more minutes we were in the parking space outside her apartment, a lower unit of a three-floor brick modern. I helped her from the car grateful for the absence of puke on the carpet. I held her around the waist as she tripped unsteadily to her apartment and propped her against the door while she fumbled through her purse for her keys.

"Gottem," she finally announced, lifting the ring triumphantly and turning to stab at the lock. She missed several tries and I took the keys from her and opened the door. I'd not been in her apartment before and it took a moment balancing her against the door jamb to find the wall switch which lit a table lamp. A sofa and matching armchair faced the door and I walked her to the sofa and let her slide onto the cushions. Whereupon she immediately fell asleep.

I lifted her feet to the couch, slipped off her shoes and, as she snored loudly, covered her with a throw from the armchair.

It had been a long while since I'd nursed a drunk friend, and even longer since I'd needed such assistance myself. But I thought I probably should stay to make sure she wasn't going to vomit and choke herself. I closed the outside door, nestled into the easy chair and ….

I awoke with a start and looked first at the empty couch and then at my watch. Nearly five a.m. Water was running in a back room. "Yuk," she announced, and I could hear her brushing her teeth and spitting into the sink. Then came the whine of a blow dryer.

When she appeared she hugged the door frame, her hair still damp from the shower. She wore only pink bikini panties and matching low-cut lacy bra. Neither afforded much exercise for the imagination. *Yeah, she's stacked all right.*

Her smile in imitation of a movie seductress was slightly unfocused but she was no longer woozy drunk. "I really appreciate your helping me. You want to stay with me?" She held out her hand.

I shook my head and said softly, "Jeni, go get a robe or something on and we can talk."

She stared for a moment as a frown wrinkled her mouth but then did as I'd asked. When she returned her fluffy blue terry robe was loosely tied and she sat languidly on the arm of my chair, careless of her exposure. "Don't you find me attractive?"

"Jeni," I said. It was a struggle to keep my eyes averted, just as I struggled for the words I hated myself for saying. "Jeni, you are a very *beautiful* young woman. But I seldom find drunk women attractive."

Her eyes darted to mine and I couldn't tell whether it was hurt or anger in them, but the glistening soon betrayed her. "I'm not drunk anymore. Don't you want me?"

"If I let myself, I could want you very much. You're desirable as hell – but you obviously know that," I said, avoiding her eyes. She smiled in tight-lipped satisfaction and awkwardly stroked at my hair.

Then, in one of those clumsy moments for which I'm famous in my own mind, I rose from the chair too suddenly and she slid off the arm and plopped on the floor beside me. I cleared the huskiness from my throat to croak, "Dammit, Jeni, this – this isn't the right time. And for us -- there won't *ever* be a right time."

Chapter 17

"What you doin' here so late, Miss?" Oren asked as Angela stopped in the doorway labeled Maintenance. Having combed the floors above looking for him, she finally caught up with him in the basement, mid-way through a sandwich on his lunch break.

"I think I might have a problem, Oren, and I'm hoping you can help me."

"Why, Miss, you knows ah'll do anything ah can for ya," he said, folding his wrinkled hands on top of the table at the center of the large maintenance workshop.

"I – I don't know how to say this," she began, "and – and – I don't want to make you mad at me. But – can I ask you something? Just between us?"

Offering her a benign, almost toothless smile, he said, "Sure, Miss. Whattaya need?"

"Can you tell me -- honestly -- if you've left messages recently on our department voice mail?"

His smile vanished as his wrinkled lips turned downward; he hesitated and then said, "Oh, Miss, you don' wanna go an' ask me that."

"So it *was* you. What did you mean, Oren? What happened? I've got to know."

"Miss, please don' ask me that. I don' wanna git in no trouble."

"You're not going to get into any trouble. This is just between you and me. I promise."

"Well, ah dasn't tell you nuthin', Miss, cuz we was told not to talk 'bout it to nobody."

"Talk about what, Oren? Please, I've got to know. It's very important – for the good of the hospital – and for me."

He hesitated, lowered his head and wrung his hands for a long moment before speaking. "Awright, Miss, I kin tell ya, but ya gotta promise not to let on how ya heerd it."

"I won't, Oren. I won't tell anyone you told me. You know you can trust me."

"Yes, Miss, ah bleeve ah can."

"Go ahead. I promise no one will know I heard it from you."

"'Bout tree weeks ago it was, Miss. Bout 2 a.m. in the moanin'. Security fella calls me to that patio in back and tells me sweep up glass from winnow was broke out. An' den wash down the seement. An den nex day the day crew, dey haf to help put new winnow on Flo' Tree."

"Third floor. Hmm, but a broken window doesn't mean someone fell out," Angela said.

"No, it don't, Miss. But patient in that room weren't there no mo, and paper say he die. An' when we ask, we told nothin' happen. An' not say nothin' 'bout it."

"Who told you that?"

"That big numma two security fella. An' ya don' argue wit him."

"And it was you who left messages on my phone."

"Yes, Miss. Ah din't know it were gonna be you hear it. Don' want cause no trouble fer you, neither, Miss. But ah knows there's gonna be trouble. Cain't keep no secret like that. Not fer long, no how."

Angela reached across the janitor's desk and squeezed his huge hands between hers. "Thank you for telling me this, Oren. I don't know how, but I've got to get to the bottom of this." She walked to the door and then turned back and said, "No one will hear it from me that we've talked about this."

She'd have to think carefully about whom to talk to next, but that would have to wait. Her first stop had to be the ladies room where she left behind what little she'd eaten. Her intestines gripped by an icy hand of fear, she left the hospital, walked quickly to her car and headed to the secure cocoon of her apartment. Maybe by Monday she'd know what to do.

Chapter 18

My deskmate was already seated at her computer that next Monday and as I walked into the newsroom she turned her head away.

"Morning, Jeni," I said, hoping to break the ice.

She mumbled in return something that might have been "morning" but then was silent for many minutes. I scrolled through a weekend's accumulation of e-mails as she straightened papers on her already orderly desk.

I looked around the newsroom to make sure no one was within earshot. "You wanna talk about it?"

"No, uh -- no, I'm -- I'm okay."

"You know, of course, that going home Saturday morning took all the willpower I had."

"Forget about it," she said, her face still averted.

"Okay, it's forgotten. But I want you to understand it."

"What's to understand?" she said, looking up with a crimson flush to her neck and face. "I was drunk and made a damn fool of myself. End of story."

"No, not end of story. There is no story."

"What do you mean?"

"Look, Jeni. You're a damn good looking woman. The easiest thing in the world would have been for me to stay with you."

"Then why didn't you?"

"Several very good reasons I can think of."

"Yeah? What?" She turned away again, as if not wanting to hear the answer.

"One, when I sleep with a woman, I sort of like it to be my idea. And, two, I'm already sorta spoken for."

"Oh. I -- I'm sorry," she said, looking at me directly for the first time. "I didn't know you and your cop had gotten that far."

"We have and we haven't. Nothing official. We're taking it slow. But we have an understanding. At least the intent is there."

"Oh -- well, good for you. I'm happy for you both," she said with something approaching sincerity. She looked away again and there was another long silence as she shuffled through a stack of pink phone messages.

"You said there were several things," she said at last, frowning and hanging her head as though she were expecting a verbal beating. "Anything else?"

"Yeah. It's not a good idea for co-workers to get involved."

She had no answer to that, and I paused to let the words sink in.

"I wanted you to like me," she finally said.

"I *do* like you, dammit," I said, my voice louder than I intended.

"You don't show it."

I looked around the room again, leaned toward her and whispered in exasperation. "I don't have to sleep with you to show I like you." I regretted saying it so bluntly as her eyes clouded and lips trembled.

"I guess I deserved that. Let's just say it was misplaced gratitude for your helping me."

"Look, I like you just fine, and you don't owe me a thing. Helping you is my job."

She stared straight ahead blankly.

"Look," I said, "you're better than that. Maybe I've spent too many years under Jerry. I've seen an awful lot of bright young men and women come and go – many of them not as smart and talented as you. But after the thrill of bylines wears off and the reality of long hours and low pay sinks in, too many leave before they're ready. And a lot of *them* opt out of the business for higher pay in PR or law school, whatever."

"I'm not going anywhere. I love what we do."

"I'm not in any position to give moral advice – maybe not even professional advice. But this isn't college anymore. And the stakes are much, much higher. Besides, you're too good for that -- to give yourself so easily. And for a one-nighter. Especially with me. Hell, I'm what, 12 years older than you?"

She stared at the ceiling for a moment, her eyes welling, and then managed a semblance of a smile. "Oh, you're not so old," she sniffed.

"Well, maybe not. And if you hadn't been drunk I'd have been flattered as hell. Really. But I think too much of you -- and of your potential. And, bottom line, I guess, of myself."

She looked at me directly again and shook her head. "Most guys I've met would've just taken it and run."

I feigned a goofy, lecherous grin – well, maybe not feigned -- and pumped my eyebrows. "Gotta admit it was damn tempting. One of my rare moments of self-restraint."

She smiled back and turned away to focus on the papers on her desk. But after a moment she got up, walked around to my side of the desk, looked around to see if anyone was looking and, tears in her eyes, leaned over and kissed me on the cheek. "You're sweet," she said. And then, "I'm glad you're my friend."

Chapter 19

Angela had no clue what she'd do with the truth – whatever it was – when she got it. But she was determined to find out whether her employer deserved the pride she had invested in working for Memorial.

Cassandra Potter was head nurse of the night emergency room. Angela had worked with her when getting information for some news releases and ads touting the hospital's new urgent care and night pharmacy.

Of all the people Angela had met at Memorial, Cassie was the one she felt she could most trust to be honest with her – or at least not report her inquiry to Ruth or Mr. Blanchard, which by now she concluded was what Willie Bostic had done. *The fink! And a fellow Kenton grad at that.* Her weekend's agonizing, solitary musings had left her convinced that her "performance" raise was actually a clumsy attempt by Blanchard to buy her silence. "Loyalty" to the team was what he called it. *But for what? And was Ruth in on it too?*

Angela waited until 10 o'clock that evening and dropped by Emergency. "Cassie around?" she said to the inquiring glance of the intake clerk.

Cassie was a black woman in her late 40s who proudly bore her scars from battle in almost all of the hospital's departments. A nurse who gave back to the doctors and administrators as good as she got, she was an outspoken non-comformist who always asked the unpopular question on everyone else's mind at staff meetings. And, she had a knack of just plain pissing people off. Too many, it seemed, because Angela had heard Cassie's tenure as Memorial's head of nursing years ago had been brief. But she'd been at Memorial too long and made too many friends on the staff and in the community to be fired – or so the scuttlebutt said. And, of course, the fact she was a minority had to be considered, too.

"Got a minute?" Angela said softly when she poked her head into the cubicle the clerk pointed to.

"Sure, Angie girl," Cassie boomed with a welcoming smile, gesturing toward a chair. "Set yourself down. Whaddaya need?"

Angela remained standing and looked around nervously. "Can – can we – uh -- step outside – just for a moment?"

The heavy-set nurse looked hard at Angela, shook her head, shrugged her shoulders, rose and led the way out the automatic doors to the canopied entrance. An EMT lounged against his ambulance smoking a cigarette, and Cassie walked a few steps further out of his earshot and into the shadow of the building.

"Guess you heard -- that it, girl?"

Angela's eyes widened. "Just rumors. But I know *something* happened. What can you tell me?"

"You sure you want to get into this, girl? You're kinda low on the totem pole, ya know."

"You mean my job could be at stake if I ask the wrong questions of the wrong person? Yeah, I know that. That's why I'm asking you."

"Oh – what -- you think just 'cause I been here 25 years I can't get canned? This midnight trick ain't the choicest assignment, you know," the nurse said.

"Oh, I know. I'm sorry, but I thought of all people you might -- you know -- give it to me straight."

"Wonderful. My reputation precedes me," Potter said, wrapping her arms around herself in the late night chill. Her long pause led Angela to conclude she'd lost the other woman. But then the nurse said, "All right, this didn't come from me, okay? But I'm glad someone is learning about it, and what you do with it is up to you. But telling you gets it off my chest."

The nurse took a deep breath and then said, "It's freezing out here so listen up, 'cause I'm only going to say this once. Far as I know, here's what happened."

The story Potter related was the flip side of what Angela had heard from Oren. "I was working on some charts at the desk. Security guy came racing in, grabbed an orderly and a gurney and away they go down the hall to the back door. Few minutes later they come back and wheel this guy into one of the emergency bays yelling for a doc. Doc says DOA and they whisk the guy back out. That's all I saw."

"But who was the patient?" Angela asked. "What happened to him?"

"I know what I've heard, and you must have heard the same things or you wouldn't be here. But I'm not gonna speculate on whether it's true or not. Only thing else I know for sure is we're all told – no, ordered -- not to talk about it. And if anybody asks, I ain't said a thing."

Potter spun on her heel, leaving Angela standing alone and shivering outside the hospital. The PR assistant realized, however, that the chill that gripped her was not from the late March freeze.

Chapter 20

The four days since Danny and I had seen each other were not unusual, given the busyness of our careers. But I was glad when she returned my call and agreed to dinner on Tuesday night. We skipped the workout at Fitness First and dinner at Applebee's. After our mattress calisthenics, we sat at her kitchen table over steaming mugs of tomato soup and the butter-fried toasted cheese sandwiches I had made.

"Mmm, good," she said.

"Yes, it was. Thank you very much."

"I was speaking of the sandwiches."

"Oh, yeah – me too. Hits the spot. Takes me back to when I was a kid."

"So, your mother didn't have any more regard for your arteries than you have."

"Considering our recent activities, let's not invoke the image of my mother."

"I missed you," she said, her hand over mine.

"Me, too. But you could probably tell that."

"Yeah -- your needs are sort of -- obvious."

"No, I mean it. I missed *you* – not just *it.*"

"That's good to know. It's nice to have something – someone -- to depend on."

"We could, you know, make it so we don't have to miss each other anymore."

"I know. Let's just not go there right now, okay?" She squeezed my hand and smiled.

"Okay. Okay. Besides, I need to talk with you about something."

I'd already decided to not discuss the episode at Jeni's. There was nothing to it, and strangely I didn't want Danny to think badly of the young reporter – now that we were "friends."

"What is it?"

"Could be nothing. But figured I'd better mention it to KPD's next detective."

"I hope."

"Well, what do you think of this? Two independent sources – to remain nameless – tell me that the demure Mrs. Gordon is something of a dentist office tease."

"Meaning what?"

"Meaning she -- allegedly – comes on to men while cleaning their teeth."

"Hmm. That's interesting -- I guess. If it's true. What's it mean – comes onto?"

"Obviously, I have no – um – direct experience. But she supposedly wears loose or unbuttoned tops and makes no attempt to conceal her – assets – while bending over them when they're in the chair."

"Sounds like you might have some horny sources – or at least with vivid imaginations."

"No doubt -- they're guys after all. But one guy says she actually came onto him – asked him if he wanted to see more."

"Again, interesting – if true. Maybe even *very* interesting.

"Well, have your detectives picked up any sense of inappropriate conduct in their interviews?"

"Not that I've heard of, but I'll check it out. Even if she's been a bad girl, it might not have any relevance to her husband's murder."

"True. But given our anonymous 'cherchez la femme' letter and a couple guys saying she's a heavy flirt, what else have you got to look at?"

Chapter 21

An icicle clung to Angela's spine and the hot bath and tumbler of chardonnay she downed while soaking failed to melt it. Torn between concerns of job and conscience, she was facing a critical dilemma. She knew the wrong choice could kill a career that had barely begun.

She was certain now that something bad had happened at Memorial and the powers-that-be wanted to hush it up. *That didn't mean the hospital did anything wrong,* she reasoned. *Bad things happen and they're not always someone's fault. But if there was no fault, why would there be such an effort to cover it up?*

And if the hospital was at fault, and somebody had died because of it, where should her loyalty be? To her employer – who signed her now-growing paycheck? Or to the family of the deceased patient? Or to that fragile commodity called the truth – the black and white one so easily discerned in the safe cloister of journalism school but that seemed more and more gray and elusive in the real world?

The mixture of wine and fear had slowed her thinking, but the recognition came with a jolt.

Raymond Owens! Of course. That's got to be it. There couldn't be two such disasters at once. That has to be why the family was raising such a fuss. And no wonder Blanchard wanted all questions directed to him. But just to be sure, I'll check the patient roster in the morning.

***

Records confirmed that the date cited by Oren and Cassie matched the reported demise of Raymond Owens. And the patient directory for that date listed Owens's room on the third floor. The man apparently had fallen to his death from his window. So the death was not, as reported, from his accident injuries – at least not directly. *It certainly could be a liability for Memorial if he had fallen. Or could he have taken his own life? Or, my god, could he have been pushed! But while a homicide would be embarrassing, that didn't prove the hospital had done anything wrong.*

For the next several days, whether at her apartment or at work, the weight of what she'd learned left her exhausted. Curiosity and a sense of justice told her she needed to continue to at least try to put the pieces together. What actually happened? Was anyone at fault? Why the cover-up? Practicality said, "Play it safe and forget the whole damn thing."

If she let it drop, she wasn't sure she could live with herself, much less continue to work as enthusiastically for Wilkes Memorial – if at all. If she continued to push for the truth, she knew she'd have to be very careful or risk losing her job. But her focus in J-school had been advertising and public relations, not news-editorial. She knew how to write interesting news releases and design ads to reach multiple audiences, but she also knew she was no investigative reporter. Who could she safely talk to? And how should she go about it?

She needed to talk to someone, but her best friend in Kenton was Jeni Jermaine -- *a reporter for god sake.*

Chapter 22

I was kicked back in my usual deep-thought mode – feet on desk and fingers laced behind my head, savoring the previous night with Danny. But my sensual reverie was interrupted by photographer Jim Rogers.

"I know you were working the Gordon killing," he said. "Just wanted you to know I've moved the photos I shot at the scene into the archive. You can find them there anytime but I thought you might want to see them all together while you're still working the story." He gave me the file name in the news server.

The electronic file of stories and photos – and anything else relevant to the community that could be scanned into the computer – had become *The Chronicle's* memory of all things local. I called up the photos Rogers had taken at the Gordon home. The same images I had seen before scrolled across the screen and I compared them in my mind's eye with what I had witnessed at the crime scene and in the cop photos Danny had borrowed.

Disheveled bed, broken closet door -- everything but the body of Stanley Gordon. It was a wearisome task, however, especially because studying an actual paper photograph is far different from staring at a computer screen. I sat back, yawned and rubbed my eyes.

I had just closed the file when something – I couldn't quite define it – snagged my subconscious. I brought the photos back to the computer screen and scanned them again, but the thought that nagged me remained elusive. I called Danny. "Hey, you know your Gordon crime scene photos we went over last week?"

"Yes?"

"Any chance we can look at them again?"

"Why? You onto something?"

"I dunno. I've just got a feeling after looking at our own shots again that we're missing something."

"A feeling? You want me to risk pissing off my future detective colleagues for a *feeling*?"

"I can't put my finger on it. Something just sticks in the back of my mind and I thought that if we could compare your photos and ours side by side it might come to the surface."

"Okay. I know we need to respect intuition. Lots of cases have been solved on hunches – or so I've heard. Let me see what I can do."

While I waited for Danny to call back I asked Jim to pull prints of the Gordons' bedroom. He wasn't delighted at the request since *The Chronicle* no longer used physical photo prints, working instead off the computer. But we still had instant printing capability to fulfill readers' requests for copies of the images captured by the paper's photographers – mostly high school athletes and cute kids.

"Okay, Brock. But you owe me a beer for this," Jim said.

"Yeah, sure, okay." There was no telling if comparison of the photos would result in anything, but a beer would be cheap if only to ease my mind that we hadn't missed something.

Danny called back and said she'd bring the photos over after her shift change at 3:00. We met in *The Chronicle's* conference room and spread both sets of photos out -- cops' on top, Jim's below -- around the long conference table that spanned the width of the room.

There were many more police photos, so we lined up only those with a common view. Because Jim had been forced to shoot from a distance, the cops' shots were closer and with more varied angles.

"What are we looking for?" Danny asked.

"I don't know. Maybe nothing. But something caught my eye that didn't seem quite right and I thought maybe if I looked at them again together I could summon whatever is lodged in the back of my brain."

"Yeah, well, in that case, maybe nothing," Danny jibed.

"Funny. I appreciate your support."

We looked at the photos one by one, starting from opposite ends of the table. When we met in the middle, I couldn't resist her closeness and put my arm around her waist and nuzzled her ear. When she turned to face me I pulled her to me and we kissed.

She returned the warmth of my kiss, but then stepped back and smiled. "Hey, I thought this was supposed to be business."

"Nothing wrong with mixing business with pleasure. I could lock the doors?"

"Back to work, Mister."

We completed the circuit of the table, looked at each other and shrugged in unison.

"One more time," I said. "I can't shake that feeling it's here."

Midway through the second pass, it came to me. "There it is – I think."

"What? Whattaya see?"

"Look. That spot on the closet door. I noticed it before." I pointed to the small dark blotch toward the top of the damaged bi-fold panel that was hanging askew from its hinge. "Remember? I asked you whether it could be blood, but you said no because there wasn't any spatter. We guessed it might just be a chip on the paint."

"Yeah, I see it," she said, pulling the picture out of my hand for a closer look. "But I guess I don't see it."

"Look at your shot taken straight on, and ours further back at an angle. Yours looks just like a black spot in the paint – maybe a half-inch wide. But ours from the side shows depth – like it's a nick in the wood – or maybe a hole."

She asked, "You sure it's not just a speck on the lens or something in the printing process?"

"Possibly. But you know what? If it is a nick, or a knothole, that's what bothers me. *You* saw the inside of that house. Everything was just so – the décor and furniture unexpectedly lush for a house in that neighborhood -- and everything impeccably clean except for the mess in the bedroom."

"But so what? So maybe Mrs. Gordon isn't a perfect housekeeper after all? Or maybe the door got dinged in the struggle."

"I wouldn't rule that out. But whether or not it's got anything to do with the murder, it would be good to find out if it's just incidental damage or what."

"Which leaves us where?"

"Bear with me here, okay? Your detectives haven't figured out any motive for Stanley Gordon's murder, right?"

"Unfortunately not."

"Well, Cass Street is a dead end – hardly a place a psychopath just passing through on the highway is going to stumble onto."

"That's true enough – which makes it all the more mysterious."

"And nothing of value was taken, right?"

"Right again. So?"

"So absent robbery or an itinerant maniac, it seems that maybe Gordon was a specific target. If it's not random, then it's deliberate, right?"

"Okay, for the sake of argument," she said.

"So, ruling out for the moment a random crazy, the one thing that doesn't fit in the picture is that spot on the closet door. I've got an idea, but there's no sense going into it now. Again, just a hunch, but I think we need to check out the exact nature of the mysterious black spot."

"*We* – meaning *me*?"

"You – or us. Whoever has the most plausible excuse to get back into that bedroom and check things out. What if one of us went back to the house and asked Mrs. Gordon to see if we dropped something in the bedroom – say a prized pen or a camera piece or something that might have rolled under the bed?"

"One of us – again meaning *me*?" she asked.

"Well, no. Not you. But maybe your photographer."

"It might raise less suspicion if it was yours – not an official visit."

"But we didn't even get into the bedroom," I said.

"Okay, but does the widow know that?"

"Right. Probably not. She was busy being questioned. Let me see if I can prevail on Jim to pay a call on Mrs. Gordon."

Chapter 23

Jeni thought Angela's voice was unusually soft and hesitant over the phone. Even though her friend was inherently shy, she had affected a bubbly gregariousness perfect for her job in hospital PR. Now, Angela seemed so subdued.

"Hi, Jen. uh -- ," she stammered. "It's – uh -- been a while since we – uh --talked. I thought maybe we could – uh -- get together for a bite to eat one of these days?"

"You okay, Angie? You sound kinda down."

"Oh, no," she said, although Jeni thought she didn't sound very convincing. "Just need to – uh -- reconnect."

"Well, I'd love to, Angie. When do you have in mind?"

"Well – I was thinking -- uh, maybe tomorrow?"

"Let me look. Uh-oh, can't tomorrow. Have an assignment. But – let me check. Uh -- hey -- how about tonight?" Jeni said.

"Tonight? Oh – I – uh – hadn't expected anything so soon. But – that -- that would be great." Her voice brightened. "Say about six? The Brass Rail?"

"Cool," Jeni said. "See you there."

The Brass Rail, Jeni thought, remembering Brock's big-brother lecture. *Well, no, not lecture exactly. But his words had stung even more than if they had come from Mom or Dad. But that's only because I had made such an ass of myself. Thankfully they'll never know about that.*

She knew Brock was right, though, about being careful of her reputation in their small town. She loved working for *The Chronicle,* but she also had her sights set higher. She hadn't given up on the *Journal, Business Week* or *Forbes* and she'd need another stop or two and a string of stellar recommendations if she was going to get there. Angie wasn't one of The Rail's after-work fun crowd – too introverted as well as seemingly always tied to her hospital desk. And, Kenton was Angela's home town, after all. But Jeni had to remind herself to limit her drinks. Three at most, she promised herself.

When she arrived at The Rail, Angela was already seated and nursing a white wine. The brightness of her voice had faded and the usual smile on her face was now transparently forced.

"Well, nice that you're so glad to see me," Jeni teased. "You look like you lost your best friend. Is it a guy thing?"

"Oh, sorry. No. Nothing like that – I wish. Just the job. I'll be all right."

"Well, good. Because it's been too long since we had a girls' night out."

The waitress came and went with Jeni's order of a glass of sauvignon blanc. Angela remained subdued and responded with only short answers to her friend's queries. Jeni ordered a salad, raspberry vinaigrette on the side. She took note that Angela, normally calorie conscious, succumbed to the carb comfort of fettuccini Alfredo.

"All right. Out with it, girl. Something's heavy on your mind, and this is looking like a downer of a night if we don't get this thing out of the way."

"I hoped it wasn't that obvious."

"I was afraid maybe the waitress would have to bring tissues instead of napkins."

"Okay, I did ask you here for a reason," Angela admitted, nodding to herself. "But it's not --easy. For starters, I need this to be confidential – you know, just between the two of us? Okay?"

"No problem. I thought we could tell each other about anything. You're not pregnant or anything are you?"

"Oh, god no," Angela blurted, grinning for the first time in the evening.

"Well, good. So then it can't be *too* bad, right?"

Again she said, "I wish."

Their meals delivered, the waitress asked, "Another glass of wine?"

"Better bring us the bottle," Jeni said, begging her own dispensation from the promise to limit her intake. It was, after all, in the name of helping a friend.

"Okay, just listen to this, 'cause I'm gonna need your best advice," Angela said.

"I'm here for you, Angie. You can tell Doctor Jeni."

"You remember calling me about the death of a man who'd been injured in a car accident?"

"Oh, yeah. Raymond Owens -- the guy who died a month after his accident. Obviously a hot potato. The family was calling us saying something happened at the hospital, and Brock talked to your boss. And then Blanchard even called our publisher to say there was nothing to it."

"Well – uh," Angela hesitated, pursed her lips, closed her eyes and shook her head. "Not so."

"How do you mean?" Jeni said, leaning in to catch Angela's near whisper.

"Look," Angela said, eyes darting around to assure they weren't being overheard. "This can't come from me. You understand? I'd lose my job in a minute if they thought I'd talked to you – much less been snooping around behind their backs."

"What are you talking about? What happened?"

"What happened – best I can determine – is that Raymond

Owens did *not* die from his car accident. He died after a fall from a third floor window."

Jeni's eyes widened as she blurted, "You mean at the hospital?"

"Shhh," Angela rasped, ducking her head to look furtively around the room. "Yes, at the hospital. The night before we reported he died from his accident."

"But why would they say that?"

"That's what I don't know -- and -- I guess -- why I'm talking to you. If I'm gonna keep my job I just can't afford to do any more digging."

Chapter 24

The price for Jim Rogers' intruding upon Valerie Gordon's grief had gone up from the last favor he'd done for me.

"Do you think you can bring it off?" I asked him after laying out the ruse.

"Of course I can," he said. "I was, after all, the lead in my senior class play."

"Yeah, a regular thespian, no doubt. Again, I'll owe you. Make it a six pack."

"Six pack, hell. It's gonna be a *case* for this."

I waited in the car outside the Gordon home when Jim went to the door. When the widow answered the photographer rummaged through his camera bag to show his Nikon was missing a lens cap. She let him in.

As pre-arranged, after a minute I called the Gordon house on my cell phone to provide the distraction for Jim to do his work.

"Hello, is Robert Gordon in?"

"I'm sorry, there's no Robert here," Valerie Gordon said.

"Isn't this the Robert Gordon residence?"

"No, you have the wrong number. This is the *Stanley* Gordon residence."

"Oh, no, I'm sorry. I was calling the Robert Gordon residence. Must have copied the wrong number from the book."

"Yes, I think there might be a Robert Gordon across town, but no relation."

"Well, this is Excelsior Replacement Windows and I was calling to see if the Gordons might be interested in a free in-home estimate. We have a wonderful discount this month on energy-saving triple-pane insulated windows and free installation. Could I interest…"

"No, I'm not interested." She hung up.

In another minute, Jim bounded down the front steps holding the lens cap he had palmed when he fished under the bed.

"Well?" I asked.

"Hey, I found my lens cap," he shouted loud enough for Mrs. Gordon to hear as she stood at her open door.

"Okay, what about the closet door?" I said when he was in the car.

"Well, it was a close call in there," he said, breathing heavily and almost giddy in excitement. "But I managed to get a look at that door."

"And – and?"

"And, well, sorry, pal, but there's no hole there."

"No hole? Then what was the black spot?"

"There's no black spot either – *now!* But there obviously was one, and it's been patched and painted over – both sides."

"Bingo!"

***

"Okay, okay," Danny said later at her apartment. "You were right about a hole in the closet door. It wasn't a blemish in the paint, or a knot, but a hole that has since been patched."

"And what does that say to you?"

"The widow is getting ready to put the house where her husband was murdered on the market?"

"Come on," I said, trying to squelch my impatience. "You know where I'm going with this. We already know – or think we know – that Mrs. Gordon is a tease, showing off her -- endowments, as it were. And maybe even asking men if they want to see more. So what if she was more than just a flirtatious, frustrated housewife? What if she really does get it on with some of Dr. Schmidt's patients?"

"Or, what if this is all just wild speculation based on the fantasies of your horny informants? Why does it have to be the woman? *Cherchez la femme* and all that. Maybe he was the one getting it on with some other woman – or even a man."

"Sure, either one's possible," I said. "But since the wife angle is the only thing we have even a hint of, let's follow the dental assistant scenario for now."

"Okay. So, say it's her. Obviously, she's not going to do it in the dentist's office. Which leaves a choice of motels or the back seat of patient Joe's car – neither of which seems very discreet or safe in a town like Kenton. So maybe it's in the privacy of her own home."

"But what's at home?" I asked. "Her husband, who's either in the house or out in his garage studio when he's not out on some appointment."

Danny nodded. "That *would* make sexual adventures a bit inconvenient."

"But what if they weren't clandestine? Maybe the husband was in on it. Maybe even kinky stuff like group sex."

Ignoring my pumping eyebrows and leering grin, she hitched on to my train of thought. "Or, maybe just to watch – voyeur stuff, getting off on watching his wife have sex with other men. Talk about kinky. And that would explain the hole in the closet door."

"Or -- getting back to his business -- to take pictures."

"For later enjoyment – if he was a voyeur. Or, maybe even to sell – internet porn?" she said.

"So maybe someone discovered he was being photographed or filmed and he killed Gordon in a rage."

"Possibly, except for the fact that Mrs. Gordon spent the night of the murder at her elderly mother's house across town."

"And your department verified that?"

"Yes, the mother -- a Mrs. Ellis, I think – confirmed that her daughter stayed with her that night."

"So if Mrs. Gordon wasn't home, there wouldn't have been any sex – much less filming – going on."

"Yes, that's right, and no shocked dental patient surprised he'd gotten it on for the camera. So that leaves out a sudden crime of passion – so to speak." She paused and frowned in thought. "But – but – what if it wasn't passion. What if it was -- a cold-blooded, calculated murder."

"For what? Back to the gossip mongers' scenario of a disappointed lover -- his or hers?"

"No! The pictures!" she shouted. "Blackmail! That's more plausible. Now *there's* a motive for *murder*."

Chapter 25

Exhilaration over our mental gymnastics in her kitchen fueled subsequent ones in her bedroom. Danny lay in my arms afterward and we mulled over our deduction of a possible motive for Stanley Gordon's murder.

"I've been thinking. You know our interviews with neighbors disclosed no unusual traffic or visitors to the Gordon home," she said.

"Okay, but how closely do you monitor visitors to your own neighbors' houses? And besides, even though he wasn't the most successful photographer in town, there had to be relatively frequent traffic to Gordon's photo studio – even at night. Studio sessions, customers choosing which poses to print, picking up their orders."

"You're right," she said. "People wouldn't know if visitors were anything but business clients. So an occasional male caller was not going to seem out of the ordinary."

"Assuming that Stanley Gordon wasn't just a sicko voyeur, he could well have been using his wife's assignations to bolster his photography income. According to my friend Rudy, Gordon's studio business appears to have been only marginally successful. But their home and furnishings showed some very expensive tastes."

"Mixing business and pleasure? You think she did so willingly? Or he forced her into it?" Danny wondered.

"As mousy as she seemed the one time I met her – granted it was right after her husband's murder – I'd guess it might have started out forced, but the two guys I've talked with didn't make it seem she was overly shy. Who knows how many times she did it? Maybe she came to enjoy the attention. The thrill of the game. Or even the sex," I said, rolling toward her.

"Yeah, there is that *remote* possibility," Danny laughed,

dodging my grasp and holding me at arms length. "But aren't we getting way ahead of ourselves here? As fun as it is to speculate, all this is still just supposition."

"Exactly. But assuming this isn't just a flight of mutual delusion, how do we go anywhere from here?"

"I'm not sure I like the sound of *we*." she said. "I'm not even a detective yet. And *you* don't have *any* authority to be talking to people trying to solve a crime. You could be charged with interfering with an investigation."

"Not to put too fine a point on it, but *what* investigation? Seems to me your guys are pretty much at a dead end."

She nodded reluctantly. "From what I've heard, that's so. But I'm not privy to everything. You need to be careful. *Very* careful."

"I know, I know. And you're right, no official authority. But I'll resist rubbing your nose for the umpteenth time in the First Amendment."

"Thank heavens for that," she rolled her eyes and affected a grimace.

"But people *do* expect us to investigate things. There's nothing to stop us from at least asking the right questions of the right people."

"And who would those people be?"

"Well, for starters, there would be Dr. Schmidt's male patients."

"He's my dentist and he's very busy. You're probably talking hundreds," she scoffed.

"Maybe more. I think my dentist told me his patients total something like 2,500. But given the population, there are probably more women than men, so if Schmidt also has that many, it could be about a thousand, eleven hundred."

"Oh, great," she said. "But we probably can eliminate boys and the elderly."

"What, you think teenagers and old men don't like sex?" he laughed.

"Oh, I'm sure they do," she smiled. "But kids don't have any money, and even if they did there'd be no leverage for blackmail – except maybe anonymously tattling to their parents. And one would hope older men – say those past 60 or so – would have more sense. So we'd have to look at men – probably family men -- between mid-twenties and mid-sixties."

"That might be a decade too young. But for the sake of argument, excluding elderly skirt-chasers like Hugh Hefner, let's say you're right. Would you be able to get a list of those men?"

"For starters I guess we could just ask the doctor for a list of his patients as part of the murder investigation," she said.

"Without going into details, or letting Mrs. Gordon know, maybe you could say you need the names to cross-check for those who might have a record of violence or mental illness."

"I think it might raise suspicion – *if* she's involved -- if I go in there as a cop and ask for a list of patients."

"Maybe you could speak with the doctor during a checkup – or privately at his home."

"Let me run this by my detective friend Clint Wilson," she said. "If he thinks there's merit, we can ask for the names voluntarily – confidentially. Worst case, the department could always subpoena them."

Chapter 26

Sitting at their table at The Rail, Jeni knew three things about what she'd just learned from Angela. First, if what her friend said was true about what may have happened to Raymond Owens, Wilkes Memorial was in for a lot more controversy than James Blanchard wanted. Second, she'd have to tell Brock; after all, Owens's death was his story. And finally, she couldn't tell him or anyone else where she'd gotten the information; she'd given her word to Angela.

What I don't know, she thought, *is if there's any way to make this my story. After all, Angie is my source. Maybe Brock will give me at least a share of the byline.*

Both she and Angela had had one glass of wine apiece and then split the bottle of sauvignon blanc. Jeni had kept her promise to herself after all – well, almost. She insisted on paying their bill and the two women paused outside the bar's front door.

"Don't worry, Angie," Jeni said as she gave her friend a hug. "Your secret's in safe hands. We'll get to the bottom of what happened to Mr. Owens and no one will ever be able to trace it back to you." The women parted, Angela for her apartment and Jeni back to *The Chronicle*.

Chapter 27

It was nearly midnight and Jeni was at her computer when I walked into the newsroom.

"Keeping late hours, aren't you?" she said. "Danny working tonight?"

I felt myself blush and wondered why I should feel embarrassed. "Actually, if you must know, I just left her. Thought I'd better get an early start on tomorrow."

"Me too," she responded. "But I've got something to tell you. I was just finishing an e-mail to you outlining what I heard tonight."

"Oh, what's that?" I said. I was tired and tried to look interested, leaning back in my chair and, in Jerry's absence, rested my shoes on top of the desk.

With a flourish she stabbed ENTER on her keyboard. "You can read it yourself, but the short of it is that James Blanchard lied to you when he said there was nothing unusual about Raymond Owens's death."

"What? How do you know that?" I spun to face her.

She offered a tentative, smug smile. "We feature writers have our sources, too, you know."

"So, what happened?"

"My source," Jeni smirked, "says that Raymond Owens fell from a third-floor hospital room window the night he supposedly died of his accident injuries."

"What? Are you serious? Who is this source? How do you know whoever it is isn't making it all up?"

"I know you wouldn't want me to reveal a confidential source.

Let's just say it's highly reliable."

"Well, given it's the hospital, I probably can guess it's your friend. But, okay, it's confidential – and, if it's who I think it is – arguably reliable."

"Thank you."

"I've thought, at most, if anything we were talking about a mix-up in medication."

"No," she said, "I think what we're talking about is a cover-up at the highest levels of the hospital."

"And maybe even the cops and coroner, too."

Chapter 28

"And that's what I think we have so far," I said the next day as we sat across from Jerry and Goldman. Jeni sat beside me at *The Chronicle's* news conference table.

"Damn," Jerry said. "You two *have* been busy, haven't you?" I glanced at Jeni and we both nodded.

"Have you been to the police with either of these – ah – scenarios?" Goldman asked.

"On the Gordon case," I said, "Sergeant Morgan is consulting with KPD's detective division for them to decide if there's enough substance for them to go forward on what we've learned and our sources have told us."

"And on the hospital matter?" Goldman said. "Owen -- or what's the name again?"

"Owens," I said. "Raymond Owens. The police and/or coroner might be a party to the cover-up. Too soon to tell on that. They may or may not be involved; it could be only the hospital. But our source tells us that what happened came from two different people inside the hospital."

"And who is this source," Goldman asked.

"I can't -- reveal that," Jeni said, the words catching in her throat. "I had to – uh -- grant confidentiality to get the information."

"Well," Goldman said, glaring at her youngest staffer, "we're certainly not going to risk libeling who knows how many people and smear the reputation of the hospital without at least *my* knowing who we're basing our story on."

"Look," I said, "we're not even sure it *is* a story. We've got a lot of work to do yet – only beginning really. We just wanted you to know what we're working on, because I'm going to need Jeni's help to chase down some leads."

"Brock's right," Jerry said, turning to Goldman. "There's plenty of time to vet the sources as well as the facts if it comes to that." And then to me, "How much time do you think you'll need?"

"Hard to tell. Right now, while some things percolate, we can work around our other duties. But it might come to one or both of us needing released-time on one or both of these stories."

"Okay," Jerry said. "Just keep me posted."

"One other thing," I said, looking directly at Goldman. "Right now we need to keep this hospital thing within this room."

She took the challenge. "You mean *not* telling the publisher? He's got a right to know what we're working on, and I have to tell him of things that might impact the paper in the community."

"But you know as well as I do, Graham is tight with the hospital administrator who might be at the very heart of this thing. And frankly I don't trust Dam-Gram to not run out and tell his buddy Blanchard what we're working on."

She stiffened. "Well, as long as we're being frank, you've made your contempt for the publisher very clear." Her clipped words and ultra-erect posture were a pretty solid clue to where her loyalties lay.

"That's not the half of it," I said.

"Well, I don't want to hear it. It's insubordinate."

"Hey, don't get me wrong. I'm not challenging his authority – or yours. Only his objectivity – well, and his competence. But when it comes to letting us cover the community, I've worked here a lot longer than you have. He's got a long track record of shilling for his friends and their special causes – and an inclination to at least try to squelch anything negative about them."

"I'm not going to argue the point. But frankly your attitude is not career-enhancing."

Heat swelled up my neck and I couldn't restrain myself from taking the bait. "Are you really threatening my job over this? You want my …."

"Look, people," Jerry interrupted, "let's not get our undies in a twist over something that might come to nothing." He leaned across the table, his arms outstretched like a boxing referee holding the combatants apart. Looking at his boss, he said, "I think what Brock is saying is that we don't want to put the publisher in the uncomfortable position of having to maintain confidentiality when his daily dealings bring him in contact with a possible subject of our reporting."

"Yeah, right," I said. "That's must be it."

"All right, all right," Goldman said softly, raising her palms outward. "I can see – Brock -- that you feel very strongly about this. I respect your passion for a story. And I agree, the publisher doesn't need to know right now what we're working on."

"Thank you, We done here?" I said.

"That doesn't mean we won't inform Graham before we publish," Goldman recovered. "Understood?"

"Of course," I said. "Just let us get the work done before risking getting it short-circuited by the crony system."

***

"Jesus, Brock," Jeni said as we walked back to our desks. "I thought you were going to get fired -- maybe both of us."

"Not a chance," I said, not as certain as I sounded. I had to admit to myself I hadn't quite learned how far to safely push Goldman's buttons. "If she's half as good as she thinks she is, she knows damn well this could be one helluva story."

"But she's got to answer to the publisher. She could lose her job if she goes behind his back."

"Look, I know she's got a job to do, and I don't envy her

having to put up with that dilettante asshole. When it comes to the news he couldn't find his butt with both hands."

"That may be. But while I'm a newcomer and all that, I know it's the publisher who has the final say. If you force her to choose between your job and her own – well, there's only one way that's going to end."

"I know, I know. You're right. She's not all that bad – pretty good, actually. I've seen worse. But it doesn't hurt to remind her that the news is what we're here for."

"Well, just don't get us fired in the process."

"As the saying goes, I was looking for a job before I found this one. If it comes to that, I can do the same thing anywhere else – and in all modesty probably for a lot more money."

"Yeah, well what about me?"

"Oh, you don't have to worry. I'm the one who's the pain in the ass."

"Well, just don't get me tossed out with the bathwater."

"To mangle a metaphor," I said, and we both laughed.

We were silent for awhile, occupied in our own thoughts; then Jeni asked, "So do I really have to tell her who my source is?"

"If she wants to know, she has a right. Your guarantee of confidentiality binds the paper to not disclose the source publicly. That's not in question. But it doesn't bind the paper to use the information you got from your source. Goldman has to be able to judge whether the information you got is accurate and credible."

"You said yourself my source is reliable. Doesn't she trust my judgment?"

"It's not a matter of trust; it's her responsibility. Goldman is right in that much at least. I guessed who your source is, but Goldman doesn't know who it is. She's not going to risk a libel suit unless she is convinced your source knows what she's talking about. That's her job as editor – the publisher's last line of defense. You see the difference?"

Jeni hesitated and then said, "I guess. Okay, so where do we go from here?"

"We divvy up the duties as best we can. We've got some digging to do to nail down the Owens situation before we confront Blanchard again. I'll help you where possible while I work on the Gordon case. But the hospital source is yours and I think at least that part of it should be your story."

She beamed quietly at that and I continued. "If it comes to any police involvement or charges to be filed over the Owens case, that's my beat."

"Can't we just go to Blanchard now with what we've got?"

"You mean ambush him with what we *think* we know? Not unless you want to burn your source. If Blanchard just denies everything again and blows you off, what are you going to say? A little bird told you? You've got to try to get what you've heard on the record yourself. Either the same people who talked to your source – if she'll tell you – or someone else."

"Okay – I guess," she said. "You may need to give me some help on who to talk to – and what to say."

"No problem. You've done fine so far. A lot of what we do is just asking a bunch of questions of a bunch of people until we stumble on something useful. In other words, a lot of hard work – and a little bit of luck. Meanwhile, I'll work the police and coroner again to see if I can break something loose there."

We settled back into our own work, but after a few minutes had passed, she said, "Brock?"

"Yeah?"

"Thanks for letting me have the hospital story."

"No problem. You've earned it. You'll do fine."

She got up and walked around the desk to me.

I looked up. "You're not going to kiss me again are you?"

She peered around, saw no one in the newsroom was looking, and said, "Try and stop me." She planted her lips loudly on my cheek. I didn't mind.

Chapter 29

"Are you crazy?" Angela demanded in a hoarse whisper, leaning across the table toward Jeni. "I told you these things in confidence, and now you want me to tell you who told me? I can't do that. I swore I'd never reveal they had talked with me – and I won't."

"I understand," Jeni said softly, glancing around to make sure they weren't being overheard. They were at The Rail having drinks again, Jeni's invitation only grudgingly accepted by a now-suspicious Angela. "I told you I wouldn't reveal *your* name, so I wouldn't ask you to betray a confidence either."

Angela took a deep breath and dropped back against the padded booth. "Well, thanks for that, at least."

"But look," Jeni said, reaching her fingers across to touch Angela's hand. "You *could* ask them if they'd speak with me – also in confidence. Or tell me others who might know the same things, couldn't you? Your name would never enter the conversation. Would you do that?"

"I don't know," Angela said, her lips pressed into a pout and arms folded in defense. "I'll have to think about it."

Silence hung over their table for several long minutes while Angela sat, eyes downcast and slowly shaking her head while spinning the stem of her wine glass between her fingers. At last she said, "I know for sure – or at least was told – that our security and emergency staffs were involved. The assistant head of security went to high school with me – a real jerk. I don't know if he was the one who answered the emergency call that night, but he's apparently the one who told people to keep it quiet."

"You think he'll talk to me?"

"Sure, you're a woman. He'll talk to anyone with boobs, but don't necessarily expect any answers. He was the first one I talked to and he denied everything. Tried to make me feel like a fool for even asking."

"Maybe I could get more out of him if he thinks we already have the story."

"Well, if you talk to him just keep me out of it. But -- on second thought – stay away from him. He might just assume I've talked with you since I already asked him about it. I don't want it coming back on me. I think he already ratted me out to Blanchard after I talked to him."

"I can make it seem like we're just following up on the family's continued concerns."

"You might want to keep your distance. He thinks he's quite the ladies man. He's asked me out several times, and with your looks…"

"Don't worry. I can take care of myself," Jeni smiled. She studied her friend for a moment and then asked, "Ah – back to your sources. Would you -- ah – at least consider asking them if they'd talk with me on their own?"

"I'd hate to even ask them that. They took quite a risk just talking to me."

"I understand how sensitive this is. But you came to me, remember? If I'm going to get this monkey off your back I need some help here, Angie."

They sipped their wine in silence for several minutes before Angela spoke. "Let me think about it. I don't know if I can ask my sources to talk with you, but I'll try to come up with a list of people *you* can contact."

Chapter 30

The look on Danny's face the next day when I let myself into her apartment told me the news wasn't good.

I knew better than to ask and waited for her overture as we sat at her kitchen table over cups of coffee.

"Well, it's no go," Danny said, her eyes downcast.

"Why not? Your detective friend didn't think it was plausible?"

"Worse than that," she said, biting her lip and shaking her head. "Clint went to the chief of detectives who told him to tell me in no uncertain terms to mind my own damn business. Only he didn't say damn," she smiled ruefully. "There probably goes any chance at detective."

"Why? I thought promotion was based on results of the exam."

"It is – mostly. But if you get on the chief's shit list, there are a million ways a promotion can be delayed – or lost. Or even if you make it, they can make life miserable for you."

"That seems awfully petty. Just because you suggested a different approach to a stalled investigation?"

"That's about it."

"Sounds to me like turf protection at its worst."

"Well, I guess I can see their point in not wanting someone bumbling into their case uninvited."

"Well, does that mean they won't at least check out Valerie Gordon's possible extracurricular activities?"

"I don't know. I guess we'll just have to wait and see."

"Come on, Danny. The case is getting colder by the day. It's already been – what – six weeks? Can't you still follow it up on your own?"

"What – it's not enough to sacrifice my promotion? I've got to get myself fired for insubordination?"

"How can they fire you? You don't work for the chief of detectives, so his response has no direct bearing on you."

"True, but all he has to do is talk to the head of patrol division – or the chief -- and my butt is cooked."

"Your very nice butt," I offered in flimsy encouragement. She ignored me.

"I've worked too hard to get this far. I'm not going to flush it just on the remote chance that some bimbo's lover offed her husband."

"You didn't think it was so remote when we talked the other night."

"You know what I mean. Sure, it's an intriguing possibility – no, speculation. But I can't take it any further – at least now. Not when I'm so close to taking the qualifying exam."

"I understand that. I don't want you to get in trouble either. But – and I'm just thinking out loud here – couldn't you at least ask Dr. Schmidt for that patient list? I could take it from there."

"You really sure it's worth all the effort – and *my* risk?"

"I wouldn't even suggest it if I didn't think so. And if you ask the good doctor right away, you could say it was before you were told hands off."

"But what would you do with the list? You can't just go around asking hundreds of Kenton men if they've slept with Dr. Schmidt's dental hygienist. And certainly not let on that you got their names from KPD."

"Hey, give us more credit than that. If there's one thing we know how to do it's ask people questions in a way that won't put them on guard. And, to tell if their guard goes up without cause. We talk a little – and listen a lot. In that way at least, we're not a lot different from cops."

"Somehow I don't think the chief would see it that way."

"Look, I promise I'll do everything possible to not bring this back on you. What do you say?"

"Brock, I could lose my job."

"Remember, I've got another job in mind for you anyway."

"I'm not kidding, dammit," she said, shaking her finger in front of my nose. "You get me screwed over for this and I'll never speak to you again."

"All right. All right." I raised my hands in surrender. "You know I wouldn't hurt you for anything. Whatever you think is best."

She breathed in deeply and glared at me.

Hours later, as she lay with her head on my chest, she dug me in the ribs, looked up and said, "Well. I guess it's time for me to schedule my annual dental checkup anyway."

Chapter 31

"Did you read today's obits," Jeni asked when I arrived at my desk the next morning.

"Here early again? You turning over a new leaf?"

"Yes – and no," she said. "Well, sorta."

"Huh? What are you talking about?"

"Today obits. Did you read them?"

"Yeah, skimmed them as always. Didn't see anyone I knew. Why?"

"Mrs. Elnora Ellis, 77, 421 North Elm?"

"Didn't know her. Yeah, so what?"

"Survived by her only child – Valerie Gordon."

"*Our* Valerie Gordon?"

"Lives in Kenton. How many could there be?" she said as I grabbed my paper. "Wow, that's tough. Loses her husband and mother within two months. Poor woman."

I turned to the obituary page and studied it for a moment. "Well, I'll be damned."

"Probably," she quipped. "But why?"

"You see who memorial contributions are directed to?"

She grabbed her paper, scanned it, looked up and smiled. "Wilkes County Alzheimer's Association. You -- you thinking -- what *I'm* thinking?"

"Yeah. Our grieving widow's airtight alibi for the night her husband was killed just bumped into a pinprick of doubt."

"Doesn't mean the old lady had Alzheimer's," Jeni said. "Maybe it was just a favorite charity. Husband, friend or whoever might have had it."

"True. But if Valerie Gordon's mother did have dementia, she might or might not have actually remembered when her daughter spent the night. Maybe all Valerie had to do was plant the suggestion after the fact and the old lady backed her up."

Chapter 32

Angela sat at her home computer, an elbow on each side of the keyboard and head in her hands. The e-mail she was typing was short – very short. Only three names to be exact: Emelda Paradiso, John Robertson, Richard Carter.

Paradiso was Wilkes Memorial's night nursing supervisor, Robertson head of maintenance and Oren's boss, and Carter chief of security and Willy Bostic's boss.

Another natural source for Jeni to check were the emergency room doctors on duty the night in question. But Angela didn't know their names. Emergency was staffed by a contract outfit so the docs weren't on Memorial's payroll, and she wasn't about to draw attention to herself by trying to find out who was on duty when Raymond Owens plunged to his death.

Angela also had met a nursing assistant who worked the night shift on the third floor, but in the stress of the moment couldn't think of her name. Maybe she'd remember later.

Conspicuously absent from her list – at least in Angela's mind -- were the names of Cassie Potter and Oren Williams. Stabbing the keys deliberately, she added them to the list, stared at the screen for a few moments, and then deleted them.

No, Jeni Jermaine was her friend, but Angela wasn't going to betray her co-workers' trust in her. If Jeni stumbled on them in her own research, so be it, but she wasn't going to even ask them if they'd speak with *The Chronicle*.

Chapter 33

The two-story brown brick at 423 North Elm Street was of a vintage near downtown Kenton that evidenced the city's prior prosperity as a railroad and manufacturing center. Stately homes built in the late 1800s and early 1900s were now struggling against the elements and gravity. Next door stood the white frame two-story of the late Elnora Ellis, chipping paint and sagging eaves attesting to the straitened circumstances of the area's fifth generation owners and renters.

I mounted the broad concrete stairs to the porch and paused before the massive oak door, trying to peer inside but my view was blocked by a lacy curtain that covered the oval leaded glass. I pushed the button for the doorbell but heard no bell or buzzer sound inside. My second push was also rewarded by silence, so I followed up with a loud knock. After a lengthy silence I saw a shadow approaching the door and then it was opened by a short sixtyish woman with a mop of frizzy, grizzled hair and a cigarette hanging from the corner of her mouth. She started to speak but then held up a hand and convulsed into a wet-sounding smoker's hack that made me glad I'd skipped breakfast. The woman reached into the pocket of her pink-flowered house dress, fished out a tissue and wiped something from her mouth.

"Sorry 'bout that," she croaked. "How can I help you?"

Self-consciously not extending my hand, I introduced myself and she said, "Oh, a reporter?" as if flattered, and then alarm set in. "Uh – why do you want to talk to me?"

"I understand your next door neighbor, Mrs. Ellis, died yesterday?"

"Oh, yes, poor dear. Whyddya ask?"

"Well, as you know, her daughter recently lost her husband, and now her mother. I'm starting to gather background for a follow-up story -- before I talk with Mrs. Gordon."

"Oh, really? Well, don't ya -- think it's -- a little soon?" The words were interrupted by more spasmodic coughing. "I mean – the old lady isn't even – not even in the ground yet. I'm sure – her daughter wouldn't want – to be bothered just now."

"Oh, of course we'd not trouble Mrs. Gordon for some time. But there's a powerful human interest story of grief and loss that might help others – you know – who might be undergoing similar – but less tragic circumstances"

"Oh, I see. Well, ya might as well come in."

She led the way through a long hallway, her skinny legs and slippered feet shuffling softly on a threadbare oriental runner that covered hardwood darkened by many coats of varnish. We passed a traditional parlor on one side and formal dining room on the other on the way to a kitchen last remodeled in the 1950s. She motioned to a chrome chair covered in red vinyl set at a white porcelain dinette with chrome legs. Aside from a drainer full of dirty dishes, the place seemed clean enough, but everything reeked of smoke.

"Coffee?" she asked.

Thinking of the hand that held the tissue, I started to demur but she was already setting a filled china cup and saucer in front of me.

"Cream and sugar in front of ya," she said, resting her elbow on a small square of carpet remnant that hinted at many hours spent in the same position. A half-filled ashtray bedside her betrayed the source of the cough.

"Black's fine. Now, about Mrs. Ellis?" I prompted, taking a tentative sip. *Not bad.*

"Oh, yes. Well, she suffered so -- you know. It was really a – a blessing that she passed so suddenly." More fits of coughing, followed by lighting of another cigarette.

"Suffered? How do you mean?"

"Well, first there was the diabetes. Affected her heart -- and then legs, ya know. Poor thing could hardly get around for years. Depended – depended on her daughter for about everything. And I tried to help out every now and then. Driving her to the doctor – doctor, and that sort of thing. We all need to do what we can for each other – don't ya agree?"

"Oh -- uh – of course. But you mentioned 'at first.' Was there more?"

"Well, toward the end, you know, poor thing -- just didn't have much a mind left -- if ya know what I mean."

"Tell me."

"Well, whether it was the diabetes or whatever – don't know if there ever was a formal diagnosis of Old Timer's."

"Alzheimer's?"

"Yeah -- I know. But it's more fun to just call it Old Timer's."

I nodded and waited as she told her story between hacking interruptions.

"Got so bad that she had to go to that – that adult daycare during the day. Not that she'd wander off in her condition, ya know. But she couldn't – couldn't take care of herself. So the past year or so I'd drive her over in the morning and then Valerie – that's her daughter, ya know – would pick her up after work and bring her home."

"Did you know Mrs. Ellis long?"

"Long as I been in this -- house – near 35 years. She was just the -- sweetest thing. Such a shame. I'm gonna miss her. Course, with her mind gone, it was like she was – she was gone a long time ago."

"And did you know her daughter – Valerie? I gather she was an only child?"

"That's right. I guess Mr. Ellis left right after she was born. Valerie was about five when Elnora moved in here. Rented the bottom apartment all those years. Darn place was fallin' down around her ears and you think the dang landlord would fix anything? Not hardly."

"About Valerie? What kind of daughter was she?"

"Oh, the best. Such a nice girl. And a top – top student – considering they didn't have a dime to spare. Made her mother right proud. And so loyal – taking care as best she could to the end."

"If Mrs. Ellis was so bad off, why didn't she go to a nursing home?"

"Neither Elnora nor Valerie would hear a -- word about it. Elnora always said she could – she could die at home just as well as in an expensive nursing home. And between me and Valerie and the adult day care, she did just fine."

"How about Valerie's husband -- the late Mr. Gordon. Did you know him?"

"Not well. And that was fine with me."

"How so?"

"Well, he was just hard to --- hard to get to know. Sorta stand-offish, if ya know what I mean. And it – it seemed Elnora just tolerated him because Valerie loved him so. I gathered he was just so demanding – controlling, ya know. But I guess Valerie would do about anything for him."

Chapter 34

Jeni timed her call at Emelda Paradiso's home in Kenton for 2:45 p.m., a good hour, she figured, before the night nursing supervisor nurse would have to leave for her 4 p.m. shift at Memorial. On consulting with Brock, Jeni had decided that an oblique approach to the contacts on Angie's list might be more productive than a direct frontal assault at the hospital. She had gleaned enough about Mrs. Paradiso from *The Chronicle's* archive to know that she was both the widow and mother of Kenton physicians. Her husband, a Filipino émigré, was a long-time general practitioner before his death five years ago. Her daughter, Constance, had followed her parents into medical training and had an apparently thriving OB-GYN practice.

The mother's condo was part of the upscale new Fox Glen development on the east side. Ribbons of blacktop bordered by sloping white concrete curbs and sidewalks wound through the development of dozens of single-story duplex garden condos. The units were ostensibly identical except for the different colors and textures of facades in brick, field rock or flagstone. The Paradiso colonial style red-brick front was adorned with a gleaming white door with brilliant brass hardware. A brief wait followed Jeni's touch of a button that set off a Westminster chime inside. The white-clad woman who answered the door had long raven black hair held back by an ornate silver comb on each side. Mrs. Paradiso, also apparently of Asian origin, had gorgeous, smooth skin and a perfect smile, but Jeni figured the mother of an established physician had to be at least 60. The nurse obviously had finished her makeup and was ready for work.

"Hello, can I help you?"

"Yes, I hope so, Mrs. Paradiso" Jeni said, offering the woman her card. "I'm Jeni Jermaine from *The Chronicle.* May I speak with you?"

"With me?" the woman said uncertainly. "I need to leave

soon."

"This won't take long. May I come in?"

The woman hesitated for a moment and then said, "Of course," graciously stepping aside and with a slight bow and broad sweep of her arm inviting Jeni inside.

In contrast to the American colonial exterior, the interior was populated by ornate furniture in natural bamboo and light woods atop deep plush beige carpeting. The bamboo settee into which Jeni was waved was upholstered with square-cornered white cushions. Mrs. Paradiso sat in a similarly designed chair, folded her hands on her knees and looked expectantly at her visitor. The room was darkened by dense gold draperies over the front window, making it hard for Jeni to see her host clearly. Sensing her guest's squint, Emelda Paradiso leaned over to turn on an elaborately carved wood lamp with white parchment shade, and then said, "How can I help you, young lady?"

Overcoming her own hesitation, Jeni blurted, "I – I need to speak with you about the death at Memorial of a man named Raymond Owens."

The older woman's face remained impassive but the blink and widening of her eyes betrayed an obvious alarm. "I'm afraid I know nothing I can tell you, Miss Jermaine," she said.

"Look," Jeni said in a soft, even voice. "I'm not trying to put you on the spot, but we have solid information that Mr. Owens died as a result of a fall from a window at the hospital – and *not* from his auto accident injuries."

Mrs. Paradiso had pulled her hands into her lap. *A sure sign of defensiveness,* Jeni thought. The woman squirmed almost imperceptibly in her chair and said, "I'm sure I wouldn't know about that."

"But we're told it was on the third floor. Aren't you the night nursing supervisor? Surely you'd know if something like that happened on one of your floors."

"I've already told you I can't tell you anything."

"Can't – or won't?" Jeni pressed, surprised at her own chutzpah.

The woman's features hardened but she kept her voice level. "I'm sorry, Miss Jermaine, but I'm going to have to ask you to leave. I need to get to work."

Sensing it was pointless to pursue it any further, Jeni rose and said, "I'm sorry to have bothered you. Thank you for your time."

When the door closed behind her, Jeni checked the time on her cell phone and punched in Brock's number. As soon as Mrs. Paradiso got to the hospital she'd surely put the administration on alert. If Jeni was going to get anywhere with the sources Angie had given her, she'd have to get to the hospital before Blanchard shut them down even more.

"Hey," she said when Brock picked up. "I need your help." She explained her fruitless encounter with Emelda Paradiso and said, "Can you get to Memorial in five minutes and talk with Richard Carter, head of security? I'm headed there to talk to John Robertson, the head of maintenance, and I think we might quickly become *personae non grata* once word gets out we're not letting this thing go."

Chapter 35

Our cars nearly collided entering the Memorial parking lot at ten minutes after three o'clock, and when Jeni exited hers I said, "Good job, Jermaine. Sounds like the rabbits are running."

Once inside the hospital's main doors we split, she for the elevator to the basement and I for the security office on the first floor.

"Hi," I said to the black-uniformed young man sitting in the outer office. "I'm Brock Andrews from *The Chronicle*. Is Mr. Carter in?"

"He's busy," said the burly fellow whose chest bore a plastic name tag proclaiming Will Bostic, Security. "Perhaps I can help?"

The door to Carter's office was partly open, and I could see a man sitting behind a desk. He was leaned back in his chair, arms folded, staring straight ahead. There was no sound of conversation, so he apparently was in thought.

"I'll wait for Mr. Carter," I said.

Bostic's scowl made it clear he didn't like the implied dismissal of his position, but he said in a controlled, uninflected voice, "Can I tell him what this is about? I'll see if he can see you."

"I'd prefer to address that to him, if you don't mind. Please tell him I'm here."

Bostic stared blankly at me for a moment, seeming to decide whether to make an issue of the challenge to his authority or let his boss handle a smart-aleck reporter. At length he got up, came from behind his desk, spun on his heel to enter Carter's office and closed the door. A moment later he came out and said, "The chief of security will see you now."

Chapter 36

Jeni padded warily down the long, dimly-lit corridor, unfamiliar with the Memorial basement but following the sign indicating the direction of the Maintenance Department. When she got there the double steel doors were open allowing the bright light inside to bisect the darker hallway. The large room was lined with steel cabinets, cluttered work benches and pegboards festooned with all manner of tools. In the center of the room were racks of spare parts and used equipment in various stages of disassembly. Behind a desk in a glassed-in area in the corner sat a man of perhaps 50 dressed in dark green work clothes. As Jeni approached she could see his sleeves were rolled up and his head was bent over a large spreadsheet. A roughly chewed pencil was clenched between his teeth.

"I'm – I'm sorry. Mr. Robertson?"

"Yes?" He looked up from his desk and smiled as he arched his back and stretched his arms above his head. "What can I do for you?"

"I'm sorry to bother you, but I'm Jeni Jermaine. From *The Chronicle?*"

"No bother at all. We don't get too many nice young ladies down here, and – no offense – but I'll take about any excuse to set aside this budget."

"Mr. Robertson, I'll get right to the point. We have information that a man died as a result of a fall from an upper story window here at Memorial, and I'm trying to confirm what actually happened. It was a Thursday night, March second."

Robertson looked down at his desk, shook his head, looked back up at Jeni and said, "I'm sorry, Miss. We're just the maintenance staff down here. You'll have to ask the medical folks about any of that."

"But if a window was broken out you'd know about it, right? You'd have to clean up the breakage, as well as install a replacement window, wouldn't you?"

"If that had happened, you're right. We would have done as you say. But you'll have to talk with the medical staff – or, no -- Mr. Blanchard, the hospital president. Have you spoken with him? I think you should start with him."

"We have spoken with Mr. Blanchard, but frankly all we're getting is denials that anything happened. We know *something* happened, and the family of the deceased patient is not going to let this go until the truth comes out. I won't quote you or anything. Can't you just confirm for me what happened so we know the right questions to ask to get official confirmation?"

"Let me call Mr. Blanchard. Maybe he can clear this up." With that, Robertson punched in a speed dial number and apparently reached the CEO's desk directly.

"Mr. Blanchard, there's a reporter from the newspaper here asking about a patient death last month. Can you speak with her?"

Jeni's stomach clenched, knowing she had opened a can of worms that inevitably would spill onto the desk of her publisher.

Chapter 37

The man in the gray pin-stripe suit who entered the maintenance office was easily 6'4" and 240 pounds. "Hello, Miss Jermaine," he said in a deep voice. "I'm Jim Blanchard. I don't think we've met before."

She reflexively reached for the beefy hand he extended and felt hers disappear inside one that was surprisingly soft, warm and sweaty. She stilled a squirm of revulsion.

"Uh – no – I don't believe so," she said, aware of her own discomfort as he loomed a bit too closely.

"Well, pleased to meet you," he said with a thin smile and low, flat tone that made her doubt his sincerity. "Now, what is it you wanted to know?"

"I – uh – we, *The Chronicle,* have been told that a man named Raymond Owens died on or about March second as a result of a fall from a window here at Memorial."

"I'm sorry, Miss Jermaine," Blanchard said as he shook his head and his face reddened, "but we have already answered that question for one of your reporters. And, frankly, I don't appreciate…"

His rising volume was interrupted by the ring of the desk phone that Robertson answered and then held the receiver out to his boss.

"Oh -- yes, I see. Yes, I'll be right there," Blanchard said. Looking at Jeni, he smiled a grimace and said, "Miss Jermaine, will you come with me please?" Without speaking further he led the way out of the maintenance room and down the corridor to the elevator. When the door opened, he motioned Jeni inside and followed her, punching the button for the first floor.

Jeni said nothing, staring straight ahead at the polished steel door, willing her insides to stop churning as she shared an elevator with an imposing and obviously angry administrator. When the door opened again, he said only, "Follow me, please."

A right turn out of the elevator and only a few steps down the first floor hallway found them at the door marked Security. In the anteroom sat a muscular young man in a black service uniform who Jeni deduced was Angie's "friend" Will Bostic. His name tag confirmed it as he stood when they entered.

"Inside, sir," Bostic said, letting his eyes shift from his boss to take in Jeni. Based on what Angie had said about his "god's gift" arrogance, Jeni tried to hold his gaze, but his eyes flowed her full length and back to her face where he squinted, arched his eyebrows and graced her with what he must have thought was a lady-killer smile. A chill rippled up her back.

"Please join me, Miss Jermaine," Blanchard said.

Chapter 38

Richard Carter was standing behind his desk with arms folded, and I was across the desk matching the pose when Jeni and Blanchard arrived. There were only two guest chairs in the office, but neither Blanchard nor Carter made a motion for anyone to be seated, indicating a brief meeting.

Instead, not bothering with introductions, Blanchard stepped to me and, hands on his hips, said, "Mr. Andrews, I spoke to you earlier about this matter of Raymond Owens, and our community relations staff has spoken with Miss Jermaine. But apparently my word was not good enough. Now, here you are again, and I have had quite enough of this harassment by *Chronicle* reporters. Mr. Graham will hear of it, I assure you."

Blanchard had at least two inches on me and maybe 40 pounds. His posture and proximity indicated he meant to be intimidating.

"Now, Mr. Carter, would you please show these people to the parking lot? Other than for medical treatment they are no longer welcome on Memorial property." He fixed both of us with a stern stare and said, "Is that clear?"

Jeni's eyes bulged, her hands were held stiffly at her side and she appeared to be holding her breath. I, however, had taken Blanchard's tirade with what Jeni later described as an eerie smile. I'd be damned if I was going to be the first to back away. I let my arms drop slowly and rocked slightly forward on my toes so my face was only inches from Blanchard's. I took a deep breath and then said evenly, "What is *very* clear -- Mr. Blanchard -- is that you've got a dirty little secret that you're trying to hide. You go ahead and call the publisher – *again*. But I promise you it *will* come out. And when it does, it may be *you* who is no longer welcome on Memorial property."

Blanchard self-consciously backed away several inches but

said nothing for a long, awkward moment. Realizing his superior height, bulk and anger had not worked to intimidate me, he turned instead to Jeni, and then to Carter. Jerking his head toward the door, he ordered, "Get them out of here."

"Don't bother to show us the way," I said. "We're going."

Carter and his boy Bostic followed us to the hospital's main entrance and we headed for our cars. I didn't realize my stride had out-distanced Jeni until I heard her call out, "Hey, wait up. My god, Brock."

"What?"

"*What?* I was afraid for a second you were going to deck the guy."

"Nah. I got in his face just to show we weren't going to be buffaloed by him and his security goons. Besides, the printed word is a lot more potent than the fist. The guy knows he screwed up and he's scared as hell he's headed for a fall. But he'll try to bully his way out of it if he can."

"You mean with Graham?"

"Yeah, Graham."

"Where do we go from here?"

"I think we'd better brief Jerry and Goldman so they're not blindsided by Graham."

"Good plan," she nodded with a grin. "Gotta admit I was a little scared in there, but it was kinda fun too."

"Me too," I grinned back. "Now you're catching on."

***

"Well, what do we actually have that we didn't have before this – this fiasco?" Goldman asked when she and Jerry had heard our account.

"Look," I said in as conciliatory tone as I could muster, "I know it's a pain in the ass to have to tell the publisher that we've just pissed off one of his buddies. But before Blanchard calls, Graham also needs to know the background we've gotten from a well-placed source."

"But we can't tell him who our source is," Jeni blurted, looking to me for support. "I'm – I'm not saying he'd do so intentionally, but if Graham and Blanchard are friends he might reveal her identity inadvertently," Jeni said.

Goldman whirled to her. "*Her* identity? I think it's time you let me in on whose word we're basing this investigation on."

Jeni look at me and I nodded. She bit her lower lip, breathed in deeply and said, "Angela Lawrence, PR assistant at Memorial."

"Why on earth would the hospital's PR assistant be feeding you damaging information about her employer?" Goldman demanded. "This smacks of possibly a disgruntled employee – or maybe an unbalanced one."

"Or just as possibly – no, even more likely," I said, "a conscience stricken one who has learned something she can't keep to herself."

"And we can't have her lose her job just because she's talked to us," Jeni said. "And it's not just her word. She says she's gotten the story from at least two other people."

"All right, all right," Goldman said. "Obviously we're still a long way from nailing this down – *if* it's real. We need to talk to these other people. But we'll protect your initial source. Graham's out of town this weekend, so I'll brief him first thing Monday on what's going on -- and nail him down on not tipping our hand to Blanchard."

I smiled at her tacit acknowledgement of the publisher's naivete and abundant community conflicts. It was her first outward admission that she knew what a doofus her boss was. She might be beholden to Graham for her job, but maybe her news instincts were kicking in ahead of concerns for her next career move. She caught my expression and frowned, shaking her head and raising an admonishing index finger.

"Who do you talk to next?" she asked.

"Well, obviously Blanchard has got the first tier of managers muzzled. We'll need to go deeper," I said. "Plus, I'll need to probe harder with cops and coroner to see if they're at all complicit. So far, it appears they might be out of the loop on this entirely."

"God, let's hope so. It'd make a helluva story, but we've got to live with these people afterwards," Jerry said, the conservative editor speaking up for the first time.

I couldn't help but bristle at the comment. "If these people conspired against the family's learning what really happened to Raymond Owens, we need to make sure they're no longer in positions where we *have* to live with them."

Chapter 39

It was almost six on a Friday afternoon, which meant that while Memorial was a 365 day, 24/7 operation, more people would be easier to catch at home off work for the weekend.

"Can you get Angie to give you a roster of hospital employees?" I asked Jeni. "Preferably by department and shift – with phone numbers if possible?"

"Sure, I suppose – if she hasn't left already." She reached for her desk phone but was stopped by my raising a cautionary index finger.

"It might be safer – for her – if you call her from your cell phone from now on."

"You mean in case Blanchard monitors phone records?"

"I have no doubt, now that he knows we know what happened, that he'll do everything he can to try to find and plug the information leak that had to come from inside."

"Oh, my gosh. Angie and I have called each other several times over this."

"That can't be helped now. Besides, lots of people at the paper – not just you -- call the hospital and vice versa. Angie handles advertising as well as news releases, doesn't she?"

"Yeah, that's right."

"Well, from here on you'll both just have to be more circumspect. Cell phones only."

"Okay," she said. "What are you going to do?"

"I've got to get back on this Gordon thing, and for starters I need to see if a certain cop I know has been to the dentist."

***

Danny had let her long black hair down that evening so that it covered the shoulders of her white sweater. She smiled broadly and gave me a warm welcoming kiss.

"You get to see the doc?" I asked.

"Well, so much for foreplay," she said.

"Huh? Oh, yeah, sorry. I've just been so preoccupied with both the Gordon and Owens things."

"You *might* be forgiven, I'll decide later."

I brought her up to date on my and Jeni's visit to the hospital and she nodded approvingly. "Sounds like something's coming to a head."

"Yeah, shouldn't be long now. How about you? Any luck? Did you get a chance to talk to Doctor Schmidt?"

"I had a bit of a time catching him at home," she said. "He's a busy fellow. Bottom line, he was all too willing to cooperate. He said Valerie Gordon is the best hygienist he's ever had and he's sick over what happened to her. Hopes she doesn't wind up leaving him. From the behavior he described, I'd say she is genuinely grieving."

"Doesn't mean she and her husband weren't involved in blackmail together. Her mother's neighbor said she seemed devoted to her husband. But the most telling remarks were that he seemed very controlling and that she'd do about anything to please him."

"That *might* explain the situation."

"Is the doctor going to give you the list of his male patients?"

"He said he'd have it for me on Monday. He was kind of dubious about it at first. Naturally, he couldn't imagine that any of his patients would do such a thing. And he didn't want them dragged into an unpleasant situation. But I promised him we wouldn't be contacting people indiscriminately – just cross-checking to see if any likely matches popped up from our records search."

"Be nice if it were that easy. You didn't by any chance get any hint the doc himself might have a relationship with her?"

"No, not at all," she said with a touch of irritation. "He just seemed concerned about her both as an employee and a person he has come to value. Jeez, not every male-female relationship has to come down to sex."

"Just a thought – but you've got to admit, often it does," I said, pulling her close. I looked down into her eyes and said, "How about you? You feeling okay about this approach?"

"You know, lover boy," she said, wrapping her arms around my neck, "I'm taking a helluva risk just asking after I was warned off the case. But, yeah, I told him I was working independently and asked him to talk only with me about the patient angle. I think I'll be okay."

I nuzzled her neck, slid my hands up under her sweater and, massaging her back, whispered, "Well, just think of what a hero you'll be if we come up with something."

"Yeah, right," she scoffed. "But -- speaking of coming up with something…"

***

I decided to spend my Saturday morning canvassing the Gordons' neighbors along Cass Street to see if they could recall over a month later anything not shared with police at the time of the crime.

I knew it was a long shot, but the Gordons had few neighbors on their semi-rural, dead-end street. Each of the houses was of the same post-war bungalow vintage but none as updated and expanded as the Gordons' had been. Given the Gordons' extra-large lot, there were only four houses on their side of the block, six on the opposite side. Sizing up the task, I decided to work the long side first.

No one was home at the first house on the far corner with cross street Walnut. *Not a promising start,* I thought. But I learned from the young woman who answered the door of the second house that her neighbors on each side were Florida snowbirds. Both couples were away at the time of the murder and not back yet. The smiling but bedraggled dishwater blonde had a girl of about four clinging to her left leg while she balanced a boy toddler on her right hip and showed a tummy bulge that I took to be another on the way. She said she and her husband had lived on the street only a year, didn't know the Gordons, and had no recollection of anything unusual.

Two doors down, an elderly couple named Hershberg invited me in and started my pulse racing when the husband said, "Well, you know, there was always something strange about that house." But it soon became apparent that the old man's fascination was all about the various addition and remodeling projects. "Why a couple with no children would need all that room is beyond me," he pronounced with finality. They admitted they spent most of their days – and nights -- with the front blinds drawn watching TV in a back bedroom turned into a den.

Next door to the Hershbergs was a vacant white-frame house with a for-sale sign and enough evidence of neglect that I assumed it had been empty at the time of the crime.

The last house, directly across the street from the Gordons', was owned by an octogenarian couple named Bryant. They were a cute and mutually supportive pair who proudly showed me their sixtieth anniversary photo. They said they were shocked at the demise of their neighbor but could recall nothing they had not told police. "They were pleasant, but not really open to neighboring," Thelma Bryant said.

Most of the visit I was regaled by Walter Bryant, aided by his wife's memory for names, with an elaborate history of the neighborhood they had lived in since it was built. The almost chronological litany of move-ins and move-outs soon had me mentally clawing the walls for escape, which I finally managed by thrusting my card at them and extracting a promise that they'd let me know if anything else occurred to them.

So, I assessed my morning: *No unusual comings and goings. No disturbances. No lurking vehicles that didn't seem to belong. No signs at all that the Gordons weren't just your average middle-aged working couple with no kids.*

I caught a quick lunch at the counter of Elly's Tap, a decidedly tacky and tattered eatery in the nearby factory district. Its record with health department inspections indicated it was none too clean, but I was a frequent diner, savoring both the informal atmosphere and the fact Elly (actually Elmo – go figure) served the best pork tenderloin sandwich in the county. I ordered my hammered-thin tenderloin grilled – not fried – and with mayo, pickles and onion. I'd had just taken the first bite when my cell phone rang.

"Just checkin' in," Jeni said. "Angie said she can get the employee list for me, but not until HR opens on Monday. She said she'll spend the weekend cooking up some plausible excuse for needing the information – like something about promoting how Memorial employees represent the whole county."

"Good," I said. "I've canvassed half the houses on the Gordons' block, but so far nothing useful. I'll finish up this afternoon. Unless the sky falls, I'll see you on Monday."

***

The handicap ramp at the house next door to the Gordons' was not encouraging, nor was the sight of the frail, white-haired woman who opened her door while leaning awkwardly on a walker. She looked at least 90, wore dark-tinted glasses and, after asking me to repeat my introduction twice, volunteered, "I don't see or hear very well." The living room she ushered me into was darkened by shades. It smelled suspiciously like the nursing home where I'd visited my grandmother before she died. The Seventies-style furniture, in shades of orange and avocado, was threadbare where it wasn't frayed. I shouted self-consciously the purpose of my visit but when she just shook her head I didn't have the heart to question her closely about what she might have seen or heard from the Gordons.

The rest of the block bore no more useful information and I had decided to pack it in for the weekend when the cell phone vibrated in my pocket. I didn't recognize the number and answered, "This is Brock."

"Mr. Andrews?" the shaky voice of an elderly woman asked.

"Yes, who is this?"

"It's Thelma Bryant. You know, you visited with us this morning?"

"Oh, yeah, sure. How can I help you?"

"Well, Walter and I got to talking after you left, and one thing did occur to us that you might be interested in."

"Oh? What's that?"

"Well, it's not anything to do with the murder, I'm sure. And I don't want you to think we're nosy neighbors or anything…"

"Oh, no, I wouldn't think anything like that." I rolled my eyes.

"You asked about whether we'd seen any strange cars?"

My pulse quickened. "Yes."

"Mind you, not that we actually *watch*, but we have been a little more aware of goings on since the – you know…"

"And?" I asked, trying to submerge impatience.

"Well, not before, but since then – we have seen this large, dark-colored four-door sedan stop at Mrs. Gordon's -- I don't know, maybe up to several nights a week."

Chapter 40

"Whattaya think?" I asked when I related the Bryants' tip to Danny that evening at her apartment.

"Be worth checking out."

"How would you recommend we do that?"

"There you go using that *we* again. Since it's *your* tip, how about *you* follow it up? Remember, I'm not supposed to have anything to do with this case any more."

"Okay, okay," I laughed, "how would you recommend *I* follow it up? Seriously."

"Maybe it's nothing, but if the grieving widow is having regular visitors of the male persuasion, it could be significant. You could maybe cruise by a few nights to see?"

"What's your guess? Male or female?" I asked.

"Women are more social animals. Could be her women friends are just keeping her company, helping her through the grief process. But if it's a man..."

"Unless it's a minister or lawyer or something, it could be a relationship, and it seems pretty soon for that to be happening," I said.

"There's no set timetable for grief; just social convention. Maybe she forms attachments quickly," Danny said, and then realized the implication of her words.

"Exactly. Since neither she nor her husband had a brother, if it's a guy..."

"Just see if you can get a make, model and license number. I can run it for identity and then compare against the patient list from the doctor to see if there's any connection."

Chapter 41

"Jeni, call me," was the voice message on her cell phone Saturday afternoon from an obviously anguished Angie.

When Jeni returned the call, her friend didn't bother with a greeting, only a demand. "What the hell did you and Brock do to Blanchard?"

"Well, hi, glad to hear from you, too," Jeni said, consciously trying to defuse Angie's tension.

"Yeah, well, I mean it. All hell has broken loose here."

"Tell me about it. I was there – as you no doubt have heard."

"No, you tell *me* about it. I know you were here -- *now*. But why didn't you mention it when you called me yesterday for the staff list? I've got to tell you I'm feeling a little – no, a lot -- used in this situation."

Jeni realized she had been thoughtless toward her friend the afternoon before – just intent on relaying Brock's request for the list of Memorial's employees. "I'm sorry," she confessed. "I see now I should have told you about our confrontation with Blanchard. I was just so keyed up afterward, and then trying to catch you before you went home for the weekend."

Silence on the other end of the line made Jeni sense the imperative to repair a relationship she unthinkingly had taken for granted. "Look, I apologize, Really, I didn't mean to shut you out. I hope you'll forgive me."

"Well, I spent half of last night and all this morning sitting through one Blanchard tirade after another," Angie said.

"Directed at you?" Jeni asked, feeling the alarm and guilt apparent in her own voice.

"No, thank goodness. If it had been at me I'm sure I would

have been fired."

"What happened?"

"First, last night after hours it was just a general meeting of department heads, plus the administrative team. All about how the paper was out to smear Memorial for something that wasn't our fault. And warning that no one – *no one* – from *The Chronicle* was to be spoken with outside of his presence for any reason.

"And then today, Ruth and I spent three hours listening to him bluster about how unfair the paper was to the hospital. And we're supposed to come up with a media plan by Monday to reinforce Memorial's positive image – and to discredit the paper."

"Discredit the paper? How?" Jeni asked.

"That's not clear yet, but he mentioned asking employees -- as individuals -- to cancel subscriptions and write letters to the editor about how the paper is a negative force in the community. And also withdrawing all of our advertising dollars -- and urging our local suppliers, and board members, to do likewise."

"A boycott?" Jeni asked incredulously.

"Well, not publicly, I'm sure. But on the QT – all of it predicated, I guess, if Blanchard can't get your publisher to make you back off on this story."

Chapter 42

Jeni knew that I and the editors needed to know the latest developments out of Memorial. She said later that after stewing about it at her apartment and trying to divert her nagging thoughts watching a DVD, she decided it couldn't wait until Monday.

She finally got me about 9:30 on my cell phone. I had let it ring several times on the nightstand beside Danny's bed before picking it up.

"Where are you?" she said. "I need to see you right away."

"Ah, that would be a little difficult right now. How about in the morning?"

"Now, dammit. I've talked with Angie and this Owens thing is about to hit the fan."

"Can't you tell me about it over the phone? It's a little awkward right now…"

"Oh -- oh," she said, the light dawning. "I'm sorry. I didn't get it. Duh! But I really need to see you. I think we've got to let Goldman know what's coming down at Memorial so she can warn the publisher. And maybe this is something Danny would be interested in, too"

"All right. All right," I said, looking apologetically over at Danny's side of the bed. "Give me a few minutes. Uh – wait a minute, let me check something."

I covered the phone with my hand, looked over at Danny and briefly explained the issue. She nodded and then I said again into the phone, "No, make it ten o'clock. We'll meet at Danny's." I gave her the address, and then Danny and I both scrambled to get showered and dressed before our inconvenient guest arrived.

Dressed in faded jeans and light sweater but with my hair only wet-combed and in bare feet, I answered Jeni's knock at the door and said, "Come in. Coffee's almost ready."

Danny appeared smiling at the bedroom door cocooned in a fluffy white terry cloth robe, her long hair hanging in wet strands.

"Uh – you two ever meet?" I asked awkwardly.

"No, but I feel I know you already," the women answered almost in unison and then laughed. They shook hands and Danny said, "You guys go ahead with the coffee. I'll be out as soon as I dry my hair."

I set out three cups and saucers on Danny's kitchen table and poured the steaming brown brew into two of them. "Might as well wait so you have to tell it only once," I said.

Jeni warmed her hands over the cup and looked around. "Nice place. Looks like it would be -- *comfortable*," she said with a hint of a smile.

I caught her emphasis and returned her sly smile, "Yes, I find it to be."

"You two going to…"

Jeni's words were interrupted by Danny's, "Going to what?" She appeared at the table still in her robe but with her hair dried and pulled back in a pony tail.

Jeni blushed. "Sorry, just being nosy," she admitted nervously. "I was going to ask Brock if you had plans to move in together."

"Jeni!" I said, but Danny cut me off.

"No plans – but might as well – as often as he's over here."

I spun toward her with knitted eyebrows. We had talked about it, but had come to no such agreement. "Uh – well -- didn't you come here to tell us something?" I asked.

"Oh, yes," Jeni replied. When finished with relating Angela's revelations, she asked, "So what do we do now?"

"Well, for sure we need to bring Jerry and Sarah up to speed."

Jeni noted my uncharacteristic use of the executive editor's first name. "Oh, so now it's Sarah? She's gotten into your good graces now that she's running interference for us with Graham?"

"Slip of the tongue. Don't make too much of it."

"You think we should risk ruining the bosses' weekend, or wait until Monday?" she asked.

"Really, there's nothing they can do about it anyway. I say let's wait until first thing Monday," I said and turned to Danny. "Anything here of interest to your department?"

She paused for a moment and said, "I don't think so; not yet at least. We have nothing yet to indicate a crime has been committed. And, sorry – despite what you may think -- it's not a crime to lie to the newspaper."

***

Sunday night's drive-by of the Gordon residence was no more fruitful than the one on Saturday night. Since I had to make a run by Cass Street anyway, Danny and I had decided to call it a night. There was no car at all in the Gordon driveway either night, but there were lights on in the house. I concluded Valerie Gordon must be parking her Sebring convertible in the garage. I noticed also there was no longer a "Stanley Gordon, Photography" sign above the first garage door.

The gray Dodge minivan that had been her husband's work vehicle was parked on the shoulder of the blacktop in front, sporting a plastic For Sale sign along with a phone number. And when I backed into the Bryants' driveway across the street to turn around, my car's headlights picked up something in Valerie Gordon's front yard that hadn't been there Saturday -- a red and white sign proclaiming, "For Sale By Owner."

Chapter 43

"I'm telling you, Brock, this damn story of yours sure as hell had better be worth it." That was Goldman's predictable reaction when Jeni and I caught her at the office as she arrived at 7:15 Monday morning.

"Blanchard's reaction sure as hell is over the top if it's a non-story," I retorted. "I wish I could swear to you that it's true, but it sure smells that way. I'd bet my next raise on it."

"If this blows up in our faces," she said with a worried scowl, "there might not *be* a next raise."

I was considering telling her where she could stick my next raise when she said, "Wait here. I'm going to see if Graham is in yet."

The curmudgeon Jerry offered, "Of course he's not in yet; he hasn't been in before nine o'clock the whole year he's been publisher."

I offered, "Well, he obviously hasn't been contacted by Blanchard yet or I'm sure we'd have heard about it."

Goldman nodded, "Stick around, then. I'll let you know when he comes in."

It was 9:45 when she again appeared at her office door and called to Jerry across the room. "Meet me in Graham's office in five."

He walked the three steps to my desk, looked down at me and said, "Look, try to keep your wise ass remarks to yourself. If it's gonna hit the fan no sense in getting it sprayed over all of us."

We trooped from the newsroom down the long corridor to the opposite end of the second floor, and when we reached the outer office Graham's secretary intercepted us. "He's on the phone with the ad director right now, and then Jim Blanchard is on hold."

Goldman stared wide-eyed for a moment, as if stricken, but then recovered and said, "Elsie, do me a big favor, will you? We *really* need to talk to the boss first. Okay? Could you just tell Mr. Blanchard that he's in a meeting and will call him as soon as he's free?"

Elsie Bowen, long-time secretary for Graham and his father before him, raised her eyebrows and looked up at Goldman over the top of her rhinestone-rimmed reading glasses. But then she nodded and smiled, "Okay. I'm sure he won't be long. Just the weekend revenue report. It looked like a good ad day yesterday so he ought to be in a good mood."

She turned to her phone console, touched a lighted HOLD button and said, "Mr. Blanchard, sorry to keep you waiting, but it looks like Mr. Graham is in for an extended conversation." She winked up at Goldman. "I'll have him call you as soon as he's able... Yes, I'll tell him it's *very* important... Certainly. Thank you."

She looked back up at Goldman and frowning said, "This wouldn't have anything to do with Mr. Blanchard's call, would it?"

Before Goldman could answer, the light went out on her boss's phone line and Elsie said into her headset, "Mr. Graham, Ms. Goldman is here to see you."

I smiled and shook my head at the artificial formality. Goldman noticed and glared at me.

"What?" I said.

"You know," she warned.

Elsie motioned us to enter through the heavy oak-paneled door that guarded the newspaper's inner sanctum. Unlike its occupant, Graham's office was warm and inviting, in contrast to the other utilitarian newspaper offices. The interior designer who had remodeled the 80-year-old building just before Mega Media's acquisition of the paper had made sure to appeal to a publisher's ego (and not incidentally the eye appeal to any prospective buyer).

While the newsroom, ad, circulation and accounting offices were in muted earth tones, the huge head office was done up in rich shades of green and gold. The original dark oak bookshelves, woodwork and wainscoting had been carefully removed, stripped and revarnished a gleaming golden brown. The publisher's large mahogany desk was set across the room in a bay formed by windows overlooking Main Street. In the foreground, facing sofas were in striped fabrics in red and gold, and a pair of fawn-colored leather armchairs at each end formed a spacious square accented at the corners with parchment-shaded brass lamps.

"Well, well," said a smiling Graham, standing and booming his best hale-fellow welcome. He waved the four of us into the upholstered quadrangle. The tall, slender and handsome publisher as usual was dressed impeccably, that day in navy pinstripe trousers and vest. His suit coat hung neatly from a hanger on a coat rack in the corner. "To what do I owe the pleasure so soon on a Monday morning?" He obviously had no clue of the topic of our visit.

"We – uh – need to bring you up to date on an investigation involving the hospital," Goldman said quietly. She plainly was ill at ease bringing bad news to her boss, and I almost felt sorry for her.

"Investigation? Sarah, I thought you assured me that was a non-starter," he said, clearly uncomfortable with being surprised.

"We've had – ah – additional information come our way that I think has merited additional exploration," Goldman said, looking at me seated to her right.

"We – Jeni and I," I said, "have come to believe that the report we received earlier about the person who died – Raymond Owens – although denied by Memorial was actually correct. We don't have all the facts yet, but there is increasing evidence that he died not from his accident injuries but in a fall at the hospital."

"I thought this was all behind us. What evidence?" Graham demanded, clearly skeptical of anything that would erode his comfort zone in the community.

Again, Goldman looked to me for support. I continued, "Two major issues: First, the overly secretive and hostile reaction we have received from hospital management to our inquiries."

"Hostile reaction? I wouldn't regard the phone call I received from Jim Blanchard as overly secretive or hostile," Graham said.

"There's more," Goldman said. She looked at me and said, "Tell him the rest of it."

"Rest of what?" Graham demanded.

"Aside from the vehemence of denials -- it's highly unusual for any CEO, and especially at the hospital -- to personally clamp the lid on like this," I said. "So, we have continued to quietly ask questions. But nobody will talk with us. They've all been ordered to say nothing about the case; all information has to come through Blanchard."

"But he's already told you nothing happened," Graham said. "Shouldn't that be enough – when the CEO denies anything happened?"

"Normally, yes," I answered, "but that's the second thing. We've received additional input from a highly reliable source, supposedly corroborated by two witnesses, who says that Mr. Owens fell several stories to his death. So, on Friday, Jeni and I decided to visit the hospital and attempted to ask questions directly of the nursing, maintenance and security supervisors. Before we knew it, Blanchard descended on us and ordered us from the hospital property."

Graham was turning red, shaking his head and directing a furious glance at Goldman. "I don't believe it. I can't believe you went behind my back with this after I specifically…"

"No one went behind your back, sir," Goldman said, her voice rising defensively. "We did what we're supposed to do – follow a still-developing story until we're satisfied we've reached a logical conclusion."

"There *is* no story," Graham declared.

"But, sir," I said, deliberately moderating my voice to hide my disgust at the publisher's timidity. It didn't help that this stuffed shirt was five years younger than me. "You can't decide something's a non-story until we have… "

Graham cut me off, "There's no story unless I say there's a story. There's got to be an end – here and now -- to the fixation on this fiction -- something that never happened. It's over and out. Understood?"

By this time I could feel my color rising and was just opening my mouth to object when Goldman restrained me by digging her nails into my arm. She rose quickly and said, "Yes, sir. Understood, sir. But you should know you'll be getting a call from Mr. Blanchard. I understand he may be orchestrating a boycott of *The Chronicle* if we go forward with this investigation. I only ask that you consider how desperately they want to quash this story before you decide to forbid us to go further."

Mention of a boycott and the implication of lost advertising revenue seemed to take the fire out of Graham. He sat back, shook his head and waved his hand dismissively, "All right, all right. I'll see what he has to say."

Goldman led the four of us quietly back down the hallway past Elsie's desk where the secretary again glanced up with an inquisitive look. Goldman just shook her head.

"That prick…" I said as we reached the newsroom, but Goldman ordered, "Not here. My office."

"Okay," she said once all were inside and she closed the door. "We'll wait until Graham digests what Blanchard has to say."

"And what if he says no," I demanded.

"We'll cross that when we come to it," she said, obviously

wanting to at least delay a potentially career-damaging confrontation with the publisher.

"We can't let him hush up something this big," I said. "I'll tell you now, if we do, I'm outta here."

Jeni, who had been quiet so far, agreed. "Me too. This is not what I signed on for."

I looked at her in surprise, and said, "Hey, I don't want anyone to follow my lead on this. It's just…"

"Look, people," Goldman said. "I'm not any happier than you – maybe even less so, since I have to work with him…"

Jerry at last interrupted, "Hey, guys, in a way Blanchard's call could be a blessing in disguise. It maybe saved us all from saying something we'd later regret. And – hope against hope – it just might give Graham a chance to grow a pair and decide he wants to be a *real* publisher instead of just a frickin' bean counter…"

Goldman's phone rang and she held up a hand for silence. "Yes, sir?" she said. "Okay, I'll be right there." She hung up and said, "Graham wants me to be there when he returns Blanchard's call. Hang in there; I'll let you know."

Chapter 44

Jeni, Jerry and I sat in Goldman's office, alternately shaking our heads and quietly pondering next steps if Graham's ban on the Memorial story were to stand.

For Jerry the fatalist, his entire 39 years with *The Chronicle,* news had always been whatever the publisher says it is. Just get the job done, cover the community as best you can, rock the boat only as much as necessary, and have a little fun in the process. The thoughts he shared were practical ones. With less than a year before his retirement goal of 70, what would he do if Jeni and I followed through on our threats to bolt the staff if Graham acted true to form?

For Jeni, I could tell it was a fist-in-the-gut agony. Only a few months into her journalism career, and proud launch into independence from her parents, there was the daunting reality of student loan and car payments to make. Sure, Mom and Dad would gladly take her in if she needed to take a step back. But as frustrated as she was, would she really have the courage on a matter of principle to quit the first real job she'd ever had?

For me, however, still burning from Graham's high-handed spiking of the Memorial story, I was calculating which of the various editors who had tried to recruit me over the years I'd contact first. Kenton wasn't my home town, and while I'd invested 15 years here, I was confident of finding pastures as least as green if I decided to look.

When Goldman hadn't returned after 15 minutes, we went back to our desks where Jerry got busy editing stories from the other reporters. Jeni mechanically rearranged the already neat piles on her desk and then busied herself at her computer.

I found myself opening one desk drawer after another, combing through file folders until I found what I was looking for. I spread it open before me and rested my elbows on the desk to hold my chin up while I studied the contents.

***

Goldman finally emerged from the hallway to Graham's office an hour and a half later and called out, "Jerry." She made a sweeping motion of her arm which to him meant "bring Brock and Jeni."

The executive editor, usually so put together and confident, looked exhausted. Squinting from behind an unruly wisp of straight brown hair, she pursed her lips, thrust her chin forward and, as the three of us entered her office, forced herself upright in her desk chair. She managed a feeble smile, blew out a pent up breath and said, "Well, we've still got a story – at least for now."

"Well, that's good news," I said, breathing in deeply as the tension evaporated. "What happened?"

"Blanchard was so far over the top that even Graham had to stand up to him."

Jerry asked, "What'd he say?"

"Blanchard didn't mince any words or niceties. He just flat out demanded that Graham 'leash' – his words – the paper's 'attack dogs' – also his words -- or *The Chronicle* would be made to pay for it."

"Apparently the art of subtlety is lost on Mr. Blanchard," Jerry said. "I've heard of a lot of threats over the years, but seldom so blatant. Did he specifically mention an advertiser boycott?"

"Yes, in so many words. And he threatened to go over Graham's head to Mega Media if he refused to be *sensitive* to highly regarded community organizations."

"*Sensitive,*" I cried. "Go over Graham's head for that? Hell, there couldn't *be* a publisher *more* sensitive to all his cronies in the community."

"Yes, but corporate doesn't know that," Goldman said. "Obviously, if Blanchard contacts them that will raise some alarms about Graham and *The Chronicle* whether or not they're deserved."

"And what did Mr. Graham say?" Jeni asked.

The three of us looked at her over her use of the term "mister" but Goldman answered,

"At first he tried to be conciliatory, but when Blanchard continued to rant in that threatening vein, Graham just cut it short. He said, in effect, 'I'm sure you'll do what you feel you have to do, and we will do likewise.'"

"Well, good for Graham – I guess," I said. "But that must have taken all of 15 minutes. What took you so long?"

"Just holding the publisher's hand – figuratively, of course. He needed to vent about how much pressure there is to keep growing the bottom line – certainly not easy these days."

"Yeah, well, I guess that's why he gets paid the big bucks," I said, not meaning it to sound as flippant as it came off.

Goldman snapped, "I'm sure the pressures are real. Whether you like Graham or not, you might at least try to put yourself in his position."

"No thanks. I'll leave that to you."

Goldman turned to me with knit eyebrows as if to say "where's that coming from" but bit her lip to restrain a response. Instead, turning to the others, she said, "Look, if the paper doesn't make a profit, none of us has a job."

"We all know that," I said. "But giving readers the news is what keeps them buying the paper and advertisers buying ads. And there's a legitimate question of how much money is enough. Will it ever be enough for Mega Media? And will Graham ever have the balls to stand up and say we need to do this for credibility with the readers and the long-term health of the franchise?"

My universal reporter rant about corporate ownership finished,

Goldman's office was quiet for a long moment before she shook her head, rose, leaned over her desk on tented fingers and spoke with finality, "Well, he stood up today, and for now, that should be enough. Let's get back to work."

As we filed out, Goldman said, "Brock, stay behind a moment, please." Jeni shot me a quick look of alarm but as I reversed direction I gave her a knowing wink.

"Close the door," Goldman said, frowning and with an obvious chill in her voice.

"Sitting or standing?" I forced a sheepish smile.

"Sit," she said, without humor, so I slouched onto a chair across from her desk, fully expecting a "woodshed" dressing down.

"Brock, you make me tired," she began, the tell-tale flush of emotion rising from her neck belying the soft, controlled voice. And she did appear tired, her words as weary as her face appeared, dark half-circles under her eyes. Obviously her session with Graham had been draining.

I was prepared to defend myself but was puzzled by her personal comment. Usually so self-assured, she suddenly seemed vulnerable.

"And, frankly," she continued, "I thought what you said about putting myself in Graham's position was a cheap shot."

Ahh. "Oh, that. I didn't mean anything by it. I'm sorry. I didn't mean to offend you. I'm glad it's you who have to deal with him and not me."

"No, there was more to it than that," she said. "As if you think I'm bucking for his job – or another one like it."

I could offer no response, and obviously there was more to come.

"I want you to know that I am totally devoted to the news

business – and to this newspaper, however long I'm here. I have no designs on becoming a publisher – here or anywhere else. I don't expect you to always agree with me, but I've got a job to do here and I don't need to have someone – especially in your senior position – constantly second-guessing me. Sometimes I feel like we're working at cross purposes. Like you resent me – for some reason. And I'm not aware of anything I've done to you to make you feel that way."

Not to me, but to the paper, I thought. The staff cuts and shrunken news space, overlarge photos and sensational headlines. We did often seem to be working at tangents from one another. But I felt chastened to learn I'd hurt her feelings.

"I'm sorry, Sarah. I know I can be a smart-ass sometimes," I confessed with a weak attempt at a smile. "It's nothing you've done to me – and I don't mean to be a thorn in your side. I know your job's not easy – delivering on expectations from corporate – and especially dealing with a publisher like Graham."

"What is it, then? The fact I'm a woman? An outsider – sent in by Mega Media?"

Obviously I'm not going to be fired or we wouldn't be carrying on this conversation. So I might as well let it out. "I have no problem working for a women. But, truthfully, it's the partly the corporate thing, I suppose. Someone in your position should be – well – maybe more vigorous in defending our staffing and news space – and more aggressive in supporting our coverage."

She shook her head and gave a tight-lipped, rueful smile. "You have no idea."

"Well – if that's the case ---.and, again, I know you're caught in the middle somewhat. But without being disloyal to the publisher, it might not hurt to let the staff know you understand our needs and that you're in there arm-wrestling with Graham and corporate on our behalf."

"Caught in the middle is a gross understatement," she said,

again reddening. "But -- that's a point well taken. I can see that. Maybe I haven't been as communicative of my feelings as I could be."

"Oh, you've been very upfront about your agenda of bringing the paper up to date appearance-wise and being more in touch with readers. And, I respect that, without saying so, in a lot of ways you've had to work around Jerry. He's solid but old school, and to your credit a lot of people would have just shoved him aside – or out."

She nodded acknowledgment but said nothing, so I continued. "We were way behind the times and needed new leadership. I think most everyone in the newsroom understands and supports your goals. And, if it hasn't seemed so, I'm sorry, but I do too. But in a lot of ways, you know, we're constantly being asked to do more with less – and getting damn little if any encouragement from the front office."

She nodded again and said, "I appreciate your candor. Really. I do understand how hard everyone's working. And I really do appreciate it even if it doesn't show. And I want you to know, Brock, I deeply respect you both as a reporter and for your knowledge and commitment to the paper and the community. You wield a lot of influence with the staff and…"

At this I tuned her out. Was she just blowing smoke or did she really understand the impact the penny-pinching, wet-blanket Dam-Gram had on staff morale?

"…I'd like to think," she was saying as I tuned back in, "we could find a way to work together." She stopped for a moment and with an almost shy smile added, "Without it being so obviously an armed truce."

I grinned at that and decided to accept her proffered armistice as genuine. "Sarah, you can count on my support," I said, and meant it.

"Great," she said, standing, indicating the interview was over.

"I'm glad we have arrived at an understanding."

Unwilling to let her have the last word, I grinned and said, "Well, let's not go *that* far. Let's just leave it that I respect your position and will do what I can to help you reach your goals."

"*Our* goals," she said. "Remember that. *Our* goals."

Huh, she got the last word in anyway. Well, let her have it.

***

Jerry eyed me curiously but said nothing when I re-entered the newsroom from Goldman's office. Jeni was not so circumspect.

"Well," she blurted barely under her breath. "Do you still work here?"

"Relax," I said, resolving to keep my own counsel about the exchange. But when Jeni pressed I said, "Let's just say that Sarah and I have decided we can work together."

"Oh, so it really is *Sarah* now?" Jeni teased. "Bout time isn't it? Since she's been here over a year?"

"Give it a rest, will you?" I grinned in spite of myself. "It's just a matter of mutual professional respect."

"Well, hallelujah and saints be praised," she said, grinning back. She studied me for a few moments before saying, "Well, I've got some good news for you, too."

"Yeah, what's that?"

"What are you doing after work today?"

"I dunno. Thought maybe I'd stake out Valerie Gordon's street for awhile. Why?"

"Thought maybe you'd like to come along with me on an interview."

"An interview? Whom are we interviewing?"

"You remember Emelda Paradiso? You know, the night nursing supervisor?"

"Uhuh. Why?"

"She wants to talk. Privately. She's calling in sick today and wants me to be at her house at six o'clock."

Chapter 45

Emelda Paradiso stood motionless and expressionless at her door after responding to our setting off her door chimes. She again was dressed all in white, but not a nurse's uniform as when Jeni had visited before. Over white slacks she wore a long white blouse with white brocaded designs at the waist, neck and wrists. She had on delicate white slippers and her long black hair was swept back by ornate silver combs.

"Mrs. Paradiso, this is Brock Andrews," Jeni said. "We're working on the Raymond Owens story together. I hope you don't mind that I brought him along."

The woman looked to me, again expressionless, and then back to Jeni. "Of course," she said, betraying no emotion. "Please come in." She ushered us into the large living room.

The room was darkened by heavy drapes at the front windows, but our host circled the room to turn on several white-shaded wooden table and floor lamps. "Please sit -- anywhere you're comfortable," she said. We took opposing chairs while she sat tentatively on the edge of her sofa.

"Before we begin," she said soberly, "I must have your agreement that I will not be quoted as a source for your investigation. I have spent many years at Memorial, I have many friends on the staff, and I expect to retire from there in a few years. I can't have my name associated with any story you write. Is that understood?"

Jeni looked at me, I nodded and she said, "Yes, I understand. We will not use your name without your permission."

"Good – and thank you. But you will never get my permission, because I love the hospital too much to…" She halted as moisture sparkled around her dark irises. She threw her head back, took a deep breath and seemed to relax.

"Now, may I offer you something to drink? Water? Some iced tea, perhaps? I have some freshly brewed iced tea."

Eager to get on with the interview and not lose focus over refreshments, I would have demurred but Jeni said, "That sounds wonderful." So I added, "Yes it does. Thank you."

The woman nodded and for the first time allowed herself a half smile before leaving the room. Her absence gave me an opportunity to look around and take in the furnishings. "Nice place," I said.

"She and her late husband were from the Philippines. He was a doctor."

"Yeah, I remember the name. But they've lived here a long time. I guess I'm surprised they stuck with the décor."

"Whatever you're most comfortable with, I guess," Jeni said as Mrs. Paradiso swept into the room bearing a tray of drinks. This time she wore a gracious smile as though she were accustomed to the role of hostess. She placed on a coaster beside each of us a tall glass of very light-colored iced tea with a thin slice of lemon floating on top. She then sat on her sofa holding a wine glass with a cloudy liquid that might have been skim milk.

She caught my glance at her glass and said, "This is *tuba*. It's a Filipino coconut wine. Really quite good and refreshing. After you've had your tea perhaps you'd like to try one."

"Thank you, but no," I said. "I'm sure the tea will be fine."

But Jeni, taking a sip from her glass, said. "Wow, this is great. What's in it?"

"Thank you. I'm glad you like it. It's a special Filipino recipe – tea and lemon and, I have to confess, a lot of sugar. Probably not an appropriate thing for a nurse to be serving, but it was my husband's favorite. I make it now, I guess, just out of habit…" She fell silent for a moment.

"It's terrific," I said, savoring the unusual blend of sweet and sour. "We appreciate it."

"Well," she said, leaning forward, depositing her glass on the coffee table and clasping her hands over her knees. "I know you didn't come here to hear me talk about Filipino tea." She looked at Jeni and continued, "When you visited me before, I'm afraid I was rude. I apologize. But you took me by surprise and I didn't know then what I know now."

"What is that?" Jeni asked.

"I want you to know that I was on vacation at the time of Mr. Owens's death. Actually visiting my family in the Philippines. I was here when Mr. Owens was admitted, but then I was gone for three weeks. When I returned he had already died – and, while death is an unpleasant reality of my profession, nothing seemed out of the ordinary. I only heard that the family was upset and that Mr. Blanchard had asked that any inquiries be directed to him."

She paused at some length, as if deciding how – or whether – to go on. I looked to Jeni and gave her a slight tilt of my head to indicate she should prompt her source.

"Yes, we heard the same thing," Jeni said. "But what made you call me back?"

"The secrecy for one thing. Not only the administrative involvement, but also when I asked some of the floor staff about it, they said they all were told to not discuss it – not among themselves – and definitely not outside the hospital. Something had to have gone wrong."

"Why do you say that?" Jeni asked. "You mean that Mr. Owens didn't die of his accident injuries?"

"Yes."

"How do you draw that conclusion?" I asked.

"One other thing," the nurse answered. "Both the charge nurse and the nurse's assistant on the night of Mr. Owens's death are no longer employed at the hospital. The week I returned from vacation the nurse – Sharon Newhouse -- took early retirement."

"Is that unusual?" Jeni asked.

"Considering that she had never mentioned it before, was too young to start collecting her pension, and neither she nor her husband has that kind of money. They've never even taken a vacation out of town the nine years I've known her. Plus, her husband is very ill and she's their only means of support."

"So what do you think happened?" I asked.

"I don't know, and it has taken me awhile to put the pieces together. You don't want to believe bad things about the place you've invested your career with. But it's just all too convenient. I suspect it has to do with avoiding hospital liability."

"So they paid her off – the nurse?" I said. "This conspiracy of silence is about bribery?"

"They're calling it early retirement – but I suspect it's what in the business world would be called a buyout."

"They bought her off – why?" Jeni asked.

"Because -- because I now believe – no, I know – that your suspicions must be correct."

"That he fell out of a window?" Jeni said, excitement telling in her voice.

"No -- jumped," the nurse said shaking her head, her face downcast.

"Why would you say that?" I asked.

"Look, Mr. Andrews," she said in obvious frustration. "I don't know all the details of Mr. Owens's case. You will need to dig that up on your own. But I do know the way the rooms are constructed – they all have high window sills -- it wouldn't be easy for someone to just *fall* through a window. It would take a pretty determined leap to go through the glass."

"That being the case, there's another scenario, isn't there?" I asked. "That he might have been pushed?"

Her hands flew to her face. "Oh, my god, no. I don't want even to think of that. No, I can't even entertain such a notion. I won't."

"Very well, then – for now," I said in a calming voice. "But why would he want to commit suicide? All reports were that he was getting better."

"I don't know. But it wouldn't be unheard of for a patient to be depressed after being seriously hurt. Sometimes healing takes a long time, and then there's possibly a long period of rehabilitation. And it's all very expensive."

"Wouldn't insurance cover that?" I said.

"Again, I don't know the details of who was paying for what. Or of Mr. Owens's state of mind. But I'm saying that if we or the doctors felt there was a chance of the patient being suicidal, it would have been our responsibility to put him on suicide watch – or in a secure ward."

"So therein lies the hospital's concern for liability?" Jeni said.

"And thus the coverup," I added. "What about the nurse's assistant?"

"There's a lot of turnover in those positions. I haven't followed that up. But given everything else it seems just too coincidental that they both were on floor duty the night Mr. Owens died and they're no longer there. "

"What's her name?" Jeni asked, pen poised over notebook.

"Judy Galloway."

"Do you know where she lives?" she added. "Or where she might have gone to work?"

"I have no idea. Perhaps human resources can give that to you."

Jeni turned to me and smiled, "Well, I don't think human resources – or anyone else at Memorial -- will be talking to us anytime soon. But I'm sure we can find it another way." She continued, "Is there anything else you think we should know?"

Mrs. Paradiso pursed her lips, closed her eyes and shook her head. She rose, indicating the interview was concluded.

"Well, I can't thank you enough for getting back to me. I truly appreciate your trust in sharing all this with us," Jeni said.

The nurse fixed us for a moment with a firm gaze, but she looked away as her eyes welled again. "Truthfully, trusting you had nothing to do with my call. I – I just care too much about the quality and integrity of care at Memorial to see something like – this -- go unchallenged." She walked us to the door and as we stepped outside offered her hand. "But I do trust that you will keep your agreement to not use my name. I wish you luck with your story. Good bye."

Chapter 46

"Oh – my – god!" Jeni said aloud as we reached my car. "Did we really hear what I think we heard?"

"Shh," I said, looking back at Emelda Paradiso's still open front door. The nurse stood there, peering sadly out at us. "Yes, I think we did. If she's right, this just keeps on getting thicker and thicker."

I started the Camaro and pulled away, and we drove back toward the office in silence for several minutes. Finally, Jeni said, "But if it wasn't an accident, why would they go to such lengths to cover up a suicide?"

"There's still the remote possibility of a homicide – even if Mrs. Paradiso doesn't want to consider it."

"Yes," Jeni reasoned. "But so far there's no evidence of a motive for anyone to kill Raymond Owens. And what possible motivation would Memorial have to cover up a homicide? That wouldn't be anything they could anticipate or be held accountable for."

"Unless it was an employee. Crazier things have happened. But let's say you're right. Just looking at cover-up motive, accidents can happen anywhere – and bad as they can be, they're usually covered by insurance. But suicide while the patient's in the hospital's care?" I shook my head. "I don't know, but that smacks of liability – neglect or failure to diagnose. Docs, nurses – and especially administrators – all covering their asses."

"And buying off those directly involved while ordering the few who might know to keep shut about it or lose their jobs," she said. "But do the Owenses seem like vindictive people? Would they have sued if the hospital had just told the truth from the beginning?"

"Hard to tell," I said. "I don't know the family well enough to judge. The wife and daughter seemed just like reasonable people trying to deal with a tragedy. The son? Maybe a bit of a hothead there. They might have been willing to accept the bad news of a suicide, but after being lied to and stonewalled? That does tend to piss people off."

"So if this turns out to be what we think it is, and we're able to print it, what do you think will happen?" Jeni asked as I pulled into *The Chronicle* parking lot.

"My guess? Excrement hits the air circulator. Family sues. Maybe even charges are filed – although I don't know what those might be. Bottom line, Blanchard goes bye-bye."

"And if we don't print it?" she asked, stepping from the car and peering at me over the roof..

"Brock goes bye-bye."

"I was afraid you'd say that," she said, thrusting her lower lip forward in a deliberate frown. "And me, too – I guess."

***

"So where do we go from here?" Jeni blurted excitedly when I reached my desk the next morning. Her adrenalin rush was palpable and made me smile wondering when the last time was I felt that pumped about a developing story.

"I'll brief Sar--ah," I said, anticipating her lifted eyebrows. "Then I've got to get back on the Gordon case. But I'll nose around the cop shop to see if anyone remembers anything at Memorial on the night in question. Meanwhile, I think you'd better see what you can find out about the nurse and the assistant. What are their names again?"

She flipped through her notebook. "Sharon Newhouse and Judy Galloway."

"Yeah. If Mrs. Paradiso is right, Blanchard might have bought the nurse's silence, and maybe the assistant's too. See if you can talk to both of them. If you reach them, I'll join you – if you want me to."

"I'd appreciate it," she said.

"Oh, and I'll also check with the prosecutor to see what, if any, laws might be broken in falsely reporting a cause of death."

"You're going to *tell* them?"

"What, and blow our scoop? No, of course not. Just speculative, I'll say. And also I need to talk with Mrs. Owens. If her husband committed suicide, she might not have known if he was clinically depressed but she'd surely know if there were other things he might be upset about.

"And, no, to anticipate your question. I'm not going to broach the subject of suicide to her. They've had enough heartache without having to deal with what at this stage is just an informed suspicion on our part."

Minutes later, seeing that Goldman's light was on, I started toward her office.

Looking up with a sly smile, Jeni called, "Let me know what *Sar--ah* says."

***

Unsure of how to begin after our set-to the previous day, I stuck my head in her doorway and said, "Wanna hear the latest, boss?" I hadn't called her that before; and at that moment realized I probably had avoided addressing her directly by name since she'd arrived. *No wonder she felt like I resented her.*

"Come on in." She smiled. "Will I like what I'm going to hear?"

"Try this on. Jeni got a follow-up call from a nursing supervisor at the hospital. We went to see her last night. Nice lady. Anyway, her take – off the record – is that it was a suicide."

"So why is Blanchard trying to hush it up?" she said, her arms folded

"If the guy was clinically depressed the doctor and staff should have seen it and been more watchful of their patient. If the docs and nurses look bad, so does Memorial and so does Blanchard."

"That seems pretty drastic. Maybe even over the top?"

"Yeah, it does. But there's more."

"Oh, good. It gets better?"

"Better as in both the charge nurse and nursing assistant on the ward that night are no longer employed at the hospital."

"Disciplinary actions?" she asked.

"No, doesn't look that way. They're just both suddenly gone. The nurse took an unscheduled early retirement, which she likely could ill-afford. We don't know about the assistant yet. But it looks like Blanchard could be buying their silence."

"You said 'off the record.' Can we prove any of this?"

"No, not yet. We had to assure the nursing supervisor of confidentiality to get her insights to the story. She was away on vacation when all this happened, so she has no direct knowledge we could use anyway. But she seems genuinely upset over it -- and over the clampdown on information since her return."

"So where do we go to get something that *is* on the record. I can't take anything back to Graham unless we have proof – someone who knows and is willing to tell us *on the record* what actually happened."

"That's what we're trying for," I said, and then related the next steps for Jeni and me.

"Okay," she said. "Go to it."

I had gotten as far as her door when she called out, "Oh, Brock?"

"Yeah, boss?"

"Thanks for the update. I'm glad you're working with Jeni on this."

***

Georgia Owens responded late in the afternoon to the message I had left that morning on her answering machine.

"Yes, Mr. Andrews? Do you have anything to share with us?"

"Well, not exactly," I dissembled. "I just wanted you to know that I haven't forgotten about your request and I just need a clearer picture of the circumstances around your husband's time in the hospital."

"What circumstances are those?"

"Well, just some general information to start with. Uh – who was your auto insurance with? And – uh – I assume your husband had a hospitalization plan at work? Had you begun receiving bills from the hospital yet?"

The line was silent for many seconds and I wondered whether my questions had offended her – or she had hung up. "Mrs. Owens?"

She cleared her throat. "Yes. Yes, I'm still here," she said, her voice quaking. "I'm – I'm sorry. This has all just been so overwhelming."

"Can you tell me about it? I'd like to hear it."

"Oh, no, it's just the bills. Now that Ray is gone, I'm struggling to understand it all – much less know how it's all going to be paid."

"You did have insurance coverage, didn't you?"

"Well, yes, but our auto policy medical coverage was just the minimum, and his insurance from the plant wasn't…" Again, her voice broke.

"Your husband worked at LaGrange Tool?"

"Yes, but their hospital plan was pretty bare bones. Very disappointing…"

"Was he covered by life insurance?"

"Yes," she recovered. "He had a $10,000 death benefit from work, but most of that went toward the funeral expenses. And we each had a $25,000 life policy – which was doubled because of the accident. But just my share of the hospital bills is so much more than that."

"If – if you don't mind my asking -- what do they say you owe?"

"I'd have to look up the exact amount – but it's – it's still over $100,000."

"Wow. I understand. That's gotta be tough," I said, trying to reassure her. "Do you have anyone to help you sort it all out?"

"My daughter lives down in Louisville. She's a nurse so she understands these things better than I do."

"What about your son?"

"I have two sons. John, the oldest, lives in Kansas City; you talked to him before when he was here. Jimmy's my youngest. He lives in town, but he – he and Ray were – well, they were…" Her voice caught and it was a moment before she spoke again. "I guess -- the word is estranged. They hadn't spoken in a couple years -- and then suddenly it was too …" Her voice went silent amid sniffles and then she said, "But Jimmy and his wife have been very supportive since then – even though they're struggling themselves."

"That's good," I said lamely. I felt sorry for the woman, but knew I could offer her little hope or encouragement.

"As bad as it is now, I don't know what we'd have done – if Ray had lived -- to pay for all the long-term rehabilitation they were talking about. None of the children are in any shape to help me much financially – and I wouldn't ask them."

"How long was rehab going to take?"

"They were saying it could be three to four more months off work and then all the therapy..."

"Wouldn't his hospitalization from the plant have paid for some of that?"

"Some, maybe, but his benefits were about exhausted. It's a tiny company and I know these insurance plans are very expensive. I think they provided what they could afford. But there's a limit per incident, and he was near his lifetime benefit limit because of the valve and bypass surgery he had three years ago." She paused and then said, "As I guess you can see, my husband was not a well man."

"Would he have been able to retire on disability?" Brock asked.

"No, the company offered no long term disability – or pension – and we had already borrowed heavily on his 401(k). With years to go before Social Security and Medicare, if he couldn't work, we'd have had to rely on Social Security disability – and I'd have to go to work. I guess I still will. We had already taken all the equity out of our home. I'm afraid I still might lose the house."

"What kind of work do you do?"

"I don't know. I mean, I've never worked since we've been married. Ray always wanted me to be at home. And now..."

"I'm sorry this situation is such a burden for you," I said, thinking of my own mother who had given up her journalism career to stay at home while I was growing up.

"And you know what the clincher was?" she continued, now obviously crying. "To top it all off, the company said that since he was going to be gone so long they'd have to go ahead and fill his position."

Chapter 47

I had about finished explaining my conversation with Georgia Owens when the Applebees waitress delivered to our booth the dessert Danny had decided we would share. *Why can't I have my own,* is what I thought. What I said was, "So considerate of you to think of my waistline. Besides, it's so romantic to *share.*"

Her order of what the restaurant called a Maple Butter Blondie had made me wince. "Why can't these places just serve pie and ice cream?" But the first bite changed my tune. "Damn, this is pretty good."

"Glad you like it. Just remember I'm here too," she said, sliding the plate closer to her side of the table. "Now, as you were saying…"

"Well, yeah, based on Mrs. Owens's account there certainly was plenty of reason to suspect that a depressed patient facing all those hardships might think of taking the easy way out."

"Uhuh," she said. "That would be one way to look at it. But for the sake of argument, what other scenarios for Mr. Owens's death occur to you?"

"Well, the nurse seems to rule out anyone just accidentally falling out a window. I checked, and the window sills are nearly waist high. Plus, Owens was still wearing a cast and barely ambulatory."

"And have there been any other such *accidents* at Memorial – or suicides, for that matter?"

"Gotta be a first time for everything, I suppose," I said. "But you mean if it's not an accident and not suicide, it might be homicide? Sure, especially with this cover-up we can't totally discount any possibility. But there's nothing to indicate…"

"At least none that we know of," she said and paused to take a bite before the dessert was gone. "Just blue-skying here, but what about a son who didn't get along with his dad thinking there might be other relief for his about-to-be impoverished mother?"

"Jeez, you're starting to think like a detective already, aren't you?"

"Just trying to help sort out all the alternatives."

"Well, you're right. It's pretty far-fetched, but maybe something to keep in the back of our minds as we plumb the possibilities."

It was only a Tuesday night, and tempting though a return to Danny's apartment was, I left her in Applebees' parking lot to allow her to log some online study time for the detective exam. I decided to check in with Jeni on her progress.

***

I found her at 8 p.m. still at her desk in the newsroom.

"You need to get a life," I said. "Don't you have a boyfriend – or girlfriend, as the politically correct case may be?"

Her exasperated look told me I'd touched a sensitive nerve.

"Not that there'd be anything wrong with that, of course," I said.

"Not that it's any of your business, but you, of all people, should know I don't have a *boy* friend – *yet*. Not that I've had time since joining *The Chronicle*."

"Oh – yeah. Well, that's good," I recovered, looking away while failing to suppress a smile. "I mean – while you're working on a big story. Oh, hell, you know what I mean. What did you find out today?"

"I found out that Sharon Newhouse, RN, has moved from Kenton – address unknown, at least to her neighbors. She and her husband were renters and, from what the lady next door thinks, have moved to somewhere in Florida. At least that's what they always were talking about."

"Shouldn't be too hard to track down – mail forwarding, change of address, etcetera. Might even check with our circulation department – refund if they were subscribers."

"Right, I'll do that tomorrow. And maybe Angie can help out with that, too. I'm still waiting for that listing of hospital employees' names and addresses. She hasn't called me back. Hope I haven't burned a bridge there."

"Me, too. Maybe after Blanchard's tirades she's too scared to contact you. What about the assistant -- Judy what's her name?"

"Galloway. From what I've been told she's now working for a nursing home out in the county. I'll try contacting her there tomorrow."

"Good, let me know what you learn."

"Will do. How about you?"

I related my conversation with Georgia Owens, and with Danny. "Just to keep our options open, Danny thinks we shouldn't necessarily reject homicide."

"What do you think?"

"Well, obviously it wasn't appropriate to delve into that today with Mrs. Owens, but maybe the daughter in Louisville can shed some light on apparently strained relations between her father and younger brother. I'll give Teresa Wilkerson a call tomorrow."

***

The night was young, and with Danny busy and my share of the Owens story on hold until the next day, I decided to take a turn down Cass Street. It was a warm April evening and with the window down I cruised slowly the length of the street to Valerie Gordon's house at the dead end. I backed into the Bryants' drive across the street. Lights were on in the Gordon house, but there were no vehicles in the driveway. The Dodge van was no longer parked on the street so maybe she had succeeded in selling it. The house for sale sign, however, still stood in the front yard.

I drove back up the street before returning and backing into the drive of the vacant house across the street and down the block from the Gordon place. Thus parked I had a clear view of the street and Valerie Gordon's drive. I turned on the radio with the volume just loud enough to hear Marty Brenneman's play by play of the Cincinnati-Chicago game. But with the Major League Baseball season just underway, there was little to hold my interest and I nodded off.

When I awakened with a start, a cool breeze was pouring in the open window and light raindrops were pattering against the windshield. I gave an involuntary shiver and turned the ignition key to light up the dashboard clock. It was nearly eleven. I'd been asleep for more than 45 minutes. The rain started falling more heavily and I raised my window. Soon it began to pour and I started the engine to pull away, but when the wipers cleared the window I could make out the shadow of a car in the Gordon driveway. Lights were no longer visible at the front of the house, but shone through windows at the rear.

Pulling out of the driveway I nosed the Camaro slowly down the street, straining to see what I could of the visiting vehicle. As Mrs. Bryant had said, the car was a large, dark colored sedan but I could make out no details through the rain-flecked side window. I backed again into the Bryants' drive so that my headlights fell across the front of the Gordon house. Hoping to not ignite the Bryants' alarm and maybe a call to the police, I killed the lights and sat there for several minutes. The rain having stopped, I opened my door and, hunched against the raw wind, crossed the street to the edge of Valerie Gordon's gravel driveway.

The car sat in the shadow of the house – too dark to see much detail but it was an older model Crown Victoria, ostensibly all black with no chrome and no wheel covers. It was the kind of vehicle that police customarily handed down to other departments when they were still serviceable but no longer reliable enough for sustained patrol duty.

A city- or county-owned car? The license plate would tell, but I hadn't brought a flashlight. My first thought was to creep down the driveway to find the answer but my second was self-preservation. In a place where there had already been one homicide, I didn't want to be mistaken by the Widow Gordon for a prowler and shot. Curiosity won out, and I tiptoed as noiselessly as possible on the gravel to the rear of the vehicle. I was just bending down to squint at the tag number when the crunch of distant footsteps on gravel froze me behind the car. I crouched while my mind raced over the options of hiding or flight. The footsteps drew nearer and the driver's side door opened. The interior light came on and I realized that if the car started to move I would be exposed – if not run over.

There was a rustling of papers and then the car door closed without anyone getting in. The footsteps retreated across the gravel toward the rear of the house and I strained to hear the sound of a door closing. When it came I allowed myself a long-suspended breath of relief. Without taking time to recheck the license plate, I slunk back to my car. *Time to call Danny.*

Back in the car and on the cell phone, I punched in my #1 speed dial.

"Huh? What?" she asked, her voice clogged with sleep. "Jeez, Brock, it's late. What's up?"

My explanation was enough to spring her wide awake. "Better hurry. Don't know if it's an all-nighter."

I moved my car back to the corner of Cass and Walnut and awaited her arrival. As her black and white cruiser reached the intersection I flashed my headlights at her and she pulled up beside me. I was glad, for once, that the controversial policy of take-home cars gave her a plausible reason to be patrolling the neighborhood. I told her so and also complimented her thinking to wear her uniform.

"Well, if we're spotted we don't want to put Mrs. Gordon and her visitor on guard," she said. "But if one of the neighbors sees us sneaking around we don't want them calling KPD either."

As she drove slowly down Cass, she admonished me, "Just because she's got a visitor – even a male one for an overnight – doesn't mean it necessarily has anything to do with her husband's death."

"I know, I know. But it just seems suspicious so soon, don't you think?"

"Possibly. Possibly. We'll see."

She stopped with the Gordon driveway on her left. The dark sedan was still there. There was no sign of activity on the property, but lights were still on at the back of the house. She took careful aim with the handle of her spotlight so it would hit the drive behind the shadowed vehicle. She switched the light on and lifted the spot for just a moment to the rear bumper. The effort was rewarded with the reflected light blue of a publicly-owned vehicle. IN5427.

"Holy crap," she said. "I don't believe it."

"What?"

"I recognize the plate, that's what."

"And – and? Don't keep me in suspense."

"It's the coroner's car," she said. "Buster Bradshaw's."

Chapter 48

"Hard to figure Buster as a murderer," I said. "He's kind of a contentious prick, but I've always seen him as just a small-minded country yahoo – lots of bluster but not necessarily the violent type."

"There's no one type," Danny said. "Almost anyone can become violent given the right circumstance."

We were back at her apartment, where the coffee was easily better than at any of the late night places.

"But let's not get ahead of ourselves," she said, pouring from the freshly brewed pot. "All we know is that his car was there tonight."

"And according to the neighbors apparently has been a regular visitor before."

"Yeah, *if* it's the same car the neighbors have seen. I'll have to check that it's still Buster's."

We were silent over our cups for awhile when Danny offered, "Maybe she met him when he came to their home to claim her husband's body."

"Yeah, that's a great way to start a relationship."

"Stranger things have happened."

"Or maybe at the dentist's office?" I said. "Easy to check. When do you get the patient list?"

"Dr. Schmidt said he'd have it for me tomorrow. And then I'll have to check to make sure the car we saw tonight is still assigned to Buster."

"Strange, isn't it," I mused, "that the coroner seems to have a role – however minor or tangential -- in both of these cases –

Stanley Gordon and Raymond Owens?"

"Well, bodies *are* his business, right? Could be just coincidence of his official duties. What's the next step for you – and Jen-eye?"

"Hey, let's not mock her. She's earning her spurs on this one. She's done about as much as she can with her hospital contacts. Next she'll try to run down the *retired* nurse and the former nursing assistant. See if we can break anything loose from them about the fateful – and fatal – last night of Raymond Owens."

"And you?"

"I'll talk with his daughter, Teresa, in Louisville. And then, if you can confirm it was Buster's car we saw tonight, maybe I'll find a way to gig him on his new relationship."

***

Having briefed Jeni on the previous night's surveillance, I sat at my desk the next afternoon, poring over a thick sheaf of papers dropped off mid-morning by Danny. It was an alphabetical compilation of names and addresses of Dr. Howard Schmidt's male patients.

Jeni was paging through a print-out delivered by Angela Lawrence that listed Wilkes Memorial Hospital employees by department – names, addresses and phone numbers.

"You see anything interesting?" I asked across the desk.

"Well, now that I have these two women to track down, maybe I won't need other hospital contacts so much. Everybody has probably been warned off already anyway. But at least Angie's still talking to me. How about you?"

"Frankly, I'm impressed," I said.

"Why's that?"

"A dentist able to generate a list segregating patients by

gender? Dr. Schmidt must be something of a computer geek."

"Or maybe his office manager – a *woman* no doubt – knew how to get it for him."

"Touche. Actually, they couldn't just give us a list of adults. It's all male patients with date of birth in a separate field so we can use that to sort them. Danny's got a copy and is running down any known violent offenders. I just want to see if any names jump out at me."

"Well, I'll be damned," I said after a couple minutes of page turning.

"What?"

"Seems that Buster and the whole damn Bradshaw family are patients of Dr. Schmidt."

She got up and leaned over my shoulder as I pointed, "See here? Bradley J. – that's Buster, age of – uh -- 49. And Kenneth C., about 72 – that's the father who founded the funeral business. And Kyle W., 44, Buster's brother and partner in the funeral home. And these five others? Ages – uh -- 12 to about 25? Must be Buster and Kyle's kids."

"So Buster must have had contact with Mrs. Gordon on numerous occasions, huh?" Jeni said.

"So it would seem. Doesn't prove anything, but at least the murder scene almost certainly wasn't their first meeting." I went on scanning the names, running across photographer Rudolph Lipscomb and car salesman Thomas Wallace before exhausting the list. "Lots of well-known local names among the doctor's patients," I said, "but none that stands out as suspicious. No known criminals or notorious womanizers predisposed to succumbing to a wanton hygienist's chair-side wiles."

"At the very least, you've got Buster as knowing Mrs. Gordon before the murder," Jeni said. "And *if* the current night visitor is Buster…"

***

Danny hadn't gotten back to me yet on the license plate, and I didn't want to bother her on her cell while she was on patrol. I decided to use the time to call Teresa Owens Wilkerson in Louisville. I knew she was a nurse, but didn't know whether she was currently employed. I fished her cell number from the notes I'd taken when she originally called and punched the digits into my office phone.

"This is Teresa," she said cheerily, a number of voices evident in the background.

"Oh, hello. This is Brock Andrews of *The Chronicle*. I hope I'm not disturbing you at work."

"Oh, no, it's okay, Mr. Andrews. I'm in the break room at the nursing home. My mother told me you had spoken with her."

"Yes, well, I wanted you also to know that I hadn't forgotten about your request. And I have a few follow-up questions -- if you don't mind."

"Does that mean you think there's something to our suspicions? Mom got that impression."

"It's too soon to tell," I hedged, not wanting to divulge too much before we were ready to break the story – whatever it eventually was. "But there are a number of things that seem not to add up – including the fact the hospital is so hypersensitive about our inquiries. It's taking some time – but we're checking them one by one."

"Again, we appreciate your working on this. How can I help you today?"

"For starters, can you give me some insights into your parents' insurance coverage -- auto and medical? Just trying to cover all angles. Your mother seemed so stressed during my call, I didn't want to bother her with too many specifics."

"Yes, well, as you can tell it's been very overwhelming to her – both losing Dad and having to sort through all the bills -- hospital, doctors, funeral home, insurance and everything."

"That's entirely understandable. What can you tell me?"

"Without Dad's life insurance, I'm sure Mom would lose the house. As it is, it'll be tough for her to scrape by, but I think with what little my brother and I can give her she'll be able to stay in her home."

"You mention your brother. Your older brother? The one I spoke with that day you called?"

"Yes, John. He's younger than me, but the older of the two. He's in Kansas City. Just getting on his own feet financially, but between the two of us we'll be able to afford a couple hundred a month to help with the mortgage. And, of course, Mom will have to go to work – whatever there might be for a nearly 60 year old woman with almost no experience."

"I'm sure she'll find something," I said. "And it's good of you to help out."

"Well, it's not exactly like we have a choice. Unfortunately, Dad hadn't taken out any mortgage insurance – hindsight, you know. Ironically, it's almost better that he died or they both would have been out on the street."

She paused and stertorous breathing indicated she was fighting back tears.

"I'm sorry to have reopened these wounds," I said.

"No, no, it's okay," she said, sniffing. "I'm the one who should be sorry. That must have sounded terribly mercenary. But it's just the cold hard facts."

"What about your younger brother? Is he in any position to help out?"

"Oh, that's what's so really sad about this. Jimmy was the

baby of the family, and they gave him everything. But it was never enough. He and Dad had a falling out about a loan my folks couldn't afford to give him in the first place. Despite Jimmy's promises – and I suppose good intentions – he made a few payments and then stopped all together."

"That's tough. What happened then?"

"Dad had finally had enough. Told him to grow up and not to come back until he could live up to his obligations like a man." She stopped, heavy breathing again.

"And?"

"And he didn't – didn't come back home. He didn't even visit our father in the hospital after the accident. And then -- then it was too late. And at the funeral home he and John got into this big argument… It was just -- hideous."

"I'm sorry to upset you like this. What did they argue about?"

"Oh, with Jimmy, the usual. Money, or lack of it, and was he going to do anything with his life to live up to Dad's hopes for him."

"What about now?"

"Now? Jimmy's the only one in town to help out Mom, and I think all is forgiven. At least now I think he'll be there for *her*. It's a cinch she won't have any money to give him, so maybe he'll step up and be the son she needs now that Dad's gone."

Chapter 49

A call to the Golden Rest Nursing Home elicited agreement from Judy Galloway to meet Jeni at a picnic table outside the rear entrance to the home. The long one-story brick structure was off a quiet country road a dozen miles west of Kenton. The former nurse's aide at Wilkes Memorial blew the smoke from her cigarette up away from her face and nervously flicked ash onto the concrete patio.

"Thank you for seeing me," Jeni said to the woman who appeared to be about 40 years old and as many pounds overweight. The black leather jacket she wore against the outside chill didn't disguise that her white uniform was stretched to capacity.

"What do you want?" the aide demanded, her voice betraying wariness bordering on hostility. The dark crescents under her brown eyes matched her prematurely gray hair.

"I want to know why you left Memorial," Jeni said.

"Look, I don't want to talk about it. I only agreed to talk to you out here because I don't want you asking questions inside where others can hear."

"Did you have to leave because Raymond Owens died on your shift?"

"Who told you that?" the aide blurted, rising from the table and stabbing out her cigarette in a tin ashtray.

"He *did* die when you were on duty, didn't he?" Jeni persisted.

"Hey, lots of people die in the hospital all the time. It wasn't my fault. I just decided to leave, that's all. That's over and I'm movin' on."

"Were you fired, or did they ask you to leave because they wanted to keep things quiet?"

"I wasn't fired," she said, shaking her head. "If they'd done that, I would have been all over them, you can bet on that."

"So – what? Raymond Owens went through a window on your shift and you just decided you'd had enough?"

The aide's eyes widened and she stared at the reporter in silence before shaking her head and slumping back down on the bench. "Look, I didn't do nothin' wrong."

"I'm not saying you did," Jeni said. "But the hospital is trying to cover this thing up, and we're going to get to the bottom of it. You've got a chance to tell me what really happened and then I'll go away and nobody will know you even talked to me."

Again, the woman was silent, staring down at her white ripple-soled oxfords against the concrete patio. Finally she looked up and said, "You won't have to use my name? They helped me get this job and I don't want nothin' to ruin it for me."

"So they asked you to leave, but helped you find another position? Is that it?"

"Yes. They said if I left there wouldn't be any stink about what happened. And they gave me two months' severance."

"You know now that they lied about how Raymond Owens died?"

"Yeah, but by the time I heard that I figured that was their problem. He was dead and nothin' I could do about it. Again, I didn't do nothin' wrong."

"Tell me what happened," Jeni said softly, nodding at the woman in reassurance.

"Can you promise you won't tell nobody you talked to me?"

"My bosses already know I'm here. But nobody else, I promise. Honest."

"Well, all the patients – they was asleep and everything –

everything was quiet. Then we heard this crash but didn't know where it come from. We ran up and down the hall lookin' in all the rooms and in one of them there's this broken window and he's lyin' down there in the courtyard with a broken chair."

"Broken chair?"

"Yeah, he musta throwed the chair through the window before he jumped."

"So you didn't see anything or hear anything out of the ordinary? Just glass breaking?"

"That's right. And you can see it wasn't my fault, can't you? Wasn't anybody's fault if he decided to kill hisself."

"You're sure he killed himself? That it wasn't an accident of some kind?

"No, you can't just fall outa them windows. They only open a coupla inches at the bottom, and they're too high to fall through unless you're standing up on the bed or chair or somethin'."

"So if he killed himself, why do you think the hospital is trying to cover things up?"

"I ain't got any idea. Maybe somebody'd think we shoulda watched him more carefully, but we had no reason to. If we thought he was suicidal, the doctors woulda put him in the psych ward."

"Who talked to you? And what did they say when they told you they wanted you to leave?"

"It was Mr. Blanchard and the security guy – what's his name? Carver? No – Carter. They didn't tell me nothin' – just that it would be better if I left. That I'd get a good recommendation and they'd keep payin' me till I got another job."

"Not a bad deal," Jeni said.

"No, cause they called me in two days and said I could start work here right away. And after what happened with Mr. Owens, I'm glad I'm gone. And I got an extra two months' pay out of it."

"And what do you know about the departure of Sharon Newhouse? She was in charge that night, right?"

"Yes, but I don't know nothin' about why she left. I was already gone and just heard she left too, that's all."

Chapter 50

Jeni had just finished giving me the rundown on her conversation with Judy Galloway.

"That's great work, Jeni. We've still got no one on the record, but at least I think we've got enough to go to Dam-Gram to convince him we're not dreaming this stuff up."

She beamed at my approval. "And maybe to force the truth out of Memorial?"

"Who knows? They're so deep into the lie now they may be stuck with it. But we've got one more ace in the hole."

"What's that?" she asked.

"Sharon Newhouse? The nurse? Circulation didn't have a forwarding address, but they did have a local address to send their subscription refund check to. Her folks, I think. Here's the phone number. Given your success grilling the assistant, you shouldn't have any trouble finding out where the nurse ran off to."

An hour later, Jeni erupted into a loud, "All right," and waved a piece of paper in front of my nose. "Address and cell number."

"Good for you. Let me know what you get from her."

Another hour later, however, Jeni was frowning and shaking her head. "She wouldn't talk to me. She told me not to call her again and then hung up on me."

"Where's she live?"

"St. Petersburg."

"So Mrs. Paradiso was right. Retired to Florida."

"Well, I didn't get far enough to know whether she's retired. I started out telling her I was doing a feature about people who had left Kenton for southern climes – which actually is true. And she was friendly enough until I started asking about Memorial. Then she clammed up. Said she didn't want to be part of the story any more."

"Too bad. Too bad. Hmmm." My stocking feet were again on the desk as I stroked my chin.

"What? What are you thinking?

"I'm thinking -- you probably should go see her."

"What? All the way to Florida? She might not even talk to me."

"Harder to tell you no face to face."

"Isn't that kind of an expensive risk?"

"Not for a story of this magnitude. I'll check it out with Jerry and Sarah. But if I were you I'd start packing my bag for St. Pete."

***

The argument with Sarah and Jerry went pretty much the same – cost in time and money versus potential gain. Ever the watchdog over her newsroom's budget, she said, "We've already got enough to persuade Graham the story's real. We should be able to confront Blanchard with the facts and get him to confess the cover-up."

"Yes," I argued, "we've got the story pretty well wrapped up. But the nurse might show a pattern and depth behind the cover-up. And I wouldn't bet on Blanchard *confessing*. He knows it's his ass if he can't coerce Graham to back down on the story."

Sarah looked to her second in command for support, but instead Jerry said, "I think Brock's right, Sarah. The hospital's into their lies so deep, there's no turning back. If we go to Blanchard now all we have is the word of unnamed – and un-nameable – sources. It won't be hard for Blanchard to figure out who we've talked to, but with nothing on the record he can just say we've made it all up. And with no credible, identified sources, that's the stuff libel judgments are made of."

"Maybe – just maybe – we can get the nurse on the record," I said. "If not, we'll have at least tried and can demonstrate good faith efforts to get at the truth. What's a few hundred bucks for airfare compared to the ability to break the story of the year?"

"What story?" came the words from Sarah's open doorway. It was Graham, the publisher's first visit to the newsroom in months.

"We – ah – we think we need to send – uh -- Jeni to Florida to talk with a nurse who seems to have retired from Memorial suddenly after Mr. Owens died," Sarah said. "She was in charge that night and we think she was bought out by Memorial to facilitate a cover-up."

Graham pursed his lips and closed his eyes, visibly uncomfortable with the topic. "Maybe you'd better give me an update."

I did, starting with the revelations by Emelda Paradiso, the night supervisor of nursing, and concluding with Jeni's conversation with nursing assistant Judy Galloway. The publisher shook his head and said, "Maybe Jim doesn't know what's gone on behind his back. That might explain why he's being so defensive."

"Except," I said, "that the aide says the CEO and the head of security were the ones who arranged her hasty departure."

Graham just shook his head. "I find it hard to believe a person of Jim Blanchard's status in the community – and standing in his profession – would try to conceal something like this. There must be some other explanation."

I couldn't control a snort and roll of my eyes, but Sarah glared at me and Graham seemed to notice neither action.

"Well, perhaps what the former nurse has to tell us will provide that explanation," Sarah said, nodding her head reassuringly to her boss.

"Yes, well, perhaps. Go ahead and send Miss Jermaine down there," the publisher said in resignation. And then, as if to himself, "At least that might buy us some time to figure out what to do."

I shot Sarah an alarmed look but the editor quickly shook her head at me and said to Jerry, "Okay, have Jeni get the flight reservation through Elsie. Get her a red-eye so she can get to her source during the day and try to get back here without an overnight."

Chapter 51

"It's Buster's car all right," Danny said when I answered her phone call that afternoon. "Sorry about the delay, but it was a crazy morning."

"No problem. So Buster's a ladies' man, huh? Who'da thought?"

"It might not be entirely voluntary on Valerie Gordon's part," she said. "It's too soon to tell what's going on."

"But you agree it's suspicious, right?"

"Sure, but even if there's a relationship, it's not necessarily linked to her husband's death."

"Maybe I should just ask Buster if he's driving his county car on *personal* business."

"Oh, yeah," she said, "the subtle approach. We've got to be careful here – both for the sake of the case – and for me." She lowered her voice to a near whisper, "After all, you'll remember I was told in no uncertain terms to let the detective division do their own jobs."

"Oh, I get it, you're at the station. So, do you think they'd be interested now?"

"I don't know. What do we really have? Buster was a dental hygiene patient of Mrs. Gordon and now he's seeing her socially? That's a long way from implicating him – or her -- as suspects in her husband's murder."

"Don't forget, there's the bedroom blackmail angle, too. Dead photographer? Hole – perhaps a peephole -- now patched -- in the closet door? Wouldn't you think the detectives would at least be interested in talking to them now? The puzzle pieces seem to be coming together."

"For you and me, maybe, and I can drop a few indirect hints to my detective friend Clint. But I can't afford to piss off the captain of detectives again when I'm getting close to taking the exam."

"What if *I* go to him with the information we've gathered? Leave you out of it?"

"Well, it's not like they don't know we're practically engaged, you know," she said. And then, again in a near whisper, "We are, aren't we? Practically engaged, I mean?"

"I sure as hell hope so," I said, looking around the newsroom to assure that no one was listening. "I've asked you to marry me only about a dozen times."

"And one of these times I'll say yes – I promise. It's just nice to hear it now and then."

Again, glancing around, I said, "Okay, Danny Morgan, will you marry me?"

"Why, thank you, Mr. Andrews. I am truly flattered by the offer," she said affecting a southern accent that would have done credit to Scarlett O'Hara. "I'll have to think about it. Ask me again when I make detective." She laughed and hung up.

***

Jeni's direct flight to Florida was scheduled for 6:30 the next morning out of Indianapolis. She and I were having an evening skull session over pizza at a back table in Antonio's. Out of uniform, Danny was sitting in as invited kibitzer.

"What if Sharon Newhouse won't talk to me?" Jeni asked.

"You'll have one shot to get her attention," I said. "Something like, 'I know what happened with Raymond Owens, and it's going to come out, so you need to give me your side of the story.'"

"Easy for you to say," Jeni quipped. "But if I go all that way and she just slams the door in my face?"

"You can still talk to her through the door," Danny said. "Sometimes when people are afraid they'll still stand behind the door and listen."

"If nothing else, I guess I could write it out and slip it under her door or paste it on her window," she laughed.

"If she won't talk with you at her home, ask her if she'll meet you somewhere. And if she goes out, follow her until she agrees to talk," I said. "So, assuming you get her pinned down to talk, what are you going to say?"

"I'll tell her she's got only this one chance to tell her side before she winds up looking bad along with everyone else."

"That's good. And if at all possible we need to persuade her to go on the record. It's too late for confidentiality. Besides, we're running out of witnesses to quote. We don't know if she's legally liable for anything, but that's not our business. Getting the story is, and we can tell her that being up front with her side will at least make her look better."

"Assuming she promptly reported his plunge to the pavement," Jeni said, wincing at the alliteration.

"It wasn't her job to report Owens's cause of death," Danny said. "Besides, there's nothing illegal about taking an early retirement incentive."

"Even though we know it was intended as a bribe to get her out of town?" Jeni asked.

"Granted," Danny said, "it seems she must have known of the cover-up -- at least after the fact -- and gone along with it. But there was no inquest or police investigation, so at least as far as I know she hasn't even been asked, let alone had a chance to lie to officers about it."

"Isn't there something about *not* reporting a crime?" Jeni asked.

"Yeah, but remember, maybe as far as she's concerned there was only a suicide. The only crime she'd know about *might* be false reporting of a cause of death, but she didn't do that. Her bosses did."

"So what leverage do I have with her?"

"It's going to come out. She's got a chance to wind up looking good. She smelled something rotten and took the chance to get out."

"We'll see," Jeni said, shaking her head. "I just don't have a good feeling about this."

Danny shot me a look and tilted her head toward the younger reporter. I took the cue to offer encouragement.

"Look, Jeni, you'll do fine. Just be your bold and charming self. And enjoy Florida – even if it *is* only for a day."

Chapter 52

How depressing, she thought as she eased her rented Sentra onto the edge of the blacktop apron to Sharon Newhouse's mobile home park. The paint-chipped sign that swung creaking from a rusty pole spoke with unintended eloquence about the kind of lifestyle one could expect at Sunset Palms Retirement Resort. *Not my idea of a great way to spend the golden years.*

The trailer court consisted of a block deep and block wide horseshoe just off one of St. Pete's major north-south thoroughfares. Mobile homes in various stages of decline tightly lined both sides of the wide lane of crushed seashells that crunched under her tires as she made her way to #17. A row of ragged palms that gave the park its name ran along the rear of the trailers. A similar row of palms ran behind the trailers jammed into the center oval. *Like those old movies with wagon trains circled to fend off Indian attacks..*

The Newhouse home, mid-block on the left outside rim, gave no evidence it had ever been mobile. Its aluminum skin, weathered to a powdery cream with faded green trim, attested to its age. From a sagging white window box at the front of the trailer drooped nondescript plastic flowers. Peeling wooden steps led from the aluminum carport canopy to a door on the right side. A large sunroom addition with jalousie windows doubled the home's width to the left.

Up at 4:00, Jeni was already tired by the time she boarded the 6:30 flight out of Indianapolis to Florida. She felt drained and apprehensive as she touched up her makeup in the car's mirror. But as she walked deliberately to Sharon Newhouse's front door she felt a tingle of adrenaline that made her smile at her own nerves. *What can she do? Shoot me?* She fought off a chill at that thought, took a deep breath, squared her shoulders and thrust out her chin.

There was no button for a bell, but the inside door was open and she could hear laughter and applause from a TV game show. She knocked on the metal-framed screen door.

"Mrs. Newhouse?"

"She's not here," a voice rasped from inside. "She's taking her walk." The thin, reedy voice appeared to emanate from a tawny fabric recliner facing away from the open door.

"Do you expect her back soon?" Jeni asked the back of the chair.

The recliner swiveled a quarter turn and a gaunt, gray-haired man peered at her from behind thick, black-framed glasses. He had the clear plastic tubing of an oxygen cannula looped over his ears and into his nose. "Probably won't be gone too much longer. Want to come in and wait?"

Stepping through the doorway was like entering a nursing home. What had been the mobile home's small living room had become a cramped hospital room. An adjustable electric bed with a rolling swivel tray lined the back wall. Beside the man's chair was a TV tray laden with tissue box, several crushed tissues, an inhaler and a phalanx of remote controls. A walker was within arm's reach, and a large metal oxygen canister stood in a corner, attached to its user by another plastic tube that snaked across the tan carpet.

"Hi, I'm Jeni Jermaine," she said, extending her hand to the man who hoisted himself halfway from the chair before he collapsed back, gasping with the exertion. She pretended not to notice as she reached forward to grasp his bony fingers.

"Norman Newhouse," he croaked. "Do I know you? Don't think Sharon's ever mentioned you." He paused to take a couple breaths. Dry lips parted in a pleasant smile and he said, "You seem kinda young to be livin' here among us old folks. Just visiting?"

"Yes, well, in a way. Your wife and I have spoken over the phone but never met. I'd like to talk with her if I may."

"Sure, no problem. You want some coffee of something?

Should be some left from breakfast." He stopped to inhale again, labored with a racking cough to clear his throat, and then gurgled, "'Fraid you'll have to help yourself in the kitchen, if you don't mind. As you can see, I'm not much use anymore."

Jeni shook her head. "No, no, I'm fine. I don't want to trouble you." She sat on the edge of a matching recliner.

"Trouble with what?" A gray-blond woman entered the same door Jeni had used.

Fighting to calm her jumping stomach, Jeni rose and offered her hand. "Hello, Mrs. Newhouse. I'm – Jeni Jermaine."

"What?" The woman's brown eyes glinted with anger as she yanked back her hand before making contact with Jeni's. She demanded, "What do you think you're doing here?"

"Is there a problem, dear?" her husband croaked in alarm, again half rising.

Whirling to her husband, the woman abruptly shifted her attention and tone. "No. No, dear, nothing for you to worry about. I just need to talk with this young woman and she'll be on her way."

Sharon Newhouse turned back to Jeni and said, "You have come at a very inopportune time. But please come with me so you don't disturb my husband any more than you already have." And again to her husband, "We'll just take a short walk, dear. I'll be right back."

Jeni obediently followed Sharon Newhouse back out the door, down the steps to the concrete pad and onto the crunchy drive.

"You have a lot of nerve coming here like this – unannounced and uninvited," the woman hissed. "You need to leave us alone. Go away." She turned back toward her trailer.

Seeing the purpose of her trip about to slip away, Jeni stepped in front of the woman and said, "You need to talk with me about Raymond Owens. It's all going to come out, and I'm giving you this one chance to tell the truth."

Sharon Newhouse was obviously much younger and in better health than her husband. Of medium build and with short gray-blond hair, she was attractive in a care-worn sort of way, Jeni thought. *No doubt the effects of working full-time and caring for her husband. No wonder she wanted to retire.*

The nurse appeared to be about mid-fifties and at 5-foot-5 stood half a head shorter than Jeni. She took a step back and looked anxiously up and down the trailer-lined drive, as if for an escape route. "Get out of my way," she said and tried to step around Jeni, who again blocked her path.

"Do you really want to be referred to in our story as someone participating in Memorial's cover-up of Raymond Owens's death?" Jeni asked.

The woman's shoulders fell then in resignation and she shook her head. She stood there in silence for a long moment before saying, "All right, let's walk around the corner. There's a little park. We can talk there."

***

The small grassy oasis at the toe of the horseshoe was perhaps three lots wide. It offered amenities of a shuffleboard court, horseshoe pit, two picnic tables flanked by charcoal grills, and several park benches.

Sharon Newhouse slumped onto a bench, bent over and took her head in her hands. "I suppose I knew it was too good to be true."

"What do you mean?" Jeni asked.

"This," she said, looking up and sweeping her arms wide. "A peaceful retirement down here with Norm." She sucked in a breath and tears stained her cheeks. "For as long as he's got."

Not knowing what to say, Jeni said nothing, just shook her

head in sympathy and bit her lip for control.

"It didn't seem that big a deal, you know? Fifteen years? But I was 25 then and Norm was only 40. Now he's 70, nearly 71, and probably won't see 72.

"What's the problem?"

"Diagnosis of course is COPD. You must have noticed the oxygen. Too many years of smoking. Prognosis, maybe as little as six months, a couple years at most. I've seen a lot of these over the years. I'm afraid it's less than that."

"That's tough," Jeni said. "I'm sorry." She paused, looking up at the swaying palms and around at the modest homes and little park. Clearing her throat, she said, "Look, Mrs. Newhouse, I'm not here to ruin your retirement. I just need some information."

"What, so you can sensationalize this thing all out of proportion? And make me lose my pension – for doing nothing wrong?"

"Why would you lose your pension?" Jeni asked.

"Because when they offered to accelerate my retirement I told them I wouldn't tell anybody what happened."

"What did happen?"

"You said you already know about it. Why do you need me?"

"We know Raymond Owens didn't die of his accident injuries – at least not his car accident. We know Memorial has lied about cause of death. I want to hear your side of the story."

"What's to tell? He decided to end it all. Threw a chair out the window and then followed it down three stories."

"You sure it couldn't have been accidental – a fall as opposed to jumping? Or worse? Somebody pushing him?"

"Oh, my god, no. Why would you think that? It's bad enough

that he jumped on my shift."

"Tell me what happened that night," Jeni said, putting her hand over the nurse's and nodding in encouragement.

The story she heard conformed in most details to that of Judy Galloway. Once the death was discovered, top management took over, the lid of information was clamped, and within a week Newhouse's retirement deal was done.

"I saw a chance to get out and I took it," Newhouse said. "Can you blame me? Norm doesn't know anything about this – just accepted my early retirement as a stroke of good luck."

"It's not my job to blame anyone. I'm just trying to get at the facts. There's no reason for you to look bad if you tell the truth," Jeni said, again touching the nurse's hand. "You didn't do anything wrong, and no one could blame you for taking the chance to be with your husband."

"Do you have to use my name?"

"I don't make those decisions, but if you speak out before the story breaks that will lend credibility to our account and credits you with telling the truth about something you witnessed -- but that wasn't your fault.

Chapter 53

"You sure we have to use her name?" Jeni asked the next morning after filling me in on her whirlwind trip to Florida and the meeting with Sharon Newhouse.

I could tell she was hung over from her long and stressful day and she stretched back in her chair with her stocking feet atop her desk. "Her name is the lock that holds the chain together."

"I guess," she said. "I just hate to add any more stress to that poor woman. She's going to lose her husband soon. And now we drag her into a scandal that's not of her doing."

"I understand your feeling. No, I *share* your feeling just from what you've told me. But we can't publish without at least someone on the record who's been directly involved. And from what we've seen, Mrs. Newhouse has no motivation to lie – the very opposite."

"What's next then? Do we go to the police? Prosecutor? What?"

"Police, hell. First we meet with Sarah and Dam-Gram. Then, I think just to cover our butts we get a copy of the Memorial pension plan to verify Newhouse wasn't yet eligible to retire, and if possible proof that she's actually getting those checks. Maybe your friend Angie can help?"

"I don't know. I'll ask her," Jeni said.

"Good. And then -- and then we nail that SOB Blanchard to the wall with his own lies."

***

Sarah was standing behind her desk looking from me to Jeni to Jerry and back to me. The *Chronicle's* executive editor folded her arms, leaned back and nodded. "Okay, good work," she said after her briefing on Jeni's Florida foray. "Before we get too far, though,

I'll have to run this by Graham. Let me make sure he's ready for the all-out assault from Blanchard."

"How much more ready can Dam-Gram be?" I said. I could feel my face and neck reddening. "We've told the -- uh -- our esteemed publisher all about it, and now we've got confirmation on the record."

Jeni and Jerry stole sideways glances at me as Sarah blared back, "Dammit, Brock, you know Graham hasn't been comfortable with this story from the start. As nervous as he is about the grief he's gotten from Blanchard – and sure to get more? It's only fair to let him know we're ready to write. And then run it past the lawyer."

"Of course we need to get our lawyer to sign off on it, but I got a real bad feeling the last time we talked with Graham. Like he'd weasel out of it if he could."

"Jeezus, Brock, it's just common courtesy to let the publisher know what we're doing – on any controversial story, let alone one this big involving one of his friends – and possibly a boycott by advertisers," she said.

"Yeah, well, maybe this is one of those cases where it's better to seek forgiveness than permission."

"I'm *not* asking permission, dammit. It's *my* newsroom – *our* newsroom," she corrected herself.

I rocked back on my heels and held my hands up in surrender. "Hey, I'm not arguing with you, Sarah. You're the boss."

"All right then. Just let me alert Graham and then we can move forward."

***

Danny lay with her head resting on my chest, both catching our breath. She grinned up at me and said, "So, you think you're pretty smart, don't you? Looks like you've got your story, and now it's our turn."

"*Your* turn? I don't think so – not yet."

"Brock, you can't tell me you've confirmed that a probable crime's been committed and then expect me to not report it to my superiors in the department."

"I know that. You just need to give me some time to get the story done and confront Memorial's CEO with it. Once we get him on the record with his self-righteous denials, we both can report what we've learned to your detectives and the prosecutor."

"We know the hospital falsified information for the death certificate," she said. "But what about the actual cause of death? What will you put in the story?"

"Well, initially we can report presumed suicide. We'll have to follow up on that. Now that we've proved that Owens didn't die from his car accident, our main focus is a cover-up by the hospital on cause of death. That's the angle the public needs to know about most."

"That's a lot. You and Jeni have really done a great job putting it all together."

"Nice for a member of the Kenton PD to recognize that. I wish we could tell the whole story at once, but we're journalists, not cops. If it's more than suicide your detectives will have to determine that."

"And nice of you to recognize *that*," she said, digging me in the ribs.

"Well, you're not a detective yet. But maybe you'll get there quicker when I tell them how you helped us pull this all together."

"Don't you dare. I'll make it on my own or not at all. Besides, the captain would have my badge if he knew I was working with the newspaper behind his back."

"Working?" I pulled her to me. "You call this *work*?"

***

The thought of not reporting the whole story at once, however, gnawed at me all through the night, and when we awoke in the morning I decided not to mentions my misgivings to Danny. *Maybe we can get the whole story yet.*

Hours later, the morning routine rounds done, I sat at my desk, drawing on a yellow legal pad interlocking circles around the three scenarios behind Raymond Owens's death.

Suicide – serious injuries, depression, huge medical bills, physically able?

Accident – unlikely, windows too high for fall.

Homicide -- ?????, alienated son?

Physically able? That was an angle I hadn't thought to check before. Had Raymond Owens's recovery progressed to the point where he was physically capable of standing while hoisting a chair and hurling it through the hospital window and then scrambling over the sill himself? *I'll have to get Jeni to check on that.*

The paper nearly worn through from my doodling, I decided on another call to Teresa Wilkerson in Louisville.

"Mrs. Wilkerson? Brock Andrews here."

"Oh, hi, Brock. Any news to share?"

"Nothing yet. Just thought I'd like to talk with your siblings, too. Can you give me their names and phone numbers?"

She did, and within five minutes I decided to ignore the older son in Kansas City and focus for the time on the disaffected son, Jimmy Owens in Kenton.

"Whatcha working on?" Jeni interrupted my thoughts.

"Raymond Owens's cause of death. Could you do me a favor and check for anything we've run on the son, Jimmy Owens?"

Within minutes, she said across the desk, "Hmm, I think you'll find this interesting."

"What's that?"

"It would seem that all was not sunshine and roses in the Owens household."

"Why do you say that?"

"Because we've run a couple public records items indicating domestic issues."

"Owens. Owens." I thought a moment and then exploded, "Of course." I slapped my palm to my forehead. "There's a lot of them in this area, and I hadn't put it together. I faintly recall that name from the cop reports. Domestic violence? Refresh my memory."

"Six years ago," she said, "Raymond Owens was arrested on suspicion of domestic battery involving a male juvenile; neighbors called, charges never filed." She shoved across the desk a printout from the electronic archive.

"Then, three years ago, James R. Owens, 20, was arrested for domestic battery against an unnamed male, age 56, same address." She looked up from her papers, "Could be the father? Charges also never filed."

"Wow."

"But wait. There's more," Jeni grinned at her imitation of an as-seen-on-TV hawker. "The next year – two years ago – James Owens, same address, was fined on disorderly conduct and public intoxication charges after a fight at Pete's Joint. You know – that place out on the strip? Owens also was initially charged with assault but that was dropped – something about a pool cue."

"Hmm," Brock said. "No wonder there was a falling out between father and son. Seems the sister left out some of the salient details."

"Well, from what you said, she's older and married and has

lived away from home for some time. Maybe she didn't even know about all the drama."

"Maybe not. But check me on this. It would appear that we have a kid who has not only been indulged to a fault, then defaults on a loan from his parents, and is then kicked out of the home with a broken relationship with at least the father."

"Yeah," Jeni answered. "And said kid also has an apparent tendency toward violence."

Chapter 54

"Both of these cases will need to be turned over to police and prosecutor soon," I said to Jeni. "I need to spend some time mulling over how to approach the Gordon killing and the wife's apparent relationship with Buster Bradshaw."

"You mean as opposed to just asking him about his extracurricular girlfriend? He's still married, right?"

"Right, but an affair with the widow doesn't equate to murder of her husband. And Danny doesn't think there's enough to convince her detectives to look into it right now."

"And the Owens case?" she asked.

"I want to talk with the Owens's younger son. And -- I've been thinking there are a couple loose ends you might tie up with your friend Angie."

"What are they?"

"Both Mrs. Owens and her daughter told me that the younger son hadn't been to visit his father in the hospital before he died. We need to try to verify that."

"Okay, but do you think the hospital keeps a log of visitors?"

"I doubt it. That would be too easy. But someone working on that floor might remember. It's a long shot, but I think worth pursuing."

"Okay, what's the other thing?" Jeni asked.

"Hopefully easier. Had Raymond Owens recovered enough to get out of his hospital bed, pick up a chair, throw it through his window and then climb up on the sill and jump? We've been assuming suicide, but we need to verify it was even physically possible."

"Medical records, right?"

"Maybe, but you might not have to go that far. I know you don't want to get Angie in trouble for pushing too hard. Your previous contacts -- the charge nurse and assistant -- might confirm Owens's physical condition for us. But perhaps Angie can help you with a list of staff on that floor during his stay who might remember who his visitors were."

"I'll give it a shot."

***

Kenton's phone listings offered no home number for a James or Jimmy Owens, and I got no answer to my call to the cell phone number Teresa Wilkinson had given me. It was nearly twilight when I followed the address to a seedy area on the south side of town and to the even seedier Autumn Oaks Mobile Home Court. The trailer park was not an infrequent locus of police calls for domestic violence, drunken stabbings, drug busts and other crimes. "Court" was a bit grandiose to describe the jumbled assortment of the dozen or so aluminum cocoons. I pulled the Camaro into the weed-infested gravel lane that wound among the trailers.

An aging Ford Escort fronted the parking pad next to Owens's trailer, its harlequin paint scheme attesting to multiple unfinished repairs. An aged pickup of no discernible make and sporting a coat of black primer and rust was on blocks at the back of the lot.

My first creaky footstep onto the narrow aluminum stairs brought an outburst of high-pitched barking from inside the trailer. I had barely reached the door when it was opened by a corpulent young woman with dull blond hair hanging in limp strands around a pimply face. Her food-stained pink tee shirt couldn't conceal sagging, braless breasts. Between the ankles of her gray sweatpants yapped a kinky-haired terrier mix.

I couldn't see past her into the trailer, but heard from behind her a slurred male voice, "Whosh air?"

"How much did you bring?" the woman asked before I could

speak. Her open mouth revealed a row of broken, discolored teeth that made me mentally recoil. *Meth mouth.* Reports of methamphetamine use, and manufacture, had become commonplace in the area's small towns, and both the county courts and health clinic were being swamped with young men and women wasted by their addiction.

"Quiet!" the woman ordered as she bent and snatched up the snarling mutt and buried its head in her bosom.

"I – I didn't bring anything," I said. "Is Jimmy Owens here?"

"Who ish it, Carla?" again came the voice from inside.

The woman swung the door wide but stood across the opening, giving me enough of a look – and smell -- to tell him me I didn't want to go inside. The odor flowing through the open door was foul with sweat and fried food and other things inviting unpleasant speculation. Behind her to the left I could see teetering stacks of dirty pans and dishes covering kitchen table, countertop and sink. To the right a slender man lay sprawled face-up on a couch, one leg propped on the floor beside a coffee table laden with overflowing ashtrays and assorted plastic cups and beer and soda cans.

"I'm – I'm Brock Andrews – from *The Chronicle,*" I announced around the woman. "I spoke with your sister and she gave me your address and phone number. I tried to call earlier but there was no answer."

"Yeah, leave it ta her – fuckin' busybody."

"She and your mother have asked us to look into your father's death at Wilkes Memorial. I'd like to talk with you."

"Ain't talkin' with no reporter." He turned his head halfway toward the door revealing a drawn, acne covered face considerably older than his 23 years.

"Did you see your father while he was in the hospital?"

"I said I ain't talkin' with no fuckin' reporter. Now go away."

"You could help ease your family's concerns if you'd just give me a couple minutes."

Jimmy Owens lurched from the couch, his tee shirt and jeans bagging on his gaunt frame. Pushing aside his companion, he leaned against the door jamb and woozily pointed a finger in my face. Through similarly carious teeth he said, "Got nothin' to say to you or them." He paused for an elaborate belch. "Now leave me the fuck alone." He slammed the door.

They're both stinking meth addicts. I shook my head and shuddered involuntarily as I drove away. *What, do I look like some frickin' dope dealer? They must have thought I was making a delivery. But from the smells inside I wouldn't be surprised if they're cooking it right there.*

Chapter 55

From all appearances, Bradshaw & Bradshaw, Buster's mortuary business, was the most successful in Kenton. It drew funerals from the most prominent families and those who aspired to be. The long single story red brick Georgian stood a block off Kenton's main street. With gleaming white pillars, shutters and window frames it was surrounded on three sides by a massive blacktop parking lot filled with cars.

As I pulled into the lot at 3 p.m., I had to wonder how the burly coroner, brusque in at least his official capacity, could be so successful in a business dependent on compassionate customer service. *Must be the brother.*

I peeked into the main lobby where a white-on-black letterboard announced that two family visitations were scheduled for that afternoon and evening, 1-4 and 6-9. Not wanting to explain my visit to either of the somber, black-suited attendants standing outside the viewing rooms, I entered a propped-open side door where two members of a bereaved family were stealing time away for a smoke.

I nodded to them solemnly and padded down the carpeted, softly lit hallway to the rear of the building, peering in each open doorway hoping to find Buster's office and not a deceased Kentonian.

An open door at the end of the hall revealed a neat, expansive walnut desk sitting on ice blue carpet and flanked by two deep-blue leather sofas and walnut end tables with polished brass lamps. Around the desk was a semicircle of matching guest chairs. *Probably where they make the sales pitch for the expensive walnut coffins.* The room, painted to match the carpet, took on an ethereal glow from subdued indirect lighting above the white cornices. Barely audible organ hymns reinforced the other-worldly impression.

A brass nameplate placed conveniently at the front of the desk identified the occupant as Bradley J. Bradshaw, president. *Nice digs.* I decided to wait there until the break between visitations in hopes of catching Buster in person instead of being blown off over the phone. I was examining the framed prints of English pastoral scenes on the walls when the solicitious voice came from the doorway, "May I help…"

Surprised, I spun around and Buster recognized me with an abrupt change of tone. "Oh, it's you. What the hell do you want now?"

"Nice to see you, too, Buster. Just thought we could have a little chat. I'm following up on the murder of Stanley Gordon."

I did a quick double-take at the beefy mortician, hardly recognizable in his white shirt, maroon tie, black business suit and shiny cordovan wingtips. His usual attire at crime and accident scenes was windbreaker and rubber boots.

Bradshaw's ruddy complexion darkened further but he didn't speak, just stood there with mouth open and eyes bulging for a long, uncomfortable moment. He finally recovered his composure and said with contempt dripping from each syllable, "You've read my report, no doubt. Died of severe head trauma inflicted by person or persons unknown. Nothing more to say."

"Really? I figured you might be able to shed more light now that you're familiar with the grieving widow."

"What? What the hell are you talking about?" Buster yelled. "Get the hell out of here."

When I made no move toward the door, the coroner continued, "You're intruding on my family's business. We're working here – and *not* on county time. You want to talk, make an appointment with my secretary at the county building."

"I just thought, Buster, you'd like an opportunity to fill me in – privately -- on how you came to know Mrs. Gordon and the nature of your relationship with her."

Jowls flattened against his stiff white collar, Bradshaw glowered over black-rimmed glasses, shook his head and reached behind him to ease the door shut. When he spoke he did so in a soft voice starkly different from his usual bluster.

"What relationship are you talking about?"

"Come on, Buster. I know you've been keeping Valerie Gordon – company?"

"You don't know what you're talking about," he said with a dismissive wave of his bear-paw hand. "Where'd you hear that?"

"Not just heard, Buster. Seen. Your county car's not exactly invisible in the Widow Gordon's driveway these warm spring nights."

A look of realization passed across the coroner's face but he wasn't ready to admit anything. "There's lot of cars like mine in the county. All the old police cruisers are sold at auction."

"But not with your license plate number, Buster." The stricken look returned to Bradshaw's face.

Hoping to keep the conversation going, I decided to see how far I could bait my quarry. "Hey, who could blame you for being drawn to an attractive young widow? I'm sure she must appreciate your *comforting* her."

"You watch your mouth," Bradshaw snarled. "Whatever you think you know, you don't know nothing."

"Then why don't you tell me so I can understand?" I said, switching from combative to conciliatory. "That's why I'm here."

"Uh – well – uh -- okay," he said, "but not now." The pugnacious sneer had dissolved and he flexed his shoulders. "I've got two callings tonight and my brother's on vacation. Come back tonight after 9 and I can enlighten you."

***

I parked across the street from Bradshaw & Bradshaw until the last car left the parking lot at just after 9. I recognized the last two to leave as the stiff visitation room attendants I had seen earlier.

During my long supper with Danny at Applebees she had asked, "Do you really think it's smart to meet alone with someone who, for all we know, might be the killer of Stanley Gordon?"

I had scoffed then, "Oh, come on. We really don't believe that. *Do* we?"

She shook her head – at what I wasn't sure, but she clearly wasn't pleased.

"Besides, my boss and now you know I'm going there. Even if he were involved he wouldn't be stupid enough to pull anything."

"We are talking about Buster Bradshaw, right? Not exactly Mensa material, you know."

Now, a ripple of apprehension intruded as I left my car to cross the street. All lights went out at the funeral home except the massive brass lamp hanging between the front pillars. I pushed a lighted white button set into the jamb of the double doors. There was no sound and I thought maybe Buster had blown me off, but I had just reached for the button again when the door opened and there stood Buster, his shirt sleeves rolled up and his tie askew.

"Come in, Andrews," he growled, his breath redolent with something alcoholic.

We walked without speaking down the long carpeted hallway to Buster's office. Papers were strewn atop the desk, weighted down by a rocks glass half filled with amber liquid.

"Want a drink?" the mortician asked, a slight slur in his speech. When I shook my head, Buster said, "Have a seat then."

Whatever he had in mind, it apparently wasn't mayhem – at least not yet. I drew in a breath and sat on one of the blue guest chairs. Buster slouched into his upholstered desk chair.

"All right, whattaya want?"

"I'm working on a follow-up to the Gordon killing. Kenton cops are at a standstill. Now we find that you're keeping company with Gordon's wife. Pretty soon after her husband's death, wouldn't you say?"

"So I'm seein' the lady," he said, taking a swig of his drink.

Ah, at least he's given up the pretense of not knowing her.

"So, what are you? The frickin' morals police?"

"Look, Buster, it's none of my business what you might be getting on the side. But you've got to admit it raises some natural questions."

"Questions? What questions? Some kinda time limit on when a lady can have a man friend?"

"*Friend*, Buster? Do you always make such close *friends* with the widows you meet as coroner?"

"Got nothin' to do with it – bein' coroner. Look, I admit I like the lady – and she likes me. You're not gonna cook up some bullshit story about official misconduct are you? I hear you're makin' time with a lady cop. No skin off my nose."

"Again, your extracurricular sex isn't the point – nor is my love life."

"Then what is the point, dammit? I got a business and family to think of – not to mention my office. Besides, I mean, it would kill Helen and the kids if they found out."

"Maybe you should have thought of that before you started banging the widow in a murder you've supposedly investigated. Don't you think that's a raging conflict of interest?"

"Well, yeah, I'll give you that it might look suspicious. But I didn't start seeing her until afterward. And what's it to you anyway?"

I was silent, letting the weight of my questions sink in, almost hearing the gears grinding in Buster's brain.

"Look," he said. "I can break it off, if that's what you want. I mean, it's already over. Just a passing thing."

"Suppose you tell me how it started? Did you know her before the murder?"

"Uh – no."

"No? Come on, Buster. I know you're a patient of Dr. Schmidt. You must at least have had her clean your teeth."

"Oh, yeah. Sure, but I mean I didn't *know* her – if ya know what I mean."

"No, I'm not sure I do. We've heard Valerie Gordon was quite a tease to some of her male dental patients."

Buster looked away and took another slug of his drink.

"Did she come on to you in the examination chair? Is that how it started? I've heard that's what she did with other men."

He lurched from his chair and leaned across the desk and for a second I thought he was going to make a grab for me. "You watch yer fuckin' mouth! You oughta be careful what you say about a lady, Andrews. Besides, I don't know what the fuck yer talkin' about."

Is Buster really that good a poker player? Or is he an innocent dupe of a femme fatale?

"Or maybe you just saw a vulnerable woman and decided to take advantage? Was that it?"

He sat back down heavily and again sought solace in his glass. "It wasn't like that."

"Then tell me what it *was* like."

His glass empty, Bradshaw set it down and slumped back in his chair.

"I talked with her at her home when her husband died. I felt sorry for her. Then she called me a couple times. Following up the death certificate. I helped her with her insurance papers."

"And naturally she was grateful, right?"

Again, no response except a turn to the credenza behind his desk to extract a crystal decanter from which he poured a fresh drink. Sitting forward on the chair, I sensed an opening and, unwilling to stop with just a single, I decided, *what the hell; might as well swing for the fences.*

"So, you mean you didn't see anything strange in the Gordons' bedroom? The closet door off its hinges. A suspicious peephole in said door? Maybe a little voyeur sex going on? You like being in skin flicks?"

"Whattaya mean?" Buster yelled. He again sprang from his chair, knocking his glass over and soaking the papers on his desk with a spreading yellow stain. "Goddammit, what're you getting at? You think I go in for that sick shit?"

I rose and leaned on my fingertips on Buster's desk. "I don't know what you go in for, Buster. I and Wilkes County voters and your wife probably didn't think you'd go in for extramarital sex. How about bedroom blackmail? She snagged you at the office and then was making you pay for your -- indiscretion? And you decided not to take it?"

"What, you think I killed the sonavabitch? Yer outta yer fuckin' mind," he said, rounding his desk.

I admit my heart was hammering since the guy probably had fifty pounds on me and could probably clean my clock. But the heat of the hunt was on and I wasn't going to back down so we stood nose to nose for a long moment. "Or – ah -- did you see the same things I did at the murder scene and decide to take advantage of it for a little extracurricular fun? Is that it?"

Beet red and breathing heavily, Buster started to speak through gritted teeth but then drew back as a look of puzzlement replaced his scowl.

"I don't know what the hell you're talking about. And I don't think you do either. So get the fuck outta here."

Chapter 56

"I don't know what to think of Buster," I told Jeni as we sat at our desks the next morning. "He's either a lot cagier than I thought he could be, or he has no idea what he's gotten himself into."

"Maybe you've underestimated him," she said.

"He seemed genuinely clueless about what I was getting at last night. Confused. And defensive – not of himself, but of Valerie Gordon – as if he really cares about her."

"You don't think he could be mean or violent – if cornered, or maybe being surprised by his *girlfriend's* husband?"

"Sure, maybe anyone could. He was really pissed at me last night, and I'm sure he was tempted to take a swing at me, but I think he knew he was impaired by what he'd been drinking. Anyway, I've always thought the guy's a pretty blunt instrument. What you see is what you get. I don't think he could be that good an actor. How about you? Learn anything about Owens's visitors?"

"I talked again with both our nursing contacts. Judy Galloway said she'd ask her former co-workers at the hospital, but it's been two months. As far as she could recall only the one son visited."

"Any other visitors?"

"Well, she says she didn't see him, but one of the other nurse assistants said there was a tall, slender man, dark hair, on the floor one night. He was in a work uniform but no one recognized him as being on the janitorial staff. They tried to stop and talk to him but he just ducked down the stairway. But she couldn't draw any connection to the time of Owens's death."

My mind immediately jumped to Jimmy Owens, but then set the thought aside when we were interrupted by my phone. I put down the headset and nodded. "Well, looks like we're finally going to get a chance to see what Kenton cops are made of."

"Why's that?" Jeni asked.

"Because Danny's detective friend Clint ran interference for her with the chief of detectives. Since she was already warned to keep her nose out of the Gordon case, he kept her name out of it but told his boss he heard the *Chronicle* might be onto something."

"What did the chief say?"

"Wants to meet with us at our *earliest* convenience."

***

The forbidding façade of the Kenton Police Department looked like something out of a 1930s movie. Gray granite block framed the double glass doors, beside which hung large white globe lamps with POLICE painted boldly in black. Three well-worn stone steps led to the entry, beyond which a reception desk was flanked on each side by doors to the KPD inner sanctum.

In quick response to our summons, Detective Captain Chuck Simmons appeared through the door marked "Investigations" and offered me a bone-crushing handshake. The stocky gray-haired cop then escorted us to a small but orderly office and pointed to a coffee pot. "Help yourself."

We declined, at which he shrugged his shoulders and filled his own cup. When we were seated he said, "Why can't you just leave the police work to us?"

The veteran cop's tone was not unfriendly, but clearly skeptical and barbed with condescension. *He hasn't even heard our story yet.* "You really want to hear the answer?" I retorted with what I hoped was a winning smile. "We've known each other for a long time, Chuck."

"Yeah, seems like forever. What're you gonna do when you grow up and stop chasing ambulances?" he said with a half smile.

I ignored the question and said, "It's now been over two months since Stanley Gordon's death and you appear to be at a standstill. We've got as much right as you to ask questions of people who might have seen something."

The cop leaned back and folded his arms. "I'll grant you that -- short of interfering in our investigation. But since you don't know what we've been doing or what we know, you're being a bit presumptuous in thinking we're at a dead end."

"What are we – not to mention the community -- supposed to think, in the absence of anything but platitudes from the chief and mayor?"

"Yeah, yeah, I know. A *breakthrough* is just around the corner."

"Then why don't you enlighten us?"

"You know we don't comment on details of ongoing investigations."

"Oh, so the investigation *is* ongoing? All right, then, tell me this. Do you think Valerie Gordon might have been in on her husband's murder – or at least know more than she's said so far?"

"We have no reason to believe that. She seemed genuinely shocked and grieving, and she wasn't there at the time of the crime. Confirmed. At her mother's, if I remember rightly."

"So she says. But might it help you to know that her mother had Alzheimer's and died just shortly after the murder?"

"Is that right?" The cop's eyes widened, seeming to catch the possible significance to Valerie Gordon's alibi. "Uh -- I didn't think we'd heard that."

"Probably no reason for you to put it together. You know, Obituaries-R-Us? It's what we do. But there's more."

"What's that?"

Careful to avoid any hint of Danny's assistance, I related the study of crime scene photos, including the suspected peephole in the broken closet door and linking it to Gordon's profession as a photographer.

"That's a pretty elaborate conspiracy theory," Simmons said. "Might make a good novel for you someday. But as useful evidence it's pretty flimsy."

"There's something else." I told him the stories of Mrs. Gordon as a dental office tease and then added, "The Widow Gordon is seeing someone else already. And that someone just happens to be our esteemed coroner, Buster Bradshaw."

"Buster? Son of a gun. And you know this how?"

"By observation, Chuck. He's at her home several nights a week. And, I talked with him about it and he admitted he's involved with her."

"No shit," the detective said with a wry smile. "I'd like nothing better than to bust his balls – uh, sorry, Miss," he shrugged in Jeni's direction. "Buster seems to know his stuff, but he's a pain in the butt to work with. On a power trip. Likes to boss people around."

"Yeah, we've noticed," I said. "So, aside from what might be a conflict of interest for the coroner, there's a possibility of a love triangle -- or quadrangle or whatever. Is that enough for you to look into?"

"Could be. Let me think about it." He slurped some coffee and then grinned at us over the cup. "Thanks for the tip. If anything comes of it you'll be among the last to know."

"That's what I'm afraid of," I said. "But now let's talk about the death at Wilkes Memorial of Raymond Owens. Jeni?"

"Oh, yes. Clint said there was another issue," Simmons said.

Jeni related what we had pieced together about the defenestration death at the hospital and the extensive efforts to cover it up.

"Well, I have to confess that's a new one on me," Simmons said. "Cause of death accidental, but the wrong accident."

"If it *was* an accident," I added.

"Why? Another of *The Chronicle's* conspiracy theories?"

"I have to admit it's just that. But just supposing Owens had a little help out the window. There clearly was a *very* rocky relationship – and a history of violence -- between him and his younger son, who, if I'm not mistaken, is a meth addict in addition to being a leech on his parents. With a mother who seemed incapable of telling him no, he might have had an eye on his father's life insurance."

"Well, you two certainly have been busy, haven't you? And do I detect you might have had some guidance from a certain patrol sergeant?" he said to me with a wink.

"A good reporter never divulges his sources," I said, unable to suppress a nervous smile.

"Well, I'm sure Sergeant Morgan is the very soul of discretion in her relationship with – uh, *The Chronicle.*"

"I can assure you that is the case," I said with as straight a face as I could muster. "We scrupulously avoid the subject of work." I quickly changed the subject. "So, if this information is of any value to you, how do you think you'll proceed?"

"Again, we'll give it some thought. But it might be prudent to speak again with Mrs. Gordon as well as Mr. Bradshaw. On the hospital thing? I'll let you know."

Chapter 57

Late that afternoon my desk phone rang. It was Danny.

"I'm on patrol, but you probably should know that as we speak Captain Simmons is interviewing Buster Bradshaw? You wanted to know right away if that happened."

"Right. I'm on it. Thanks."

Jeni had gone out for a late lunch and I knew she'd want to be in on the excitement, so without replacing the receiver I clicked off and immediately tried her cell. I left an exasperated message and hustled to my car.

She was just pulling into the lot as I reached my car. I waved and she stopped and rolled down her passenger side window. "What's up?"

"Danny called. She wanted us to know Simmons is talking with Buster right now."

"Wow, that was quick. You'd never have known it from his reaction, but he must have really believed us."

"With luck, Buster didn't have time to tip off Mrs. Gordon. I'm thinking it's time to talk with her myself." I started to walk away.

"Hey, wait," she called after me. "I'm going too. You know, learn from the master?"

"Yeah, yeah. Forget the master crap. You're doing fine on your own. But maybe a double team *will* help."

"And a woman's touch," she grinned. "Get in."

***

The Gordon front yard still displayed the "For Sale" sign but the advancing spring had added forsythia in saffron bloom along the side yard and red and yellow tulips flowering beside the front steps. Instead of the aging gray Sebring convertible she'd had two months before, a gleaming red ragtop of the same make sat in the driveway, still displaying the dealer sticker.

"Either she's got a visitor or she's gotten herself a new set of wheels," I said to Jeni as she pulled into the drive.

"Life insurance, maybe?" she said.

Valerie Gordon answered the doorbell still dressed for work. Her white scrubs were patterned with multi-colored teddy-bears. I couldn't help but notice that despite their loose comfort the scrubs did nothing to disguise the woman's prominent bosom. From all outward appearances, the widow was doing just fine. Her hair, once long, straight and dull brown, now was shiny, curled and showed a beautician's reddish highlights. Formerly plain but pleasant looking, she now was a quite attractive. But the best gleaming smile her dentist boss could provide disappeared as soon as she recognized me.

"Mrs. Gordon, I wonder if we could have a few moments of your time," I said as we held the door open to her glassed-in front porch.

"As I told your reporter earlier, I have nothing to say. I'm sure you understand this has been a very trying time."

"Of course. If you'd just let us – uh – I'm sorry, this is Jeni …"

"Oh, you're the reporter I talked to earlier?" she demanded. Jeni nodded. "I told you then that I didn't want to be interviewed. Can't you just leave me alone?"

"This won't take long," I said. "We would like to get your reaction to…"

"Please," she interrupted. "Respect my privacy."

"Your reaction to an apparent development in your husband's murder," I finished.

Her eyes widened and mouth sagged open. "What – uh – what development are you talking about?"

The startled look. Was it relief at last that her husband's murder might be solved? Or something else? She had given no indication of letting us in when I answered, "Police are talking with the coroner, Buster Bradshaw. I believe you know him?"

She stood there staring at us for a long moment and then looked quickly around, as if checking to see if anyone could be watching even though the nearest neighbor was nearly 50 yards away. "You'd better – uh – maybe you should come in."

Regaining composure, she closed the door behind us. With pursed lips she studied her wrist watch as though calculating the seconds and said finally, "I have just a few minutes. Please have a seat."

Once again the interior decor of the home belied the modest exterior as we sat on a rich gold and cream brocaded sofa that matched the draperies. The walls were in a misty hue of light avocado, as was the deep plush carpet. Mrs. Gordon sat stiffly upright across from us, jaw tight, with her legs crossed and hands clasped primly over her knees. "Why – why would they be talking with Mr. Bradshaw about my husband's death?"

Pausing to let the weight of her question settle between us, I leveled what I hoped was a penetrating scowl as opposed to mere indigestion. "Because he was involved in the investigation of your husband's murder – and now he apparently is involved with you."

She blanched and her shoulders sagged momentarily before she recovered, took in a deep breath and said, "Why – why would you say he's *involved* with me? We hardly know each other; he's a patient in Dr. Schmidt's office is all."

"Come on, Mrs. Gordon. Are you denying that you and Buster are friends?"

"Well, if that *were* the case – and I'm not saying it is -- why would it be any concern of yours?"

"Not ours alone. Perhaps also the voters of Wilkes County who might wonder at the propriety of a coroner investigating the death of a man whose wife he's involved with."

"Oh." She paused, mulling my words. "Well, that's just ridiculous. This is a small town. Buster knows lots of people. I'm sure the voters wouldn't find any irregularity in that," she said slowly, as if trying to convince herself it was true.

"Would you deny that Buster is a frequent night-time visitor to your home?"

The mask of denial that had held her features immobile started to shred.

"And, as I said, it's apparently also of interest to Kenton police detectives."

She tossed her head back as if dismissing the idea, but gave an involuntary shiver and blinked repeatedly as if struggling for control. Her breathing was heavy and her eyes grew bright with liquid.

Unsure of what she was feeling – still grieving for her husband, concern for herself or for her new lover – I nonetheless sensed a weakness and decided to probe the exposed nerve. "And I'm sure police might also want to talk with you about your friendships with Buster and other of Dr. Schmidt's male patients."

"Me? What? What are you saying?" she flared at me, voice rising in a sudden fury that made me wonder for a moment if I had overstepped – or, that she might be moved to violence. But her rage lost force and volume even as it peaked. Turning to Jeni as if for a woman's support, she said, "I -- I don't know -- what he's -- talking about." It was as if she had stepped outside herself to see the building futility of lying.

Righteous indignation of an innocent woman? Or anger at

being exposed? I decided to close the circle. "And about that hole in your bedroom closet door?"

A temblor of realization swept over her, composure crumbling in a quake of emotion. Her shoulders drooped and she sat back in her chair. She stared silently at the wall behind us for a long moment before tears began spilling down her cheeks, carrying with them streaks of mascara. Her breath came in short, shallow gasps and her head wagged from side to side.

Jeni yelled my name, but it was too late.

Valerie Gordon's eyes rolled back showing only white as she slumped head-first onto her richly carpeted living room floor.

Chapter 58

"Oh, my god, Brock," Jeni whispered as she knelt beside the fallen Valerie Gordon. "We'd better call 9-1-1."

I was kneeling on the other side of the stricken woman who opened her eyes, blinked several times and shook her head. "Wha – what happened?"

She tried to push herself up onto one elbow but I put a restraining hand softly on her shoulder and said gently, "You fainted. Better take a minute before you try to get up."

Her eyes gradually acquired focus and her breathing became steady. With one of us on each arm we helped her rise uneasily to slump back into her chair. She lay quietly for a moment, breathing deeply as awareness of where she was and who her guests were crept across her face, and with it the realization of what we had been saying to her.

In a dry, shaky voice she managed, "I – I think – you'd better leave now."

Both Jeni and I were kneeling now beside the woman's chair. Jeni looked nervously to me but I made no motion to leave, so she said, "We will. We just want to make sure you're okay."

I looked at Jeni, tilting a hand to my mouth as if taking a drink and tipped my head toward the rear of the house. She caught the motion and said, "Let me just get you something to drink."

I waited until Jeni returned with a glass of water that she handed to the woman, but the widow sat impassive and made no effort to drink.

Fearing that the fissure of vulnerability might be closing, I said in a soft, level tone, "Mrs. Gordon, did Buster Bradshaw kill your husband?"

Her face remained expressionless but the glassy stare returned as she lay back motionless in her chair.

"Mrs. Gordon?" I said, and after a minute of her silence I repeated it, "Mrs. Gordon?"

She took a deep breath and said, "Buster? Kill my husband? Oh, of course not," she sniffed, closed her eyes and again breathed deeply.

Was she thinking, or did she fall asleep?

Jeni laid a hand softly on the woman's arm and said, "Mrs. Gordon?" and after several more moments of silence, "You can talk to us, Mrs. Gordon."

That touch of kindness was more than Valerie Gordon could take. Hands flying to her face, she convulsed into a wail that froze Jeni and me in place. The levee that had been holding back her tears and emotion suddenly failed. "No! – No! he didn't kill Stanley," she screamed. "He loves me – don't you see? He loves me -- and I love him."

A torrent of tears followed with mostly unintelligible lamentations of denial and defense of her new lover, Wilkes County's coroner. What could be understood seemed to exonerate Buster as someone who merely had stepped in after her husband's death to comfort her in her loss.

The tears stopped for a moment as she caught her breath, but when she looked up at us her remorse was replaced by rage. She jumped from her chair and with a wild-eyed glare shouted at them. "Why are you still here? I asked you to leave!"

The alarming speed of her manic shift rocked both of us back on our heels. As we got to our feet I wondered, *Has she gone around the bend?*

She again yelled defiantly, "Get out. Get out."

We both turned toward the door as if to leave, but I wasn't quite finished. Looking the widow in the eye, I said softly, "Mrs.

Gordon, you must have some idea who killed your husband. We have a pretty good idea of your little blackmail business on the side, and sooner or later it's going to come out."

She held my gaze without speaking for a long moment, seeming poised again between anger and sadness, but in the end the latter won out. The icy stare dissolved and she looked away, first at Jeni and then the floor. Her expression again went blank, rage and steam both apparently exhausted. She sagged back into her chair and, with eyes closed, breathed heavily. Jeni and I looked at each other and then back at the woman, wondering if she had again fainted. But her eyes fluttered open and she took several deep breaths before uttering in a flat, matter of fact tone, "Buster had nothing to do with it. I did it!"

All the more stunning for its lack of emotion, the admission left us both wide-eyed and speechless. We knew we had just witnessed a confession of murder and felt like trespassers on police territory.

"I did it, and I'm glad I did," she continued without facial expression but a tone that spoke of relief. "I'd had enough – the things he made me do."

Eyes darting from Mrs. Gordon to each other, we stood mute as she continued,

"Sick things. Despicable things. Damnable things! No more!"

Jeni knelt beside the woman and, without speaking, took her hand. I plucked my cell phone from my pocket and held my palm out signaling Jeni to stay. I stepped noiselessly across the carpet to the rear of the house to make the call.

***

Sgt. Danny Morgan and her partner were in the first KPD unit to arrive less than five minutes later.

"Don't leave her," I said to Jeni as I went to open the outside porch door. I spoke softly to Danny for a few moments before leading them back into the Gordon living room.

Valerie Gordon was still seated in her chair, her head back and eyes, now tearless but still red, staring straight ahead. Having exhausted her emotion, she was now breathing evenly and her look was one of almost relieved calm for someone who had just confessed to murdering her husband.

Danny had just introduced herself to Mrs. Gordon when Chuck Simmons appeared at the front door. Hands on hips and glaring at me, he said, "What are *you* doing here, Andrews? Miss Jermaine?"

I shook my head and stepped to Simmons. Speaking softly I said, "We were just interviewing Mrs. Gordon. I believe she has something to tell you relative to her husband's death."

Simmons looked at the widow and then back at us, grimaced in understanding of the situation and nodded. "Okay. I see. Well, thank you, Andrews. We'll take it from here. You may leave now."

Reflexively, I started to object, but a stern look and raised finger from Simmons was enough to close the conversation. As the officers gathered around the silent Mrs. Gordon, Jeni and I headed for her car which by now was blocked in by two KPD cruisers and an unmarked Crown Vic. We were still seated there 20 minutes later when Simmons and two officers escorted the woman, wrists handcuffed before her, to an idling squad car and departed.

The last to leave, Danny pulled the home's front door closed and checked to see it was locked. As she and her partner headed to their cruiser, she stopped to lean into Jeni's window. "My god, you two. Bet you certainly didn't expect this." We shook our heads in nervous agreement. "Well, I expect you'll have a busy night."

***

It was. By our midnight deadline, Valerie Gordon had repeated her statement to police and signed a full confession to the death of her husband.

The document revealed how, demure dental hygienist by day, she was forced into the siren role, inviting men to her bed by night. There, their episodes of stolen lust were recorded and then sprung on the unsuspecting porn stars by her husband who literally came out of the closet. In exchange for payment Gordon offered delivery of the mini-cassette tape. One night of clandestine carnality could cost as much as $10,000 depending on the mark's ability to pay. According to Mrs. Gordon, her husband never charged more than he felt the family men could hide from their wives, and he always delivered the tape.

Again, as she told it, Gordon's lust for watching other men debase his wife was not just monetary. His capacity for inflicting indignity knew no apparent limits, for whatever the marks couldn't think of themselves Gordon filled in on his own by requiring his wife to perform the next time. Finally, after the mark left on the evening of her husband's demise, Valerie had at last refused. As he had done many times before, he beat her, but that time she fought back and won. The steel tripod weighted with his hidden video camera made an effective weapon and she bounced it off his skull. One stroke and she'd hit a home run, and then camera and tripod were wiped off and returned to his garage studio.

"Widow admits killing photographer husband" was the main headline on the next day's front page, and a secondary deck noted, "Love nest was source of blackmail."

I had argued with Sarah over the use of "love nest" as lurid, inflammatory and worthy of a supermarket tabloid. But I bowed to her assertions it was factual as well as eye-grabbing. Besides, I had won enough battles over editing of the story. I wrote it, but it carried a dual byline, giving Jeni equal credit for backstopping my memory and observations of what had occurred that afternoon.

> The wife of a Kenton photographer has confessed to killing her husband after he allegedly forced her to have sex with other men as he secretly recorded them in their home. The men were later confronted with videos of their acts and blackmailed.
>
> Valerie Gordon, 40, was taken into custody by Kenton police late Thursday after confessing to his murder in early March. She revealed that

for several years her husband had forced her to repeatedly lure local men to her home for sex. She reportedly met the men while they were receiving her services as a hygienist in a local dental office.

Stanley Gordon, 42, a local photographer for about 15 years, was found slain in his bedroom at their home on West Cass Street. His wife reported finding his body on returning home from an overnight visit to her mother, who confirmed her daughter's alibi but has since died.

Mrs. Gordon reportedly told police that she finally rebelled as her husband became increasingly demanding that she perform acts to which she objected. She said she had been beaten by Gordon frequently and on the night of his death she decided to fight back.

She said she hit him with the heavy tripod that he used in the filming while hidden behind a closet door. Wilkes County Coroner Buster Bradshaw ruled the death a homicide and cause of death as skull fracture leading to severe brain damage. Police have now recovered the tripod for forensic examination.

No account of the couple's illicit income was available, but police believe they may have taken in as much as $200,000 over the past three years by bilking men of from $1,000 to $10,000 for each incident. Mrs. Gordon told police that her husband received all the money and she had kept no count of her partners, but believed the number to be several dozen.

Both Mayor Benjamin Nightlinger and Police Chief Ernest Caldwell praised local detectives for sticking with the two-month-old case to its resolution.

Gordon's death had been investigated by county and state as well as Kenton police, but officers had been stymied until recently. Detective Capt. Chuck Simmons credited a tip from a *Chronicle* reporter as leading them to focus more closely on Mrs. Gordon. An independent investigation by *The Chronicle* indicated a possible link to patients whom she would have met in her position with a local dental practice. No knowledge or involvement by the dentist is suspected, police said.

Mrs. Gordon reportedly was under compulsion from her husband to tempt family men of apparent means for trysts at her home. Such men presumably would want to avoid exposure and had the ability to pay for destruction of the recordings of their dalliance.

Police said they had received no complaints of the operation, and neighbors had reported no disturbances or unusual late night traffic at the home. For the past several years Gordon had operated his photography business from a studio in an expanded garage at his home. The video recording, however, was done in the couple's bedroom.

The Gordon home, while substantially expanded and remodeled, is similar to other post-war bungalows in the well-kept middle class neighborhood on Kenton's west side. Police said the interior and furnishings, however, show signs of significant investment in upgrades.

Mrs. Gordon is lodged in Wilkes County lockup pending arraignment later today. County prosecutors have been informed of the case but have made no decision on what charges will be filed.

I let the police take credit for their arrest but did insist on inserting the truthful statement about *The Chronicle's* own investigation.

In fairness to Dr. Schmidt and all of his innocent patients, his practice was not named, nor was the existence of a post-mortem love affair with a certain Wilkes County official. Readers were also spared the sordid details of the descent of the Gordons' marriage into virtual sex slavery.

Chapter 59

Jeni and I sat at our desks the next morning, staring at each other and at the papers strewn across our desks. Finishing our story and then planning the next steps in coverage had turned into an all-nighter. Now, we waited numbly for the jolt of our morning coffee to overcome our exhaustion.

Finally, Jeni broke the silence with, "You think Sarah has heard anything from Mr. Graham?"

"About what?"

"About our Gordon story, of course."

"Huh," I scoffed. Leaning back in my chair, I folded my arms and propped my feet on the open desk drawer. "Dam-Gram? Don't hold your breath."

"I know Sarah called him last night when we were working on the story."

"Well, *if* he's up, and *if* he's read it, it's unlikely we'll hear anything about it unless it offended his wife or one of his country club buddies."

"Well, you'd think he'd at least congratulate Sarah on her staff getting a scoop like that. I mean, it's not every day reporters break a murder case."

"Dream on." I shook my head and scowled. "He's not a newsie like his old man. You've been here – what? Going on a year? How many times have you seen Dam-Gram darken the newsroom door? Much less have something nice to say about our news report. Old Bill would have been reading over our shoulders as we were writing, then walking the floor until the presses rolled and then taken us both out to breakfast. In this case, *not* like father like son."

"Well, you're certainly a dash of cold water this morning,

aren't you?"

"Sorry. Don't mean to be. Just tired, I guess." I yawned, rubbed my eyes and re-focused on Jeni. "You ready with your list?"

"Yeah, first a couple psychologists and then a battered women's advocate," Jeni said. "You?"

"Start with the prosecutor to see what charges she'll file – if any. What's your guess? I'd say murder one is definitely off the table, maybe not even voluntary manslaughter. But I'll have to check the statutes to see the range of possibilities. Then I'll do a search for similar cases."

Again, we lapsed into silence. I got up and refilled our coffee mugs. I had just sat back down when Sarah called from her office door.

"Brock, Jeni, Mr. Graham would like to talk with us. Would you join me, please?"

Jeni looked at me and smiled, nodding with something like self-satisfaction. I just shook my head.

Jerry joined us as we followed Sarah down the hallway to the publisher's office. Jeni whispered, "Guess you were wrong."

"Doubt it; you'll see," I retorted. "Probably wants more *confirmation* of our hospital story."

"Will you two just cool it?" Sarah snapped as we reached Graham's open doorway.

"Go right in," Elsie said.

"Oh – uh -- good, good. Ladies and gentlemen -- uh -- come in and – ah -- have a seat," Graham said, obviously nervous. He seated himself behind his mahogany desk and spread his hands over the leather rimmed green blotter, an elegant anachronism left from his father's regime over *The Chronicle*. To his right was the newspaper's attorney, Winfield Ferrell. Both men were still crisp in their three-piece suits and I thought the air of formality was not a good sign. *But it's too early for Valerie Gordon or her attorney to have filed any kind of formal complaint over our story.*

Graham said, "I have asked Win to be here to lend background on an agreement we have reached with Wilkes Memorial."

"Agreement?" Sarah and I said in unison. We looked at each other before Sarah raised her hand for us to be quiet as she said, "What agreement is that?"

"I have spoken with Jim Blanchard at the hospital," Graham said, knitting his fingers atop the blotter. "He has investigated the findings of your research into a patient's death and agrees there has been an error in reporting the cause of death."

"Error?" I blurted. "There was no error. There was a monumental screw-up and then a flagrant cover-up."

Holding her hands out in a placating motion, Sarah looked at me and said, "Please, Brock. Let's hear him out."

Ignoring my interjection as if he hadn't heard it, Graham continued, "Based on your findings, Mr. Blanchard now has learned that a regrettable incident at the hospital caused Mr. Owens to suffer further injuries. But that accident and the extent of Mr. Owens's new injuries were not properly reported to Mr. Blanchard or the authorities. As a result, the cause of death was inadvertently attributed to Mr. Owens's initial traffic accident."

I exploded. "What, so they're trying to say this was all just a paperwork error?"

"Mr. Andrews, please contain yourself," Graham said stiffly, looking to his lawyer as if embarrassed by the onslaught of truth.

The lawyer, legs crossed and fingers locked over his knees in an affectation of nonchalance, took the cue and said, "The hospital is preparing a statement clarifying the cause of death and saying that those responsible for the error have been disciplined and no longer work there. Memorial's lawyers have invited the Owens family to meet with them to receive the hospital's formal apology for this regrettable misunderstanding."

"Misunderstanding, my ass," Jerry said under his breath to no one in particular.

Sarah looked nervously at her staffers and then at the publisher. "Mr. Graham, this is not at all supported by the facts that we have discovered."

"I understand your disappointment, Miss Goldman," the lawyer said, "but I have advised Mr. Graham this is the safest approach to publication. It clears up the cause of death for the family and corrects the public record. And, I might add, gives the family financial recourse for their loss."

"But it ignores contrary information from informed sources."

"I'm sorry, Miss Goldman, but your sources are far from reliable. Their truthfulness is suspect. Apparently only one is willing to go on the record, and she and another were terminated for errors and/or falsification of records to cover up their own negligence."

Jeni had watched the Ping-Pong conversation in deferential silence, but seeing her work so easily dismissed, she spoke up. "But that – that's not the truth. My sources and everyone else at the hospital was ordered not to talk about it."

"That may be, Miss – Miss – uh – Jermaine?" the lawyer said. "But without them willing to be on the record we have no certainty of their actual knowledge. Much less accuracy."

Standing now, her voice shaking and her lips quivering, Sarah said, "Mr. Graham, this isn't right."

Graham rose deliberately and splayed his fingers on the blotter as he leaned toward Sarah. "Nonetheless, that *is* your story and the one we will report in tomorrow's edition." The room fell silent, and Graham's smug expression said he believed he had had the last word.

I looked around at Jerry and Jeni and then fixed my gaze on Sarah. She had grown pale and looked back at me with raised eyebrows and a tilt of her head that signaled a shrug of submission. I couldn't believe our investigation was going to be merely dismissed and that we all were just going to take it.

I stood and cleared my throat, bile rising along with the fire racing up my neck and ears. "That is *not* the story, Mr. Graham. This is bullshit and you know it. If you don't have the balls to report the truth, then I'm sure the Indianapolis media will. The story's going to come out."

"Oh? And how are they going to find *that* out?" Graham's self-satisfied, cocked-head smirk bordered on a sneer.

"Brock!" Sarah warned.

But I already was in Graham's face, leaning over his desk and spitting out, "*You'll* sure as hell never know."

Wide-eyed shock forced the publisher to step back and raise his hands defensively by the time Sarah again said, "Brock!" She grabbed my arm and pushed herself between us to end the confrontation.

Reclaiming his composure, Graham said, "You've heard the decision, Ms. Goldman. You will publish the story as approved by counsel. And, while you're at it, you need to rid your staff of this insubordinate hothead."

Chapter 60

I was five steps ahead of the others on the way back down the hallway to the newsroom, barely seeing anything through the black curtain of rage that had enveloped me. When I reached my desk I ripped open my center drawer and dumped it out on the desktop. The clatter of pens, pencils, paper clips, scissors and stapler spun every head in the room toward me. I stopped, struggling for control. After a few deep breaths, I looked around, shrugged, and said hoarsely, "Sorry.".

Sarah called to me, "What do you think you're doing?"

"What's it look like? I'm outta here."

"You're not going anywhere."

Without looking at her I said, "Oh, come on, Sarah. You heard your orders."

Jeni stood by her desk, wide-eyed and silent, Jerry right behind her. Then shaking his head, the older editor, shoulders sagging, sidled away to his desk.

Sarah said acidly, "Don't do anything stupid, Brock. I'll work this out."

I whirled to her, irked by the sudden recovery of the command presence that had been missing in the confrontation with Graham. "Oh, yeah? How?" I demanded, louder than I had intended.

She turned to stare down the curious newsroom onlookers and the raised heads looked away. "I don't know -- yet," she said softly, shaking her head. "I need some time to think."

"Look," I said, more calmly. "I can see the handwriting on the wall here. I'm out. And even if I weren't, I can't work here any more. Your boss makes me sick." I turned back to my desk and scooped a handful of folders from a file drawer.

"Brock," Jeni said. "Listen to her. You can't just walk out on us – on me. We – we need you here."

"No one's going anywhere," Sarah said, her tone carrying less conviction than her words. "This will not stand, dammit. I'll find a way." She turned and stalked back to her office.

I called after her, "I'll need some boxes to pack my stuff in."

She turned at her office door with a set jaw and hands on her hips. Then, her lips in a tight smile, she said, "You'll get them -- when I'm damn good and ready." She went inside and slammed her door.

With his boss out of the room, Jerry returned to my side. "Sarah's right, Brock. There's got to be a way out of this. Graham will cool off and we'll find a way to print the real story – eventually. Just make yourself as invisible as possible for a few days until things settle down."

I couldn't answer, instead dumping another drawer full of files onto the growing mound of debris on the desk.

"Besides," Jerry said, "you don't want to try to get a job without having a job. Doesn't look good on the resume. Just hang on until you find another position." He paused, and then with an ironic curl of the lip added, "or -- at least until I can find a replacement for you." His words having no apparent effect on my preparations to leave, he sulked back to his desk muttering, "Damn, I figured I'd be out of here long before you."

Our corner of the newsroom fell into a tense silence and, curiosity at least temporarily sated, the other reporters and editors returned to their deadline demands. The only sound was the soft swoosh of paper against paper as, now seated, I sifted through one file folder after another. Some I set on a stack beside me; most went into the round file.

***

Morning turned into afternoon and, on returning from an

appointment, Jeni pulled her chair next to mine and said softly, "Brock."

Still bent to my file-weeding task, I ignored her.

"Brock, look at me."

When I glanced up, her eyes were welling with tears. *Dammit. Don't turn on the waterworks. This is hard enough.* I forced a smile and said, "Hey, don't get all emotional on me. Besides, it's probably time for me to move on anyway. Past time."

"I meant what I said. We need you here."

"I appreciate the sentiment, but you'll all be fine."

"Not *me*. What will *I* do?" She stood and stared down at me, lips quivering.

I looked up at her and shook my head. "Like I said, you'll do fine. You don't need me anymore – not that you ever really did."

"I told you before, if you go, I go."

"Don't be silly. You're not ready yet," I said, but then regretted the dismissive tone. "Look, Jeni, this is your first job. You need to stay awhile and build up your clip file. Then you can move on to *Business Week* or wherever."

She sank back into her chair. "But how can I go on working for a jerk like Graham?"

"You're not working for Graham. You're working for Sarah – and the readers. You can hold your head up and continue to do a good job – and then move on when you're ready."

"The same goes for you," she said. "I know this is a big deal – to all of us – but can't you at least let Sarah try to work it out?"

I could offer no response and as she sat staring at me I just continued to sort through papers and file folders, my trash can filling with the alphabetical accumulation of 15 years at *The*

Chronicle. My shuffling of papers and files continued until, after two stacks had already toppled over, I said, "I'm going to get some boxes."

Sarah intercepted me as I passed her office door.

"In here. Now," she said. As she closed her door behind us, her face was flushed red, her jaw jutted forward and her eyebrows were drawn into a tense squint. She made no motion for me to be seated, instead leaned against her desk and folded her arms. Radiating both stress and determination, she said, "Just hold off on everything, will you? I can't go into details yet, but I think it's going to be okay."

"Okay? How can it be okay?"

She blinked and shook her head. "I've been on the phone for hours. I can't say more right now. Just trust me, will you?"

"I do trust you. But you can't just blow off a direct order from the publisher. He's expecting you to print a false story in the morning. And – oh, yeah -- he's expecting me to be gone."

She shook her head. "I'm *not* publishing that story. If he tries to make me, I'm out of here too."

"But he's going to be looking for it in the morning paper. It'll come down on you if it's not there."

"Don't worry. I'll make up some excuse for a delay."

"Look, Sarah, I don't know what you're up to, but you don't want to go out on a limb for me. Graham will saw it off without a qualm. You've got a great career ahead of you. Don't ruin it on my account."

"This isn't about just you. It's about the paper and our credibility." She paused, took another deep breath and sighed. "And, in the end, it's about me and whether I'm worthy of the job."

"It's your job that I'm talking about. You must know by now

that he's an incurable suck-up. His only priorities are ingratiating himself with his hometown cronies and not rocking the boat with corporate."

She nodded. "Oh, don't think I don't know it. Just keep your shirt on until the morning, will you? Give me until then, okay?"

I had already made the mental break with the past. "But I've already about cleaned out my desk."

"Just leave it all until morning. I'll tell maintenance to leave your stuff alone. Take the rest of the day off. Get out of here and let me do what I have to do."

The passion of her appeal both puzzled and impressed me. "Okay. What's one more day? Besides, I need to talk with Danny."

***

"I think maybe it's time to move on," I said as matter-of-factly as I could after she and I finished our shared dessert. It was Thursday night and our weekly dinner, but I had moved it at the last minute from our customary date at Applebee's to The Cove, a quiet, upscale seafood and steak house where we could talk.

After alerting Danny to the change of venue, I'd spent the rest of the afternoon in a long run, an hour of weights at the gym and then a pickup basketball game. The exercise had helped clear my mind and released the tight fist clenched in my gut. And it had given me time to rehearse my opening line. My focus now was on Danny and whatever future we had with my having to leave Kenton.

"What do you mean, time to move on?" she asked, a cautious alarm in her voice. "You're not talking about us, are you?"

"No, of course not – at least I hope not."

"Maybe you'd better tell me what you're getting at," she said, her eyes searching mine as she reached for my hands across the table.

I told her then -- about the confrontation with Graham, the publisher's parting shot to Sarah to get rid of me, and the editor's plea for me to give her time to work it out.

Danny just stared at me, her long pony tail sweeping the back of the booth as she shook her head. "Oh, Brock. Couldn't you just have kept quiet and let *her* do battle with Graham?"

I smiled and squeezed her hands. "Not my style, I guess."

"Not your style?" she blurted, her eyes betraying a mix of anger and fear. "Who the hell cares about style? It's your career – and us. And you're talking about style?"

As righteous as my own anger was, I hated making her angry. "I know. I didn't mean that to sound flippant. But Sarah was dumbstruck when he ordered her to print a lie. I just couldn't let it pass."

"All right. I understand – I guess. But what'll you do now? You can't leave Kenton," she said, alarm again ringing in her voice.

I leaned across the table to her and said softly, "Not much choice there. If it comes to leaving *The Chronicle,* it's the only game in town."

"But what about me? About us?"

"That's what we need to decide," I said, nodding reassurance. "I won't have any trouble finding a job, in Indy or elsewhere -- and probably for a lot more than I'm making now. And career-wise, it's probably past time to make a move."

Tears rimmed her eyes and as she blinked them back she looked side to side to see if anyone was listening. Seeing her anxiety, I continued in a hushed tone, "And if I go, I'm hoping you'll come with me. It's time for us to move on, too. Make it official, you know?"

"Oh, Brock, you know I love you. But I – I'm just about to

make detective and..."

"I know, I know. It couldn't be at a worse time." I squeezed her hands again, released them and then sat back, wishing I'd picked a less pressured moment. I fished in my pocket, took her left hand and placed in it a small velvet covered box.

She drew a quavering breath and blinked as tears slipped down her cheeks.

"I'm sorry to dump this on you now, Danny. But for the umpteenth and maybe last time – whether we leave Kenton or stay -- will you marry me?"

Chapter 61

Instead of answering, after I paid the tab and left a tip for the waitress, she led me by the hand from the restaurant to her car and drove us to her apartment. Without speaking, she led me into her bedroom where we undressed each other.

Afterward, as we lay together, she reached to her nightstand to retrieve the velvet box she had left there. Inside was a ring much like one we had looked at several times at a jewelry store in downtown Kenton. Its diamond was elevated by four slender prongs above a thin gold band and even in the dim bedroom radiated myriad points of light. She pulled the ring from the box and slid it on her finger.

"Oh, Brock. It's beautiful," she whispered.

"I'm glad you like it."

"And it's so big."

"Why, thank you," I said with a smirk.

"The ring, Brock. The ring. Can't you be serious even at a moment like this?"

"Oh, yeah – the ring." I blinked and cleared my throat in mock solemnity.

"Well, it must have cost a fortune."

"Over a carat. But you're worth it." And then in earnest, "We're worth it,"

She beamed, wrapped an arm around my neck and pulled me to her lips.

"Does this mean yes?" my voice tighter than the dozen or so other times I'd asked before.

"Yes – and -- no."

"What's -- *that* supposed to mean?" I said, no longer flippant.

"It means yes, I love you very much and want to marry you. But will I marry you now? No, not unless you ask me again when you don't have all this uncertainty hanging over you."

"I'm okay, Danny."

"I know you're okay. And so am I – whatever happens. We have each other – I hope forever. But with so much turbulence now, I don't want you to just grab onto -- us -- like an anchor to hold onto."

I attempted a laugh. "Oh, you mean like any port in a storm?"

"Be serious. But, yeah, sort of like that," she said, digging me in the ribs – and then lower.

We lay together for more long minutes before the sound of distant sirens broke the spell. Propped on elbows, we looked at each other, expecting at any moment our phones to summon one or both of us to the latest emergency as they had many times before. But then I flopped back on the pillows and said, "Nope, not tonight. I don't work there anymore."

She smiled indulgently but then, suddenly serious, she said, "Brock -- will you do just one thing for me?"

"What's that?"

"Promise me you'll give Sarah a chance to make things right. I know you have no respect for Graham, but you've learned to work with Sarah. And maybe respect and trust her? If she's able to work out something you can live with, at least consider it? For both of us?"

I stared into her earnest eyes and felt my resolve to leave the paper slipping away.

"Please?"

Despite my determination, I couldn't resist a smile. "So this is how it's going to be? Your plying me with sex to get your way?"

"As long as it works," she grinned, and wrapped a leg over mine. She paused and then said, "Stay the night?"

"Love to. Besides, Sarah made it pretty plain she didn't want to see me until the morning – if then."

"What do you think she'll do? She can't just ignore an order from Graham."

"No, but I'm learning you women have your ways," I said, enveloping her in a tight hug. "She thought she had come up with something, but I have no idea what. Maybe without me there to wrap up details on the Memorial story there's an excuse for at least a delay."

"She's risking her job for you."

"Yes, I know. But not just for me. For herself too – her professional self respect and that of the news staff. And, long term, of the paper. If *The Chronicle* prints Graham's fiction, the true story is bound to come out, and when it does people will know we collaborated in a lie."

***

No mention of Wilkes Memorial was on *The Chronicle's* front page that next morning – not that Graham would have tolerated a banner headline on what the publisher was now prepared to dismiss as merely a "clerical error."

I was up before Danny, making coffee when I heard the slap of the paper tossed outsider her front door. I thumbed through the pages quickly and smiled wryly at finding nothing about the hospital. Then I returned to the front page where a short story below the fold snared my attention.

Ah, the sirens last night, I thought as I caught the headline: "Trailer fire fatal to two."

Yet another fire in a mobile home. The scene at Autumn Oaks trailer park as described by the night reporter was all too familiar – residence fully engulfed in flames by the time firemen arrived, two bodies retrieved, burned beyond recognition, victims not named pending positive identification and notifying next of kin.

It was the final line that grabbed me in the gut: "Cause of the blaze was undetermined, but police are following up a suspicion by the fire marshal that the trailer might have been a lab in which the occupants manufactured illegal methamphetamines."

I shook my head. Danny was standing in the bedroom doorway, barefoot, her dark hair falling to the shoulders of a white terry robe. "What's there?" she said, walking to me and resting her chin on my shoulder.

"Not even a word about the hospital. But I think there's a good chance our theory about Raymond Owens being assisted out his hospital window just went up in smoke."

Chapter 62

"What's going on there today?" I asked Jeni over the phone.

"Where are you? Are you coming in today?"

"Actually, I'm at Danny's. Just wiping the shaving cream off my face. She left for patrol and I'm here alone – trying to plan my *busy, busy* day." She offered no satisfying response to my sarcasm, so I said, "Figured I'd better check in before wandering back into a hornet's nest."

"It's like a morgue without you here," she said. "Refreshingly quiet for a change, I must say."

"Yeah, yeah, I'm sure. Go ahead and have your jollies at the fired guy's expense."

"No, seriously. I miss you being here. It's just kind of weird today – like the quiet after the storm."

"Or *before*. What's happening with the Memorial piece? It's your story now that I'm gone."

"You saw the fire story?"

"Yeah. Jimmy Owens, I presume?"

"We've determined it's his trailer at least. Coroner has to confirm idents of the two bodies."

"Well, that pretty much closes out that angle."

"How inconvenient," she said with her own touch of sarcasm. "I know how you hate loose ends."

"You're right. But it's probably just as well for Georgia Owens. If this is Jimmy -- losing both a husband and son?"

"Yes, I'd hate to load suspicion of murder on top of that. The wife and sister sure don't need that. I'm just as glad."

"All the better to focus on Blanchard, right? If we – you -- ever get to tell the truth. Speaking of which, what's Sarah saying about that?"

"Haven't spoken with her. It's strange. She was here for a short time – dressed to kill, I might add. But then she left, saying only she'd be back in later but not sure when. If something came up we could reach her by cell phone."

I shook my head, a jolt of alarm surging through me. "I hope she's not doing anything rash just because of me. Like interviewing somewhere. What'd she say after I left? What's the plan with how to handle Graham and the statement from the hospital?"

"Like I said, it's been quiet. After you left yesterday she put a note on your desk for the janitors to leave everything as it was. Then she holed up in her office with the lights off and blinds drawn – probably hiding out from Graham."

"Anything more from him? Has he shown his face today?"

"Nope," she said. "No sign of him either. Oh – wait a minute…"

The line went silent and then muffled sounds, as if a hand was placed over the receiver. I strained to hear a faint cluster of soft thuds like heavy footsteps across a floor.

Jeni came back on in a near whisper. "She just came in with three guys in suits. I don't recognize any of them but – hold on…"Again the line went dead, no muffled words or noises. *Damn, she must have put me on hold.*

After what seemed like an hour but was less than three minutes the phone clicked once again and she returned with an even softer whisper. "Brock? You still there?"

"Yeah. What's going on?" I whispered back unconsciously.

"Sarah took one of the guys into her office, closed the door and drew the blinds. And the other two -- they're heading for *Graham's* office. Something's going on. Let me find out and I'll call you back."

***

Shirt and tie, or the casual "unemployed" look? I muttered *"screw 'em"* and had just reached for the flowered tropical shirt I kept in Danny's closet when the phone rang.

"Brock, you need to get down here now." It wasn't Jeni's voice, but Sarah's.

"Why, what's going on?"

"I can't talk now, but I need you to be here."

"Okay, I'm about ready. How'd you know where to call?"

"Jeni gave me the number. Hurry, please." Click.

I finished dressing and checked myself as I started to sprint to my car. *No need to hurry, dammit. I don't work there anymore.*

Driving past the front of *The Chronicle* building I almost slammed on the brake in a rapid double take at the gleaming white stretch limousine parked at the curb. *What the hell?*

I turned into the alley and found my parking place empty – *at least my former parking place.*

The newsroom was eerily quiet – tomb quiet – despite the dozen reporters and editors bent to their computer screens. Not even the normal insistent ringing of phones to break the silence. Several heads turned my way; a couple nodded to but most looked furtively away. Jeni was nowhere to be seen, but Jerry spun his chair around, smiled enigmatically and jerked his head in the direction of Sarah's office. "In there."

The door was shut and the blinds were still drawn, but I could hear voices. I knocked and Sarah opened the door. "Have a seat," she said as she closed the door.

Inside were Jeni and one of the "suits." This one I had seen before – Norman Jenkinson, Mega Media's senior vice president for news. I had met him when the entourage of Mega executives made the obligatory visit after buying the paper from the senior Graham.

Sarah said, "Brock, I believe you know Mr. Jenkinson?"

"Sure, we've met," I said. *What the hell did she do? Rat out her boss to corporate? Damn woman's got balls, I'll give her that.*

Clearly deferential to the corporate news boss, she sat upright behind her desk, dressed in her most formal navy business suit, with gray silk blouse and a string of pearls.

Jenkinson rose, offered a half smile along with a firm handshake, and then took over. As he had been in our previous meeting, the corporation's news exec was sixtyish, trim and distinguished looking, almost gaunt from his legendary regimen of long distance running.

"Brock," Jenkinson said, "I'm here to explore what Sarah has told me about this business with your local hospital. I've heard what she and Jeni have to say, but now I want to hear it from you." His blue eyes peered out over skinny tortoise shell reading glasses and fixed me in a no-nonsense stare. I guessed I was supposed to be intimidated.

I couldn't suppress the smile that curled across my lips as I looked at Sarah and then Jeni. Managing to subdue the nervous chuckle that rose in my throat, I nodded to Jenkinson. The corporate newsman shed his conservative gray suit jacket that I surmised would cost me at least two weeks' pay. Loosening his maroon silk tie, he leaned toward me with elbows on knees.

"I'm sure what I have to say will conform to what you've already heard," I said. "I will tell you that this is the most high-handed abuse of power I've seen in my 15 years in the newspaper business."

"Brock," Sarah said. "Please no editorial comment. Just tell

Norm what's happened."

"Sure, sorry. But that's part of the story." Stifling my emotions as best I could, I told Jenkinson about Raymond Owens's accident and subsequent death in Wilkes Memorial, the family's entreaties for more information, and the encounters with James Blanchard and then with W. Damron Graham.

"That about covers it. Bottom line is the publisher ordered Sarah to print a knowingly false story, and when I objected he ordered her to fire me."

Turning to Sarah, Jenkinson said pointedly, "Have you in fact fired Brock?"

"No – no, I – I have not." She appeared uncertain of his meaning. "In – in part – that's why I called you."

Having sat silently through Brock's narrative, Jeni said, "It's not fair. Brock's the best we've got."

Jenkinson looked at her with pursed lips and then returned to stare at me over his reading glasses, either sizing me up or weighing what he'd heard or both. Then to Jeni and Sarah he said, "Anything more from either of you?"

Jeni shook her head and Sarah answered, almost inaudibly, "No," and then cleared her throat for a definitive, "No."

Irritated by the news exec's noncommittal mien, I said, "That about what you heard before?"

"Yes. Yes it is," Jenkinson said, his head now lowered as he removed his glasses and pinched his eyes between thumb and forefinger. He sat silently for a long moment and then leaned back, crossed his legs at the ankles and raked thin fingers through thick brown hair that turned to gray as it curled over his ears. He shook his head and frowned.

"So what now?" I asked, the impatience in my tone drawing a scowl from Sarah.

Jenkinson looked up and again fixed me with a stare and said, "Thank you for coming in, Brock – and Jeni. I appreciate your candor." He then turned to Sarah and said calmly, "I need to confer with my associates." He spun on his heel, opened the door and left the room, turning down the hall toward the publisher's office.

The three of us remaining looked at each other and drew deep breaths. I was the first to speak. "My god, Sarah, what have you done? Who else has he got with him?"

"President of the newspaper division and VP for HR," Sarah said, more pale than before.

"Are you going to be okay," I asked, "now that you've gone over Graham's head to his bosses? How can you continue to work with him? Where is this going?"

She broke a nervous smile and said, "Where is this going? I can't say for sure. But I'm hoping the three of us will still have a job at the end of the day. Graham? I wouldn't bet on it."

Chapter 63

Breaking the grave spell that seemed to have sucked the air out of the room, Sarah announced lightly, "Well, guys, I think we should all go to lunch. On me."

I have to admit I was astonished. "What! Go to lunch? I mean -- yeah, you know I'm always up for a meal – especially if you're buying. But -- *now*?"

"Much as I'd like to stay around, I think our absence for an hour or so right now might be most therapeutic."

Jeni and I looked at each other with raised eyebrows and mouthed silently, "Oh."

Sarah dialed Graham's secretary and announced, "Elsie, I'll be out until 1:00 but you can reach me by my cell or at the Brass Rail."

At shortly after 11 a.m. we were early for the lunch crowd, and the popular watering hole that was highly energized after work was now almost empty. The noon patrons that dribbled in after us were a mix of lawyers, business people and the city hall and courthouse crowd. Libations leaned more to iced tea and soft drinks than alcohol.

Jeni and Sarah ordered salads, I the cheese steak and cole slaw. I looked at Sarah and half whispered, "You've really put yourself out on a limb on this, Sarah. I'll be honest – I didn't expect it. But I want you to know I appreciate it."

Jeni nodded, "Absolutely."

"But where do you see this going? I sure as hell hope it doesn't backfire on you."

"Look," Sarah said, "neither of you knows Mega as well as I do. As a huge corporation it's a lot of things, and by far not all that we'd like it to be. But..." She hesitated as her eyes watered and she cleared her throat, "Unless I'm grievously mistaken, the one thing they will not stand for is knowingly publishing a lie."

"You and I know it's a lie," I said, "but will Jenkinson and his superiors see it that way? You've put them in a situation where someone has to lose – and lose big. Never mind me. I just hope it's not you."

She wrinkled her brow and nodded, "I appreciate your concern, really. And I wouldn't have done this if I didn't think it was worth it. But in a way, it really is a case of life and death – Raymond Owens's death and our responsibility to tell what we know to the living. Besides," she said with a nervous chuckle, "as I think I've heard you say, I was looking for a job when I found this one." But then, reassuringly, "But I'm sure we're all going to be just fine."

"Famous last words," I said. "I think that's what they said just before the Titanic went down."

"I sure hope you're right, Sarah," Jeni added with a laugh of bravado. "Paying off my student loans depends on it."

***

"Mister Graham has left the building," Jenkinson told the three of us solemnly when we returned at his phoned summons to Sarah's office. "He – uh -- will not be returning."

Jaws dropped in unison.

"*What?*" I said.

"What happened?" Sarah asked.

"I'm not at liberty to discuss particulars," Jenkinson said. "But the company will be naming a new publisher very soon. Now, Sarah, please come with me. We will need to draft a statement for the morning paper." With an admonition of silence about what he'd told us until a formal announcement to employees, he opened the door to allow Jeni and me to leave, and then he and Sarah left for the publisher's office.

Back at our desks, Jeni burst out, "Oh my god, Brock." Her face was flushed and her lips trembled. The newsroom curious turned to stare and Jerry arose from his chair and ambled over.

"What the hell have you done now, Andrews?" he barked.

I shook my head and answered with a sly grin, "Well, I'm not ready to swear to it, old man, but I think we just might have struck a blow for truth in publishing – assuming Mega Media is capable of that. Hopefully the sword isn't two-edged."

His only comment was a skeptical "hummpf" and then a quizzical, "Do all of us still have jobs? I was hoping to make it until the end of the year, and it's not even half over."

"Yeah, what about us?" Jeni asked, "Sarah – and you -- and me?"

"That's the other shoe to drop."

It dropped exactly one hour and 47 minutes later.

Jenkinson with Sarah at his heels returned from the executive wing, opened the door to Sarah's office and called, "Mr. Andrews, would you join us in here, please?"

He closed the door and then sat on the corner of Sarah's desk and motioned me to have a seat.

"For the record, Brock, you are not fired. I'll let Sarah fill in the details."

"What about the Memorial story?" I asked. "With Graham gone, does that mean we're free to tell the whole story?"

"Given that your local counsel is already involved and an agreement had been reached with hospital officials, I think we'll need to have our legal staff review the story. Ultimately, the decision will be up to your new publisher."

"Okay," I shrugged. "That seems reasonable -- I guess. I'm sure you'll find the story is supported by the facts." I rose to go, but Jenkinson stopped me with, "Just one more thing before you leave. We need to have an understanding."

I started to speak, but Jenkinson lifted his hand. "Hear me out. Sarah has persuaded me that your reportage, on this story and throughout her time with *The Chronicle,* has been highly thorough, accurate and ethical. That coincides with my impression over the years since we acquired *The Chronicle.* Your work seems to aspire to the high standards of our profession – and our company."

A smile started to crease my lips but behind Jenkinson's back Sarah glared at me and shook her head vigorously.

Jenkinson continued. "And – *and* she has *almost* persuaded me that your conduct toward your publisher, while understandably passionate, was not insubordinate to the point of meriting dismissal.

"However, let me caution you: Henceforth, please do not go out of your way to antagonize the person who signs your paychecks and who is our company's designated representative in Kenton. For the good of the newspaper – and your career. Do you understand?"

I took a deep breath, looked into Jenkinson's eyes and nodded, "Yeah. Yeah, I do."

"Good, good then," Jenkinson said as he relaxed his shoulders and allowed himself a smile. "In that case, let me introduce you to your new publisher." He stepped to the door and I rose beside him, waiting to traipse down the hall to the publisher's office. Instead, at the door Jenkinson turned back to Sarah, who had stayed seated.

I looked at her and said, "What, have you already met him?"

Jenkinson smiled as he extended his right hand toward her. "Here, Brock. I believe you already know the new publisher of *The Chronicle* -- Sarah Goldman.*"*

Chapter 64

The new publisher sat there, eyes watering but a broad smile on her lips. She rose to accept my offered handshake.

"You can close your mouth now," she said, a quiver in her voice.

"No. No, I'm – I'm delighted for you, Sarah. Really. Good for you." I looked then at Jenkinson and said, "And good for *The Chronicle* – and for Mega Media, too.*"*

The older man nodded and said to Sarah, "Now, there is some unfinished business. We need to wrap up that statement, and then gather all employees for the announcement."

I smiled to Sarah and started to leave but was stopped by Jenkinson's hand on my arm.

"Oh, but first let me step out for a moment."

I turned to Sarah, and as Jenkinson left she motioned me into a chair.

"Brock," she said softly, her voice husky. She cleared her throat and continued. "As – as you know, Jerry is planning to retire as managing editor at the end of the year."

I nodded, suddenly certain of where she was headed. I knew myself, and had told her and everyone who'd listen. *I'm no damn pencil pusher. I'm a writer and story teller and don't want to be saddled to a desk correcting other people's grammar and spelling..*

"I see where this is going, Sarah, but I'm not your man. Thanks for thinking of me, but I don't want Jerry's job."

She sighed and leaned forward to look directly into my eyes. With deliberate patience, she said, "I'm not talking about Jerry's job, Brock. I'm talking about mine."

I stared at her a moment, uncomprehending.

"I wasn't expecting something like this at all when I called Norm yesterday. I'd already told you I wasn't bucking for Graham's or any other publisher job. I don't know the details, but the company apparently has been uncomfortable with Graham for some time – maybe from the start when they bought the company and even more after Graham took over for his father. I get the impression this episode was just what they needed to leverage a decision."

Brock nodded. "I can see that. Son of the former owner and all."

"But now that the opportunity has come my way, I wasn't going to turn it down. I'm hoping the same for you."

"You know I don't want to be a desk jockey, Sarah."

"I know. I've heard your spiel. But just listen for a moment, will you? We've made a lot of progress here in the past year. We've raised our standards and expectations, and frankly a great deal of that has been a result of your example – your skill as a writer– and your energy and passion for reporting what's going on in our community."

I pursed my lips and shook my head, but she continued. "And with Jerry retiring within the year, I need someone to help us keep up that momentum. And to choose Jerry's successor to handle the desk details."

I started to speak, but again she jumped ahead. "Just think about it objectively, will you? I know you've been as impatient as I have at the pace of change. Jerry's been great and supportive, but he's – well -- Jerry. He's from another era. You could have even more impact sitting in this chair."

"What, budgets and reports to corporate and interviewing applicants?"

"Come on, you know that's not all I do."

I grimmaced. "Of course. I'm sorry. I don't at all discount what you've done. We *have* come a long way in just a year or so."

"And think of the satisfaction you'd get from carrying that progress forward, from directing news coverage that means something to our readers and our community. And, yes, there'll be budgets and reports, but the controller and I can walk you through those. It's easier than you might think."

I sat listening, deliberately impassive.

"Look," she said. "I don't want to talk you into something that you really don't want to do. And I admit I'm being selfish here. I'm going to have my hands full learning a new job, and I'd like to have someone I can depend on in this chair.

"Also – and I don't mean to be critical or insulting here -- but if you look objectively at where you are in your career, it's time to make a move. Either as a writer onto a bigger paper or into management. I'd like to think your place is here."

"I appreciate the confidence you have in me. Really. But what about Jenkinson?"

"Frankly," she hesitated, choosing her words carefully, "he's -- somewhat skeptical, given your – ah – shall we say, outspoken history with Graham." She smiled. "Not to mention your general resentment of all things Mega Media. But the decision is up to me. I'm sure we could make it work.

"And, there's a bonus," she said, folding her arms and pursing her lips in a smug smile.

"Yeah, what's that?"

"Besides a nice raise in pay, you get to work with me – instead of someone like Graham."

"Oh, of course," I grinned. "There's that." After a few moments of silence, I added, "I appreciate your offer. And I'm sure I *could* do the job well if I decided to do it. But…" I stopped, took several breaths and said, "You -- you don't need an answer right now, do you? I'd like to think about it overnight."

"And maybe talk to a certain local police officer?" Her smile told me she thought she had already won. "All right. Besides, I think one major announcement a day is quite enough for both our staff and our readers."

***

The announcement to *Chronicle* employees was made that afternoon at 4, before the dayside staff went home. The nightside staff was called in early. Everybody except Elsie, who went downstairs to man the reception desk and switchboard in the business office, filled the available chairs and stood around the perimeter of the newsroom.

James Gregg, president of Mega Media's newspaper division, appeared from the hallway to the publisher's office, followed by Jenkinson and another whom I took to be the corporate VP of HR. The latter quietly departed leaving the two men to face the expectant crowd.

Gregg was short, maybe five-six, compact, deeply tanned and crowned with thick silver curls. At the peak of his career, he was legendary for both his personal charm and drive to succeed and had built Mega Media from a string of medium size newspapers into a print and broadcast behemoth. He looked around the room, flashed an almost luminescent smile and introduced himself and Jenkinson. Then, with a straight face, he said, "Ladies and gentlemen, your publisher, W. Damron Graham, has decided to take early retirement."

The silence was punctuated by a few muted mumblings and one not-quite whispered, "Oh, thank god." Gregg showed no sign of hearing that and continued. "We wish to thank Mr. Graham and his father for aiding in the past two years' transition to Mega Media ownership. In his place, I am happy to announce that one of your own is being promoted to the publisher's position."

Gregg paused for dramatic effect and faces all around the room turned as employees tried to guess who was being tapped as the newspaper's CEO.

"We have had our eyes on this person since she joined the company eight years ago, and we are very pleased to appoint Sarah Goldman as the paper's new publisher."

The applause was immediate and sustained, with multiple catcalls of "All right," "Hey, hey" and "Way to go, Sarah." Several women from news and other departments broke ranks and rushed to offer her hugs and handshakes of congratulations, leaving Gregg standing awkwardly to one side. He took the interruption in stride, and when employees saw he had more to say they once again became quiet. He continued with a smile, "I'm glad to see our choice is so well received. I'm sure you will give her your full support. We're confident Sarah will do the job the company and the community expect of her. Now, we have a plane to catch. Sarah, it's all yours."

The crowd parted to allow the men to leave and then closed ranks again. She raised both hands high into the air to quiet her employees and then paused, took a deep breath and began. "I want to thank you all for the warm welcome you've given me the past year, and for your support in the months and years ahead. I'll have a lot of learning to do and I will rely on all of your patience and understanding during this transition."

She fixed her gaze for a moment directly on me, and I was afraid she was going to pre-empt my decision, but then she let her eyes sweep the room. "And, I hope to get back with you all very soon to announce a new executive editor to lead news efforts for *The Chronicle.*"

Chapter 65

Hospital covered up death from fall

CEO, security chief fired;

prosecutor eyes charges

Those were the headlines on a front page spread *The Chronicle* published some eight weeks after the departure of publisher W. Damron Graham.

The story detailed how hospital officials had conspired to conceal that an apparent fall from a window at the hospital caused the death of patient Raymond W. Owens. Fearful of possible liability over lack of safety precautions, hospital administrator James Blanchard and head of security Richard Carter caused the death to be reported instead from Owens's injuries from a traffic accident a month earlier.

We looked at the possible suicide and homicide angles carefully and concluded there just wasn't enough evidence to warrant speculation – much less put the Owens family through the agony such speculation would inflict.

Naturally, we notified the hospital board of our findings so we could get reaction before publication. The board quickly conducted its own investigation, quietly cleaned house of Blanchard and Carter, and issued a public apology to the Owens family. In negotiations with the aggrieved family's attorneys, the hospital also had awarded Georgia Owens a "substantial" cash settlement, amount undisclosed but rumored to be in the high six figures. We reported that, in exchange, she agreed to drop a threatened lawsuit for wrongful death of her husband.

The initial reaction by Wilkes County's prosecuting attorney, before her investigators completed their probe, was doubt that any crime had been committed, just a reprehensible deception which was a cause for civil action by the family. Owens did, after all, as certified on the death certificate, die from a cerebral hemorrhage (never mind that the fatal incident was caused by bouncing his head off the hospital's concrete courtyard and not from his car accident). Given lack of evidence to the contrary, "manner of death" was correctly listed as "accident."

I wasn't going to let it go at that. Fearful that it was all just going to be swept under the rug as a regrettable lapse in judgment drove me to re-examine the death certificate.

Information the state requires on the death certificate includes cause of death Chain of Events – "diseases, injuries or complications that directly caused the death." Under "Immediate Cause," Blanchard had ordered the entry to be Owens's late January car accident. No mention of a fall at the hospital on March 2. Under "Approximate Interval: Onset to Death," Blanchard had reported "37 days," not the instant of the fall. Similar falsifications were entered on date, time, place and nature of injury. The trusting "good old boy" Coroner Bradshaw had just signed the certificate without conducting his own investigation.

The headline on our follow-up story read: "Hospital officials falsified death certificate."

The prosecutor says she is now studying filing of criminal charges against Blanchard and Carter for deliberately falsely reporting a cause of death. Both men are looking for new jobs and have been warned by the prosecutor not to depart the community without due notice.

Whatever charges the lawyers scrape up if they do decide to prosecute, falsifying a public record is a class D felony with jail time of six months to three years. And the same penalty applies for conspiring to commit such a crime, which Blanchard and his minions certainly did.

But, hey, I'm not vindictive. We did our job and I'm happy to leave meting out punishment to the court. It would be fine with me if the former hospital administrator and his co-conspirators, whoever they all might be, struck a plea deal, were fined or even just put on probation. For their deceit they'd still carry criminal records with them the rest of their lives.

As for Coroner Buster Bradshaw, confronted with our published stories, he admitted he signed the death certificate with no independent verification. He has since announced he is not going to seek re-election due to demands of his funeral home business. The erstwhile comforter of widow Valerie Gordon also has apparently withdrawn to the confines of his marital vows.

Citing extenuating circumstances in Stanley Gordon's death, the prosecutor decided against filing homicide charges against Valerie Gordon. After two months there were no bruises to corroborate her story of spousal abuse. There also was no record of police complaints of domestic violence to buttress her claims. But after extensive interviews the authorities believed her and concluded Gordon's death was inadvertent in the act of defending herself. No charges of any kind were to be filed – not even for her supposed participation in a blackmail scheme since, go figure, none of her marks came forward to proclaim victimhood. Absent husband, mother and lover, Mrs. Gordon resigned from Dr. Schmidt's dental practice, sold her home and left the community to start a new life.

Ex-publisher Dam-Gram has moved to Florida where he reportedly has started a new career as a financial adviser – if his clients can find him on the golf course.

The same day as the hospital stories appeared, a column by Publisher Sarah Goldman explained the extensive procedures behind bringing the hospital story to print. As the dutiful new publisher, Sarah had to let the corporate lawyers tramp all over our stories before they were convinced we had done our job correctly, and in the meantime we double- and triple-checked all our facts and sources.

The stories bore the dual bylines of Jennifer Jermaine, our newly minted investigative reporter, and moi, executive editor.

Yeah, I took the job. And so far, it's been just fine. The

paperwork overhead has been manageable. The staff has been very responsive, and right now I'm interviewing candidates for Jerry's replacement to head the copy desk. And, it's also great to have a person in the publisher's office who knows what a newspaper is supposed to be.

Oh, and one other development. In today's Milestones feature, I paid the employee-discount price for an ad with a photo by photographer Jim Rogers of a smiling 30-something Kenton couple announcing their engagement and plans for a Christmas wedding on a beach on Maui.

ACKNOWLEDGEMENTS

I am grateful for the diligent critiques of Trish Bradbury, Norma Connor, Fran Crisman and Robin Verdon of my writers group at The Highlands at Dove Mountain in Marana, Arizona. My nurse friend, Dixie Van Buskirk, gave me excellent advice on hospital operations, some of which I followed and some of which fell to literary license. And thanks to my cousin Jim Rogers, an excellent amateur photographer, for lending his name to *The Chronicle's* chief photographer.

Made in the USA
Charleston, SC
02 November 2015